... ..or of over four dozen romance novels, including her sexy, heart-warming contemporary 'Animal Magnetism' and 'Lucky Harbor' series. She won a RITA for *Simply Irresistible* and is a three-time National Readers Choice winner as well. Connect with Jill on her website www.jillshalvis.com for a complete book list and to read her daily blog, where she recounts her Misplaced City Girl adventures, or visit her at www.facebook.com/jillshalvis for other news.

**Praise for Jill Shalvis:**

'Packed with the trademark Shalvis humor and intense intimacy, it is definitely a must-read . . . If love, laughter and passion are the keys to any great romance, then this novel hits every note' *Romantic Times*

'Heartwarming and sexy . . . an abundance of chemistry, smoldering romance, and hilarious antics' *Publishers Weekly*

'[Shalvis] has quickly become one of my go-to authors of contemporary romance. Her writing is smart, fun, and sexy, and her books never fail to leave a smile on my face long after I've closed the last page . . . Jill Shalvis is an author not to be missed!' *The Romance Dish*

'Jill Shalvis is such a talented author that she brings to life characters who make you laugh, cry, and are a joy to read' *Romance Reviews Today*

'What I love about Jill Shalvis's books is that she writes sexy, adorable heroes . . . the sexual tension is out of this world. And of course, in true Shalvis fashion, she expertly mixes in humor that has you laughing out loud' *Heroes and Heartbreakers*

'I always enjoy reading a Jill Shalvis book. She's a consistently elegant, bold, clever writer . . . Very witty – I laughed out loud countless times and these scenes are sizzling' *All About Romance*

'If you have not read a Jill Shalvis novel yet, then you really have not read a real romance yet either!' *Book Cove Reviews*

'Engaging writing, characters that walk straight into your heart, touching, hilarious' *Library Journal*

'Witty, fun, and sexy – the perfect romance!' Lori Foster, *New York Times* bestselling author

'Riveting suspense laced with humor and heart is her hallmark, and Jill Shalvis always delivers' Donna Kauffman, *USA Today* bestselling author

'Humor, intrigue, and scintillating sex. Jill Shalvis is a total original' Suzanne Forster, *New York Times* bestselling author

'Fast-paced ... ay' Cherry Adair, *New*

*By Jill Shalvis*

*Animal Magnetism Series*
Animal Magnetism
Animal Attraction
Rescue My Heart
Rumour Has It
Then Came You

# Jill
# SHALVIS

## Animal
## magnetism

**headline**
ETERNAL

Published by arrangement with Berkley,
a member of Penguin Group (USA) LLC.
A Penguin Random House Company.

First published in Great Britain in 2014
by HEADLINE ETERNAL
An imprint of HEADLINE PUBLISHING GROUP

1

Cataloguing in Publication Data is available from the British Library

ISBN 978 1 4722 1719 6

Offset in Times by Avon DataSet Ltd, Bidford-on-Avon, Warwickshire

Printed and bound by CPI Group (UK) Ltd, Croydon, CR0 4YY

Headline's policy is to use papers that are natural, renewable and recyclable
products and made from wood grown in sustainable forests. The logging and
manufacturing processes are expected to conform to the environmental
regulations of the country of origin.

HEADLINE PUBLISHING GROUP
An Hachette UK Company
338 Euston Road
London NW1 3BH

www.headlineeternal.com
www.headline.co.uk
www.hachette.co.uk

*To Frat Boy, Ashes, and Sadie*
*for the animal inspiration and unconditional love.*

# Animal
# magnetism

## One

B rady Miller's ideal Saturday was pretty simple—sleep in, be woken by a hot, naked woman for sex, followed by a breakfast that he didn't have to cook.

On this particularly early June Saturday, he consoled himself with one out of the three, stopping at 7-Eleven for coffee, two egg and sausage breakfast wraps, and a Snickers bar.

Breakfast of champions.

Heading to the counter to check out, he nodded to the convenience store clerk.

She had her Bluetooth in her ear, presumably connected to the cell phone glowing in her pocket as she rang him up. "He can't help it, Kim," she was saying. "He's a *guy*." At this, she sent Brady a half-apologetic, half-commiserating smile. She was twentysomething, wearing spray-painted-on skinny jeans, a white wife-beater tank top revealing black lacy bra straps, and so much mascara that Brady had no idea how she kept her eyes open.

"You know what they say," she went on as she scanned

his items. "A guy thinks about sex once every eight seconds. No, it's true, I read it in *Cosmo*. Uh-huh, hang on." She glanced at Brady, pursing her glossy lips. "Hey, cutie, you're a guy."

"Last I checked."

She popped her gum and grinned at him. "Would you say you think about sex every eight seconds?"

"Nah." Every ten, tops. He fished through his pocket for cash.

"My customer says no," she said into her phone, sounding disappointed. "But *Cosmo* said a man might deny it out of self-preservation. And in any case, how can you trust a guy who has sex on the brain 24/7?"

Brady nodded to the truth of that statement and accepted his change. Gathering his breakfast, he stepped outside where he was hit by the morning fresh air of the rugged, majestic Idaho Bitterroot mountain range. Quite a change from the stifling airlessness of the Middle East or the bitter desolation and frigid temps of Afghanistan. But being back on friendly soil was new enough that his eyes still automatically swept his immediate surroundings.

*Always a soldier*, his last girlfriend had complained.

And that was probably true. It was who he was, the discipline and carefulness deeply engrained, and he didn't see that changing anytime soon. Noting nothing that required his immediate attention, he went back to mainlining his caffeine. Sighing in sheer pleasure, he took a big bite of the first breakfast wrap, then hissed out a sharp breath because damn. *Hot*. This didn't slow him down much. He was so hungry his legs felt hollow. In spite of the threat of scalding his tongue to the roof of his mouth, he sucked down nearly the entire thing before he began to relax.

Traffic was nonexistent, but Sunshine, Idaho, wasn't exactly hopping. It'd been a damn long time since he'd been here, *years* in fact. And longer still since he'd wanted to be here. He took another drag of fresh air. Hard to believe, but he'd actually missed the good old US of A. He'd missed the sports. He'd missed the women. He'd missed the price of gas. He'd missed free will.

But mostly he'd missed the food. He tossed the wrapper from the first breakfast wrap into a trash bin and started in on his second, feeling almost . . . content. Yeah, damn it was good to be back, even if he was only here temporarily, as a favor. Hell, anything without third-world starvation, terrorists, or snipers and bombs would be a five-star vacation.

"Look out, incoming!"

At the warning, Brady deftly stepped out of the path of the bike barreling down at him.

"Sorry!" the kid yelled back.

Up until yesterday, a shout like that would have meant dropping to the ground, covering his head, and hoping for the best. Since there were no enemy insurgents, Brady merely raised the hand still gripping his coffee in a friendly salute. "No problem."

But the kid was already long gone, and Brady shook his head. The quiet was amazing, and he took in the oak tree–lined sidewalks, the clean and neat little shops, galleries and cafés—all designed to bring in some tourist money to subsidize the mining and ranching community. For someone who'd spent so much time in places where grime and suffering trumped hope and joy, it felt a little bit like landing in the Twilight Zone.

"Easy now, Duchess."

At the soft, feminine voice, Brady turned and looked into the eyes of a woman walking a . . . hell, he had no idea. The thing pranced around like it had a stick up its ass.

Okay, a dog. He was pretty sure.

The woman smiled at Brady. "Hello, how are you?"

"Fine, thanks," he responded automatically, but she hadn't slowed her pace.

*Just being polite*, he thought, and tried to remember the concept. Culture shock, he decided. He was suffering from a hell of a culture shock. Probably he should have given himself some time to adjust before doing this, before coming here of all places, but it was too late now.

Besides, he'd put it off long enough. He'd been asked to come, multiple times over the years. He'd employed every tactic at his disposal: avoiding, evading, ignoring, but nothing worked with the two people on the planet more stubborn than him.

His brothers.

Not blood brothers, but that didn't appear to matter to Dell or Adam. The three of them had been in the same foster home for two years about a million years ago. Twenty-four months. A blink of an eye really. But to Dell and Adam, it'd been enough to bond the three of them for life.

Brady stuffed in another bite of his second breakfast wrap, added coffee, and squinted in the bright June sunshine. Jerking his chin down, the sunglasses on top of his head obligingly slipped to his nose.

Better.

He headed to his truck parked at the corner but stopped short just in time to watch a woman in an old Jeep rear-end it.

"Crap. *Crap*." Lilah Young stared at the truck she'd just rear-ended and gave herself exactly two seconds to have a pity party. This is what her life had come to. She had to work in increments of seconds.

A wet, warm tongue laved her hand and she looked over at the three wriggling little bodies in the box on the passenger's seat of her Jeep.

Two puppies and a potbellied pig.

As the co-owner of the sole kennel in town, she was baby-sitting Mrs. Swanson's "babies" again today, which included pickup and drop-off services. This was in part because Mrs. Swanson was married to the doctor who'd delivered Lilah twenty-eight years ago, but also because Mrs. Swanson was the mother of Lilah's favorite ex-boyfriend.

Not that Lilah had a lot of exes. Only two.

Okay, three. But one of them didn't count, the one who after four years she *still* hoped all of his good parts shriveled up and fell off. And he'd had good parts, too, damn him. She'd read somewhere that every woman got a freebie stupid mistake when it came to men. She liked that. She only wished it applied to everything in life.

Because driving with Mrs. Swanson's babies and—

"Quack-quack!" said the mallard duck loose in the backseat.

—A mallard duck loose in the backseat had been a doozey of a mistake.

Resisting the urge to thunk her head against the steering wheel, Lilah hopped out of the Jeep to check the damage she'd caused to the truck, eyes squinted because everyone knew that helped.

The truck's bumper sported a sizable dent and crack, but thanks to the tow hitch, there was no real obvious frame damage. The realization brought a rush of relief so great her knees wobbled.

That is until she caught sight of the front of her Jeep. It was so ancient that it was hard to tell if it had ever really been red once upon a time or if it was just one big friggin' rust bucket, but that no longer seemed important given that her front end was mashed up.

"Quack-quack." In the backseat, Abigail was flapping her wings, getting enough lift to stick her head out the window.

Lilah put her hand on the duck's face and gently pressed her back inside. "Stay."

"Quack—"

*"Stay."* Wanting to make sure the Jeep would start before she began the task of either looking for the truck's owner or leaving a note, Lilah hopped behind the wheel. She never should have turned off the engine because her starter had

been trying to die for several weeks now. She'd be lucky to get it running again. Beside her, the puppies and piglet were wriggling like crazy, whimpering and panting as they scrambled to stand on each other, trying to escape their box. She took a minute to pat them all, soothing them, and then with her sole thought being *Please start*, she turned the ignition key.

And got only an ominous click.

"Come on, baby," she coaxed, trying again. "There's no New Transportation budget, so *please* come on . . ."

Nothing.

"Pretty sure you killed it."

With a gasp, she turned her head. A man stood there. Tall, broad-shouldered, with dark brown hair that was cut short and slightly spiky, like maybe he hadn't bothered to do much with it after his last shower except run his fingers through it. His clothes were simple: cargoes and a plain shirt, both emphasizing a leanly muscled body so completely devoid of body fat that it would have made any woman sigh—if she hadn't just rear-ended a truck.

Probably *his truck*.

Having clearly just come out of the convenience store, he held a large coffee and what smelled deliriously, deliciously like an egg and sausage and cheese breakfast wrap.

*Be still, her hungry heart . . .*

"Quack-quack."

"Hush, Abigail," Lilah murmured, flicking the duck a glance in the rearview mirror before turning back to the man.

His eyes were hidden behind reflective sunglasses, but she had no doubt they were on her. She could feel them, sharp and assessing. Everything about his carriage said military or cop. She wasn't sure if that was good or bad. He was a stranger to her, and there weren't that many of them in Sunshine. Or anywhere in Idaho for that matter. "Your truck?" she asked, fingers crossed that he'd say no.

"Yep." He popped the last of the breakfast wrap in his mouth and calmly tossed the wrapper into the trash can a good ten feet away. Chewing thoughtfully, he swallowed and then sucked down some coffee.

Just the scent of it had her sighing in jealousy. Probably, she shouldn't have skipped breakfast. And just as probably, she'd give a body part up for that coffee. Hell, she'd give up *two* for the candy bar sticking out of his shirt pocket. Just thinking about it had her stomach rumbling loud as thunder. She looked upward to see if she could blame the sound on an impending storm, but for the first time in two weeks there wasn't a cloud in the sky. "I'm sorry," she said. "About this."

He pushed the sunglasses to the top of his head, further disheveling his hair—not that he appeared to care.

"Luckily the damage seems to be mostly to my Jeep," she went on.

Sharp blue eyes held hers. "Karma?"

"Actually, I don't believe in karma." Nope, she believed in making one's own fate—which she'd done by once again studying too late into the night, not getting enough sleep, and . . . crashing into his truck.

"Hmm." He sipped some more coffee, and she told herself that leaping out of the Jeep to snatch it from his hands would be bad form.

"How about felony hit-and-run?" he asked conversationally. "You believe in that?"

"I wasn't running off."

"Because you can't," he ever so helpfully pointed out. "The Jeep's dead."

"Yes, but . . ." She broke off, realizing how it must look to him. He'd found her behind her own wheel, cursing her vehicle for not starting. He couldn't know that she'd never just leave the scene of an accident. Most likely he'd taken one look at the panic surely all over her face and assumed the worst about her.

The panic doubled. And also, her pity party was back, and for a beat, she let the despair rise from her gut and block her throat, where it threatened to choke her. With a bone-deep weary sigh, she dropped her head to the steering wheel.

"Hey. *Hey.*" Suddenly he was at her side. "Did you hit your head?"

"No, I—"

But before she could finish that sentence, he opened the Jeep door and crouched at her side, looking her over.

"I'm fine. Really," she promised when he cupped and lifted her face to his, staring into her eyes, making her squirm like the babies in the box next to her.

"How many fingers am I holding up?" A quiet demand. His hand was big, the two fingers he held up long. His eyes were calmly intense, his mouth grim. He hadn't shaved that morning she noted inanely, maybe not the day before either, but the scruff only made him seem all the more . . . male.

"Two," she whispered.

Nodding, he dropped his gaze to run over her body. She had dressed for work this morning, which included cleaning out the kennels, so she wore a denim jacket over a T-shirt, baggy Carhartts, boots, and a knit cap to cover her hair.

To say she wasn't looking ready for her close-up was the understatement of the year. "Do you think you can close the door before—"

Too late.

Sensing a means of escape, Abigail started flapping her wings, attempting to fly out past Lilah's face.

She nearly made it, too, but the man, still hunkered at Lilah's side, caught the duck.

By the neck.

"Gak," said a strangled Abigail.

"Don't hurt her!" Lilah cried.

With what might have been a very small smile playing

at the corners of his mouth, the man leaned past Lilah and settled the duck on the passenger floorboard.

"Stay," he said in a low-pitched, authoritative voice that brooked no argument.

Lilah opened her mouth to tell him that ducks didn't follow directions, but Abigail totally did. She not only stayed, she shut up. Probably afraid she'd be roasted duck if she didn't. Staring at the brown-headed, orange-footed duck in shock, she said, "I really am sorry about your truck. I'll give you my number so I can pay for damages."

"You could just give me your insurance info."

Her insurance. *Damn*. The rates would go up this time, for sure. Hell, they'd gone up last quarter when she'd had that little run-in with her own mailbox.

But that one hadn't been her fault. The snake she'd been transporting had gotten loose and startled her, and she'd accidentally aligned her front bumper with the mailbox.

But today, this one—definitely her fault.

"Let me guess," he said dryly when she sat there nibbling on her lip. "You don't have insurance."

"No, I do." To prove it, she reached for her wallet, which she kept between the two front seats. Except, of course, it wasn't there. "Hang on, I know I have it . . ." Twisting, she searched the floor, beneath the box of puppies and piglet, in the backseat . . .

And then she remembered.

In her hurry to pick up Mrs. Swanson's animals on time, she'd left it in her office at the kennels. "Okay, this looks bad but I left my wallet at home."

His expression was dialed into Resignation.

"I swear," she said. "I really do have insurance. I just got the new certificate and I put it in my wallet to stick in my glove box, but I hadn't gotten to that yet. I'll give you my number and you can call me for the information."

He gazed at her steadily. "You have a name?"

"Lilah." She scrounged around for a piece of paper. Nothing, of course. But she did find five bucks and the earring she'd thought that Abigail had eaten, and a pen.

Still crouched at her side, the man held out his cell phone. Impossibly aware of how big he was, how very good looking, not to mention how he surrounded her still crouched at her side balanced easily on the balls of his feet, she entered her number into his phone. When it came to keying in her name, she nearly titled herself Dumbass of the Day.

"You fake numbering me, Lilah?" he asked softly, still close, so very close.

"No." This came out as a squeak so she cleared her throat. And, when he just looked at her, she added truthfully, "I only fake-number the jerk tourists inside Crystal's, the ones who won't take no for an answer."

"Crystal's?"

"The bar down the street. Listen, you might want to wait awhile before you call me. It's going to take me at least an hour to get home." *Carrying the mewling, wriggling babies* and *walking a duck.*

He paused, utterly motionless in a way that she admired, since she'd never managed to sit still for longer than two minutes. Okay, thirty seconds, but who was counting. "What?" she asked.

"I'm just trying to figure out if you're for real or if you're a master bullshit specialist."

That surprised a laugh out of her. "Well, I *can* be a master bullshit specialist," she admitted. "But I'm not bullshitting you right now."

He studied her face for another long moment, then nodded. "Fine, I'll wait to call you. You going to ask my name?"

Her gaze ran over his very masculine features, then dropped traitorously to linger over his very fine body for a single beat. "I was really sort of hoping that I wasn't going to need it."

He laughed, the sound washing over her and making something low in her belly quiver again.

"Okay, yes," she said. "I want to know your name."

"Brady Miller."

A flicker of something went through her, like the name should mean something to her, but discombobulated as she was, she couldn't concentrate. "Well, Brady Miller, thanks for being patient with me." She reached for Abigail's leash, attaching it to the collar around the duck's neck.

"Quack."

"Shh." Then she grabbed the box of babies. It was damn heavy, but she had her dignity to consider so she soldiered on, turning to get out of the Jeep, bumping right into Brady's broad chest. "Excuse me."

He straightened to his full height and backed up enough to let her out, helping her support the box with an ease that had her envying his muscles now instead of drooling over them.

Actually, that was a lie. She managed both the envying and the drooling. She was an excellent multitasker.

"You're really going to walk?" he asked, rubbing his chin as he considered the box.

"Well, when I skip or run, Abigail's leash gets tangled in my legs."

"Smart-ass." Brady peered at the two puppies and pot-bellied piglet. To his credit, he didn't so much as blink. "They potty trained?"

"No."

He grimaced. "How about the duck?"

"She'd say yes, but she'd be lying."

He exhaled. "That's what I was afraid of." He took the box from her, the underside of his arms brushing the outside of hers.

He was warm. And smelled delicious. Like sexy man and something even better—breakfast wraps and coffee.

"What are you doing?"

"Giving you a ride." He narrowed his eyes at the duck on the leash. "You," he said, "behave."

"Quack."

Without another word, Brady strode to his truck and put the box inside.

Lilah looked down at Abigail. "You heard him," she whispered, having no choice but to follow. "Behave."

# Two

Brady wasn't an impulsive guy. Years on the streets as an untethered, unwanted kid had taught him a certain innate caution—which had saved his life on more than one occasion. A stint flying for the army and then Special Forces had only hammered it home.

But it hadn't been until he'd left the military and became a pilot for hire in places that weren't safe for so much as a cockroach that he'd really learned to appreciate his instincts.

And yet those instincts abandoned him in a blink as he offered his Danica Patrick wannabe a ride.

Luckily, she was smarter than him.

She was still standing by her Jeep, watching him carefully, clearly unwilling to just hop into his truck.

"I don't bite."

She laughed a little. Nervous, he realized. He made her nervous. She walked to his truck and peered cautiously inside. He wasn't sure what she was looking for; signs that he was a murderer or rapist maybe, and he looked into the truck as well. She straightened, gasped at how close he now was, and stumbled back a step.

Reaching out, he steadied her with a hand to her hip—which, he couldn't help but notice, was nice and curvy and warm beneath his palm. Her eyes were a clear, deep mossy green. She had a few freckles across her pert nose and the hint of a sunburn. Beneath her blue knit cap, her straight brown hair hit her shoulders, with long bangs shoved off to the side as if in afterthought. Her mouth was full but naked. No makeup for this pretty little felon. She wasn't model beautiful, but there was something undeniably arresting about her features, something that drew him right in . . . Probably it was the blatant mistrust she had all over her face. "I'm not a kidnapper. Or a woman-napper."

"And yet you do have candy in your pocket."

"If I promise not to offer it to you, or say 'Hey, little girl' in a really creepy voice, will you get in?"

Her gaze was locked onto the Snickers sticking out of his pocket, and into the silence her stomach once again rumbled with shocking vehemence.

He actually felt a smile curve his mouth. "Or maybe I *should* offer it to you. Are you hungry?" He hadn't considered the fact that maybe she was homeless, but he took in her clothes and rust bucket Jeep and wondered. He held out the Snickers bar.

Looking away, a faint tinge colored her cheeks, she shook her head. "I couldn't possibly—"

"I have another," he lied.

Shielding her eyes from the bright sun, she gave him a long, serious once-over. Not playing fair, he tore open the candy bar and wafted the chocolate beneath her nose.

"You're evil," she said, and snatched it out of his hand. She broke it in half and then slid his part back into his pocket. Sinking her teeth into her portion with a big bite, she went still, then moaned in pleasure.

"Do you need a moment alone with that?" he asked, amused. And also a little turned on.

"Oh my God." Her voice was thick and throaty. *"Good."*

"So it's true," he murmured, watching her mouth avidly. It was a really great mouth, soft, with a plump lower lip. "Everyone has their price."

"Yes, and mine is chocolate. Offer me some and probably I'd follow you anywhere," she admitted.

"Probably?"

"Well, you're still a stranger."

"I told you my name."

"I'd need more than that."

He just looked at her, smiling. They both knew he'd had her at chocolate.

Laughing at herself, she took another bite of the Snickers, licking that lower lip of hers to get a stray strand of caramel. "Seriously, I was raised better than this. Make me feel okay about getting into a stranger's truck."

What could he possibly tell her that wouldn't scare her off or deepen the mistrust? And why did he even care? "I'm a pilot," he said.

"Okay." She nodded. "That's good. I've never heard of a pilot who murders people. Who do you fly for?"

"An international organization who hires me out to places like Doctors Without Borders, the government, whoever's paying. So see? You're safe enough from me. Get in."

She looked into the back again. "What's with the camera case?"

An *observant*, junk-food-loving felon. "I'm also a photographer." Sometimes even a paid one. His photos had been in both *Outsider* and *National Geographic* this last year. Given his adrenaline-fueled life, taking pictures grounded him in a way nothing else could.

Well, except sex. Sex was always his first choice, of course. Not that *that* would be happening while here in Sunshine.

Lilah was watching him closely again. Mistrustful little thing, which for some reason, made him like her all the more. "It's just a ride," he said quietly.

"Yeah. Um, so do you ever lure women into your truck with candy bars in order to get them to pose naked for you?"

"Nah. My editor frowns on the exploitation of women. It'd have to be a side job and only if you say please."

She rolled her eyes at him but took a step closer to the passenger door. "So does being a photographer ever get you laid?"

There was no good answer to that question, but yeah, sometimes it got him laid.

Clearly reading his face, she shook her head. "Don't tell me. You trade on your good looks and that whole sort of badass vibe you've got going on, right? And women fall for it hook, line, and sinker."

"Yes, but you're on to me, so no falling for you. Plus you've got protection." He jerked his chin toward the mallard at her feet. "A guard duck."

They both looked at Abigail, who was busy preening and fussing with her feathers to get them just right. "Is it legal to own a duck?" he asked.

"I'm duck-sitting. Are you sure you're not also a cop?" Lilah wanted to know.

"Why, do I look like one?" He felt the weight of her scrutiny. He knew what she saw when she looked at him. Dark hair cut short enough to be maintenance-free—when he remembered to have it cut at all. Tanned skin and a rangy, tough build from long months at a time in places where three squares a day were pure fantasy. The nondescript clothes he'd gotten used to wearing so as not to be marked as an American in places where being an American meant certain death or far worse.

"Actually," she finally said, "you look like trouble." Her gaze touched over his features. "The sort of trouble that women actively seek out against their better judgment. It's sort of a fatal genetic flaw of my entire gender."

She was right about the trouble part, but he'd never met a woman who liked it for long. "So now that we've established that I'm probably not a murderer, what's it going to be? A long walk home with . . ." He gestured to the box on the front passenger's-side floorboards. "Two puppies and whatever that thing is, or—"

"A potbellied pig."

He looked closer. "Are you sure?"

She laughed. "Yes!"

"Okay, I'll take your word for it. You getting in or what?"

She took another bite of his Snickers and studied him from those remarkable eyes. "The road out to my place needs some work," she finally said. "It got washed out in the floods last week and hasn't been repaired yet."

At least she had a place. "I can handle it."

"I don't know . . ." Her eyes sized him up as if she were six feet tall instead of *maybe* five foot four in her steel-toe work boots. "In my experience, guys are rarely the drivers that they think they are."

In the army, he'd driven in and out of hot spots that made Iraq and Afghanistan look like Disneyland. Hell, for his more recent work, piloting for hire, he'd driven on roads that didn't officially exist. He had no doubt he could take on anything the serene mining town of Sunshine dished up.

Having apparently made a decision, Lilah slapped a hand to his chest to push him out of her way. Because it amused him that she thought she could move him at all, he let her. As she shifted past him, the scent of her hair filled his nostrils with something like . . . honey, maybe? Whatever it was, it was better than anything he'd smelled in a long time.

She climbed up into his truck, her baggy Carhartts tightening across her back end as she stretched farther to check on her box of babies. *Yeah*, he thought, *there really is noth-*

*ing on God's green earth nicer than a woman's ass*, and he took a minute to soak in the sweet view before walking around and angling behind the wheel. "Where to?"

"North straight through town."

Town was relatively quiet, and so was his passenger. The human one. Not the animal ones. The duck in the backseat hadn't shut up for more than two seconds since he'd turned on the engine.

"Quack, quack, quack . . ."

Brady finally cut his eyes to it via the rearview mirror. "Hey."

Abigail looked at him.

"I know this great duck soup recipe," he told her.

Lilah gasped.

Abigail shut up.

Not the animals in the box at her feet, though. The two puppies and little piglet were wrestling and rolling around each other, having a party for three.

At the end of town, the road went from smooth concrete to torn-up, pitted asphalt, and as Lilah had promised, it was a mess. He hit a pothole and got a little air.

"Uh-oh," Lilah said.

"What?" He couldn't look, because she'd been right—the road was bad. If he took his eyes off of it, they were going to go flying. "And Jesus, you weren't kidding about—" He broke off when Lilah clicked out of her seat belt and dropped to her knees on the floorboard.

"It's okay," she cooed softly, and crawled toward Brady, touching his calf.

He went very, very still as she leaned down even farther, reaching between his legs . . .

"I've got you." Her voice pure sex, and still in that erotic position, began to make kissy kissy noises that went straight to his . . .

"There," she murmured, lifting the potbellied piglet to cuddle against her chest.

Brady let out a very long breath and realized he was jealous of a fucking pig.

Lilah flashed an apologetic smile and climbed back into her seat, rebuckling her seat belt. "Runaway."

It took him a full sixty seconds to find his voice. "You seem to have your hands full."

"Little bit." She turned in her seat to face him. "And I really am sorry about all this. Not that it's an excuse, but I stayed up too late last night studying, and I wasn't paying close enough attention to what I was doing."

"What are you studying?"

"Animal science. I'm trying to finish up my degree on-line at night. I'd like to go on to vet school after that."

"Makes for a long day."

"Yeah. Keep going straight here."

On the outside of Sunshine now, the road was lined by forest, thick and unforgiving. Classic northern Idaho. After the glaciers of the last great Ice Age had melted away, they'd left meandering rivers and lakes of all sizes, most pristine, some more remote and intimate than any of the places in the far corners of the planet in which he'd been. Once upon a time, the vastness of those Bitterroot Mountains and the waters of the Coeur d'Alene had changed his life, given him a sense of self when he'd desperately needed it. He didn't need it now. He knew who he was.

A man not quite ready to face the past that was about to be shoved in his face.

"So what brings you to Sunshine?" she asked, smiling when he glanced at her. "Maybe I just want to know more about the guy I'm going to buy a new rear bumper for. Thanks for sharing."

"No problem." He watched as she licked the last of the chocolate off her lips. "Still hungry?" he asked, amused.

"Yeah." She licked her finger, scooping up a fleck of chocolate. He was certain she didn't mean for it to be sexual, but watching her tongue run over her lips, hearing the sweet sounds of suction as she worked those fingers, was giving him a zing nevertheless. It was hard to tell what the rest of her body was like in those baggy clothes, but apparently it didn't matter in the least.

He was attracted to her, and he handed her the other half of his candy bar.

She stared at it like it was a brick of gold. "I'm on a diet." But she took it. "A see-food diet, apparently. I see food and I eat it." She took another big bite. "I mean, I *try* to eat healthy, but I have a little thing for junk food. Uh–oh . . ."

"What now?"

"Abigail, no." She reached back and pulled the strap of Brady's duffel bag from the duck's beak. "She also likes to eat." She laughed easily, and he found himself smiling at the sound with rusty facial muscles. His shoulders loosened and he realized he was feeling relaxed.

And even more odd—at ease.

"Are you here on vacation?" Lilah asked, petting the creatures in the box at her feet.

"Not exactly."

She let that go, leaning back to watch the scenery, which was admittedly worthy of the fascination. Lush and green, the mountains loomed high thirty miles off in the distance, the exotic rock formation forming mouth-gaping canyons he'd once explored as an angry teen looking for a place to belong.

His passenger let the silence linger, which he suspected was unusual for her. When he felt her watching him instead of the landscape, he turned his head and briefly met her gaze. Yep, she was waiting patiently for him to crack the silence. A good tactic, but it wouldn't work on him.

"Huh," she finally said, slightly disgruntled.

He felt the corners of his mouth turn up. "Used to people caving?"

"*And* spilling their guts." She eyed him again, thoughtfully. "You're a tough one to crack, Brady Miller, pilot and photographer. Really tough."

Not anything he hadn't heard before. "I was thinking the same could be said of you," he said.

That got him a two-hundred-watt smile, along with a sweet, musical laugh. "True," she agreed.

The road ended, and he had two choices—the highway straight ahead, or left to head away from the towering peaks and out to ranching land, where as far as the eye could see was nothing but gently rolling hills and hidden lakes and rivers.

"Left," she said, pointing to a dirt road. "And then left again."

The road here was narrow, rutted, and far rougher. "Ah. You're bringing me to the boondocks to off me so you don't have to pay for the damages to my truck."

She laughed. She really did have a great laugh, and something went through him, a long-forgotten surge of emotion. "Not going to deny it?" he asked, sliding her a look meant to intimidate.

She wasn't. Intimidated. Not in the least. In fact, she was smiling. "Worried?" she asked, brow raised, face lit with humor.

Giving her another long look—which she simply steadily returned—he shook his head and kept driving. "I never worry."

"No? Maybe you could teach me the trick of *that* sometime."

Yeah, except he didn't plan on being around long enough to teach anyone anything.

His enigmatic passenger shifted in her seat and crossed her legs. The hem of her Carhartts rose up, giving him a good look at her scuffed work boots and the cute little black and pink polka-dotted socks peeking over the top of them.

Which of course made him wonder what else she was hiding beneath those work clothes.

The growth thickened on either side of the road, which narrowed, commanding his attention. He caught glimpses of a sprawling ranch, and then a glistening body of water, flashes of brilliance in a color that changed the definition of blue. The road narrowed again, and at the hairpin turn, two of his four tires caught air.

"Not bad," she said in admiration. "So how does a pilot get such mad driving skills, anyway? Because you're not just a pilot and photographer."

"No?"

"No. You've got a quiet intensity about you, an edge. It's why I thought cop or military."

She was good. "Army."

"Ah," she murmured, saying nothing more, which both surprised him and left him grateful at the same time. People were naturally curious, and his life choices and experiences tended to bring that curiosity out, but he didn't like talking about himself.

"Here we are," Lilah said a minute later. "Home sweet home."

The road ended in a small clearing, at the top of which sat a tiny cabin next to what looked like a large barn. The sign on the barn read SUNSHINE KENNELS.

Peeking behind the property was a small lake, shining brightly, surrounded by a meadow radiant with flowers, and lined by the not-so-distant jagged ridges stabbing into the sky.

Actually, Brady knew this land fairly well, though it'd been a long time. Emotions tangled with the need to reach for the beauty wherever he could find it, and he soaked it all in, letting it bring him something that had been sorely lacking in his life.

Pleasure.

Lilah unhooked her seat belt. "It's special."

"Yeah."

"The Coeur d'Alene Indians found it," she said. "They lived here." She paused. "The myth goes that the water has healing powers."

He slid his gaze her way, wondering if she believed it.

"They based their lives around the legend." She paused and bit her lower lip, like she knew damn well he didn't buy it. "Don't laugh when I tell you the rest."

He wasn't feeling much like laughing. Not while watching her abuse that lush lower lip that he suddenly wanted to soothe. With his tongue. No, laughing was the last thing on his mind.

"Legend says that if you take a moonlight dip, you'll supposedly find your one true love."

"Of course." He nodded. "It's always midnight. So, do you swim often?"

"Never at midnight."

He couldn't help it, he laughed.

With a slow shake of her head and a smile curving her mouth, she reached out and touched a finger to his curved lips. "You're a cynic," she chided.

It'd been a long time since someone had touched him, unexpected or otherwise. A very long time, and he wrapped his finger around her wrist to hold her to him, letting his eyes drift closed.

"For how big and tough you are," she said very softly, "you have a kind mouth."

He opened his eyes and met her gaze. "You should know it's not kindness I'm feeling at the moment."

"No?" A brow arched, and the light in her eyes spoke of amusement, along with a flash of heat. "What *do* you feel?"

Dangerous territory there. Nothing new for him. He did some of his best work in dangerous territory. "Guess."

Still smiling, she leaned in so that their lips were nothing but a whisper apart. Even surrounded by a duck, two puppies, and a potbellied piglet, she still smelled amazing. He wanted to yank her in and smell her some more, but he held very still, absorbing her closeness, letting her take the lead.

When she spoke, every word had her lips ghosting against his, her breath all warm, chocolately goodness. "I'm more of a doer," she whispered, and kissed him.

She tasted as good as she smelled. Then almost before it'd even begun, she pulled back. "Thank you."

He had no idea what exactly she was thanking him for now but he was all for more of it. Their connection, light as it'd been, had still carried enough spark to jump-start his engines. "For . . . ?"

"For driving me all the way out here." Again she was letting her lips brush his with every word. "And for not being a serial killer." She was staring at his mouth. "And for . . . everything."

Not wholly in charge of his faculties, he took over the lead, pulling her in until she was straining over the console before covering her mouth with his.

With a low murmur of acquiescence, she wrapped her arms around his neck, angling her head for the best fit, deepening the kiss.

Which worked for him.

He lost track of time, but when she pulled back, breathless and panting for air, she licked her bottom lip as if she needed that last little taste of him.

He knew the feeling. He was more than a little flummoxed by the loss of blood to his brain. She'd felt good. Good and soft and willing. He had one hand low at her back, the tips of his fingers tucked into the waistband of her pants, against warm, satiny skin while his other hand cupped her jaw.

"Gotta go," she whispered, and pulled free. Twice she tried to grab the door and missed. Leaning past her, he pushed it open for her.

"And we're still at least a hundred yards from the water," she muttered. "Imagine if we got *in* it."

He heard himself laugh. "It's not the water." He wasn't sure what it was, but he was positive it wasn't the water.

"Cynic," she repeated without heat, looking both flustered, and aroused.

An incredibly appealing combination that made him want to haul her onto his lap and show her *cynic*. "True enough," he agreed. "But it takes one to know one."

She snorted and it was the craziest thing, but hell if he didn't feel the tug of attraction for her all the way to his toes.

Yeah. Definitely dangerous territory.

"Wait here." She slipped out of the truck and vanished inside the kennels. Twenty seconds later she was back with her insurance card. "Keep it, I have another." She wrapped Abigail's leash around her wrist and grabbed the box. "Thanks for the ride, stranger." Then, with a flash of a smile, she sauntered off in those baggy Carhartts toward the kennels, looking for all the world like a princess going into her palace.

# Three

ilah Young forced herself to cross the yard and get all the way to the front door of the kennels before allowing herself to glance back at the truck.

He was still there: Brady Miller, pilot, photographer, kisser extraordinaire, slouched behind the wheel, hair still messed up from her fingers, watching her.

Letting out a low breath, she pressed a hand low to her abdomen. "Sweet baby Jesus," she whispered.

"Quack," Abigail said.

With a low laugh, Lilah opened the door and managed a smile at her business partner, Cruz Delgado. "I'm back. Again."

Cruz's perfectly toned hard body was still where it had been two minutes ago when she'd come running in—sprawled flat on his back in the center of their greeting room, with Lulu on top of him.

Lulu was a lamb that thought she was a puppy. She belonged to one of their clients who was out of town for a few days, and she sometimes needed a little extra TLC in the middle of her day. Okay, all of the time she needed a little extra TLC. Lulu was a 'ho for TLC. "How many times do I have to tell you," Lilah said to the lamb. "Cruz is mine."

From the floor, Cruz grinned, then pushed Lulu off of him and sat up. His silky dark hair fell into his face, but he shoved it back, flashing laughing melted-chocolate eyes Lilah's way. "She was feeling lonely. We were playing tag. She won." He rose to his feet, scooped Abigail up, and disappeared into the back. When he returned without the duck, he took the box from Lilah's arms next and smiled down at the three sleeping babies. "They were good for you?"

"Not even close, the little heathens. Don't get me started."

Cruz looked out the window at the truck turning around in the front yard. "So where's your Jeep?"

She didn't really want to talk about it, not when she could still hear Brady's truck's motor, just the sound making her nipples hard. "The Jeep's on Main. Don't ask. Today's crazy enough. We have a full house, and I have a message that there's a new rescue at Belle Haven."

She and Cruz had rotating shifts that allowed the kennel to be open for enough hours in the day to be effective. They traded off between two shifts—six A.M. to two P.M., and noon to eight P.M.—with part-time help from high school kids on the weekends and as needed.

Lilah typically took the early shift because Cruz didn't do early. But he had a gig tonight in Coeur d'Alene, where he moonlighted as a bass guitarist in a cover rock band, so he'd come in at six o'clock.

Along with the kennels, Lilah was the go-to person in town when there was an abandoned animal. There was no official humane society in the area, so if an animal needed temporary shelter, she was it. This came mostly from her inability to bear seeing anything suffer and the fact that she got far too attached to every animal she met. The rescue part of the business was extremely nonprofit and depended on grants and donations, so Lilah—along with Cruz—worked hard to keep the kennels afloat.

Their only source of income. A typical workday began at the crack of dawn with the day's client files spread out in front of her. She reviewed all the pets coming in or going out and decided where they would be kept. The facility had several sections: the outside pens, the inside pens, and the inside playroom, where the friendly, well-adjusted animals could hang out together under careful supervision. The not-so-friendly and grumpy older clients, were separated out from the pack and dealt with individually. It was usually those animals that claimed Lilah's heart the fastest.

Part of the morning's record-keeping process always involved reviewing any other important events such as vet appointments, client visits, and employee notes. In today's case, there'd been an abandoned dog dumped off at Belle Haven, the veterinary center a half mile down the road.

Belle Haven was run by her two closest friends, Adam and Dell. They were holding the dog for her. She'd pick him up and care for him until she placed him in a foster home. But first she looked herself over. "I got up too late to grab a shower. I'm going to go take a quick one now before I head to Belle Haven."

"Need me to soap your back?"

She slid Cruz a long look. "Been there, done that, remember?"

"I remember it was good."

"Uh-huh." They'd dated for approximately two weeks several years back, until they'd realized they were far more suited for this, for a friendship. "Except for the part where we drove each other crazy," she reminded him.

"Yeah." He blew out a sigh. "Maybe you could work on not driving me crazy."

She laughed. Living in a small town had made it hard for

her to find a guy she meshed with. There weren't all that many to choose from in the first place, and the few that there were, she'd known a long time. Forever.

She loved Cruz, but they were day and night when it came right down to it. And the biggie: she wasn't in love with him, and she never would be.

Ditto for him. He liked to be the center of a woman's universe, and she had too many things in her orbit to give herself wholly. Luckily, they'd both survived the attempt, and so had their business. "Let me guess—Marie dumped your sorry ass again?"

He shrugged. "Little bit, yeah."

Lulu bumped her head into Lilah's thighs until Lilah bent and stroked the lamb's ears. "What did you do this time?"

He sighed. "I forgot our anniversary."

"What anniversary? You've only been dating a few months."

"Not that kind of anniversary." When he waggled a brow, she rolled her eyes.

"TMI. And just make it up to her. I'm sure you can figure out how."

He was thinking about that when Lilah headed out. She lived in a small cabin next door, and when she slipped inside the small cozy place, she sighed. It was neat and clean and warm, and unlike just about everything else in her life, all hers.

But.

But even with the three years that had gone by, it was still too quiet without her grandma's cheerful voice.

"Mew."

Lilah looked down at the three-legged black cat winding her way around her ankles. There were rescues coming in and out of her life, waiting patiently for the right home, but Sadie was her favorite. Lilah knew that wasn't fair, but tell that to her heart. Twice she could have placed Sadie with a foster home, but she hadn't been able to do it.

Whenever there was even a hint of an animal being fragile, she had a hard time letting it go to an adoptive family. And though Sadie wasn't fragile, she was special.

Okay, so the truth was, they were all special to her. She couldn't help it, she just couldn't make herself abandon anything, ever. After all, she knew what that felt like.

"Mew," Sadie said, bumping her little head to Lilah's calf.

Lilah scooped her up and nuzzled her close.

Sadie was deceptively small, and it made her look like a kitten even though she was full grown. The mistake was in thinking that she had a kitten's temperament. She didn't. She was ornery as hell.

"Miss me today?"

Sadie blinked up at her sleepily, the rumble of a purr thick in her throat as she leaned in—and bit Lilah's chin.

"Gee, hungry?"

"Mew."

Rubbing her chin, Lilah moved to the window. Brady's truck might be gone, but the memory of his mouth on hers was not. "He was a bit more attitude-ridden than I usually go for, but trust me, it worked for him." She met Sadie's narrowed gaze. "Hey, don't judge me. It's been a long time for me."

And she'd been lonely.

The truth was, she needed . . . something.

Actually, someone. She needed someone. But Sunshine was small, and the problem wasn't helped by the fact that Adam and Dell tended to watch over her like they were her big brothers, making it clear that anyone with less-than-honorable intentions were risking life and limb.

Which had left her with slim pickings and a secret yearning for a guy with some not-so-honorable intentions.

Like Brady . . .

She knew why Adam and Dell did it. They'd been the ones to help her pick up the pieces when she'd come back to Sunshine during her second year of college to quietly and completely fall apart. The reasons had been complicated, but in short, her grandma had died and she'd let a guy devastate her. It'd taken a while, but eventually she'd picked up the pieces and moved on. Gotten stronger. Adam and Dell knew this, but old habits were hard to break. "Is it so wrong to want a guy in my bed?" she asked Sadie.

Sadie just stared at her with those pale green eyes, and Lilah sighed. Much to her annoyance, she'd been fairly unsuccessful at getting any man she knew to cross Adam or Dell. *Fairly*, because certain guys were just good at being sneaky and getting around the watchdogs.

Cruz, for one.

But she didn't count Cruz because she didn't ache for him.

She wanted to ache, dammit.

Her thoughts drifted to Brady and she shivered. "He kissed me," she told Sadie.

Actually, she'd kissed him first, and then he'd taken over. And oh boy how he'd taken over, with that bone-melting aggression that had seriously rocked her world. It'd taken her right off her axis, in a good way, a way she'd been unconsciously needing quite badly.

And she'd hit his truck. "God," she moaned, and covered her face. "I am such an idiot."

"Mew."

"Okay, no opinions from the peanut gallery, thank you very much." She pulled out her cell phone and speed-dialed Dell. The three of them had gotten tight a few years back, when the guys had bought the property down the road from hers and built the animal center. They had no family to speak of and she'd just lost her grandma so they'd created a tight-knit family of their own.

Dell's phone went right to voice mail, so she tried Adam. Same thing. "I had an *I Love Lucy* moment," she admitted in her message. "A doozy. I'm going to shower, then head over to get the rescue dog and I'll tell you guys about it then. Oh, and I'm sort of going to need a little help with the Jeep."

The Belle Haven center was close enough to Coeur d'Alene and neighboring smaller towns like Sunshine to serve domesticated animals but it was also ideally located in ranching country to specialize in bigger animals, both wild and ranching-based as well. Dell ran the place with a growing staff and a reputation that had spread to the entire northern state area. Adam was in search and rescue. He trained and bred dogs for S&R teams across the country and was also extremely well known—much to his discomfort.

Lilah set her phone down and stripped on her way to the bathroom, passing her kitchen table in the process, which was still strewn with her laptop and books. She'd fallen asleep there sometime past midnight and had woken with a page from her biochem book stuck to her face.

She still hadn't finished studying and had a paper due and a midterm coming up in both physics and animal biology, but that would have to wait. She let the baggy, grungy work clothes fall where they might. They'd suited their purpose this morning cleaning out stalls, but they sure hadn't suited her purpose to meet an enigmatic stranger. She wondered what he'd thought of her, then told herself it didn't matter.

Besides, he'd kissed her—so how put off by her appearance could he have been?

She let the water pound over her body and then turned to her shelf, filled with her guilty pleasure—soaps and scrubs of all scents. Coconut, she decided. She felt like being a coconut today.

As the warm scent permeated the bathroom around her, she relaxed, standing there under the spray for long moments, dragging it out as long as she could, in no hurry to get on with the rest of her day.

"Ack!" she screeched when the water went suddenly icy, as it did every day thanks to her ancient water heater. Shivering, she stepped out of the shower and onto the mat of her teeny bathroom, banging her knee on the toilet, which was the last straw. "Shit!"

Sadie, sitting in the sink prissy as could be, smirked.

"*Shit* doesn't really count as a bad word," Lilah said in her own defense as she grabbed a towel. "It's practically a legitimate adjective."

Sadie lifted her back leg to wash her lady town.

"Yeah, yeah." Lilah bent for her clothes and shoved her hand into the front pocket to pull out a dollar. She walked it to the kitchen and dropped into her swear jar on the counter. The jar had been Mrs. Morrison's idea, the owner of a parrot who'd stayed with Lilah for a week last month when Mrs. Morrison had gone on a Mexican cruise. When she'd come home, her parrot had a new vocabulary made up of "crap," "shit," and "Dammit, Cruz!"

The jar had at least fifty bucks in it.

When it reached two hundred, Lilah was going to splurge on a spa day. At this rate, she'd have it by next week.

She pulled on fresh jeans and a scooped-necked T-shirt, then dropped two pieces of bread into her toaster, one of them being the heel because she needed to go grocery shopping, a chore she put up there with cleaning out the crates at the kennels. When the toast popped up, the lights in the kitchen flickered and went out. She'd blown the fuse again. She swallowed the very bad four-letter word on the tip of her tongue because she was broke and grabbed a new fuse from the stack in the drawer.

The cabin needed work more than she needed her next breath of air, but for now, with business loans hanging over her head and school debt looming, Lilah was like a drowning victim going down for the last count. She replaced the fuses as they blew—which was all the time—because it was still cheaper than trying to redo the entire electrical in the place, something that needed to be done sooner than later. Just thinking about it had her chest tightening.

*Save the stress,* she told herself, *for when you have a spare pint of double-fudge ice cream to go with it.* Sighing, she looked at the toast. She had to skip the butter because it was healthier that way—and also because then she could justify the ice cream later. But she did add strawberry jelly, because hey, that was a fruit.

Stepping outside, she started walking to Belle Haven. The trail was drenched from the heavy rains of the night before, and the rough terrain gave beneath her boots like live sponges. She loved being outside after any rain, and she inhaled deeply the scent of wet nature. Her very favorite scent of all.

The lake was backed by rolling hill after rolling hill, and beyond those, the towering peaks of the Coeur d'Alene's, the colors so deep and mesmerizing the whole setting looked like a painting.

The trail ended at the center. The building itself was a two-story sprawling place, with several pens and a large barn alongside, with several more smaller buildings for equipment. Lilah walked through the parking lot and saw Adam's and Dell's trucks. Adam's was freshly washed and shiny as always, and Dell's was covered in a fine layer of dust and filled with work equipment, sporting gear, and whatever other stuff he'd put in there and forgotten. She might have smiled. After all, just being here filled her with a warm peace. Except that right next to their trucks sat a third.

This truck's back bumper was cracked and dented, as if someone in a Jeep—a very tired, overworked someone—had rear-ended it.

Oh God. Brady was parked in the lot next to her best friends as if he belonged in their world right alongside them.

And that's when it hit her. Where she'd heard his name before. An odd mixture of dread and anticipation mingled in her gut along with something else that she couldn't quite put her finger on, something that she didn't know what to do with. She walked through the front entrance and waved at Jade, the receptionist on the phone behind the big welcome desk. There was a wide-open space that greeted both two- and four-footed clients alike, and a comfortable seating area spread out strategically to encourage people to hang out in front of the huge wall of windows overlooking the land and the animals on it.

Three horses were out in one of the paddocks, a sheep in another, and on the outskirts stood a flock of geese who'd waddled over from the lake to watch the goings-on.

Inside, several people sat in the waiting room along with their dogs and cats and, in one case, a caged bunny.

Lilah walked through, heading to the offices, stopping to take a quick look out into the glorious day, the first without rain in two weeks. What she would give to be sitting on a blanket in front of the lake, the water lapping at her feet, a good book in her hand—and not her animal biology book. But it'd been a long time since she'd had enough wriggling room to just hang out and be.

"Never gets old, does it?"

She turned at the masculine voice that was as familiar to her as her own.

Dell slung a friendly arm over her shoulder. He was an outrageous but harmless flirt and could make ninety-year-old women preen and get infant girls to bat their eyelashes. One reason was his easy good looks. He was six foot two and still built like the football quarterback that he'd once been. He had the warm mocha skin that spoke of Native heritage and the sharp eyes to match. His black hair framed a striking face. He wore his sleeves rolled up, his shirt unbuttoned at the collar and untucked over a pair of well-worn jeans, and he would have looked like a college kid except for his eyes. His eyes said he'd seen too much for his barely three decades.

But his smile was pure devil. It never failed to crack her up that he broke hearts right and left and had no clue to his own power. He was the heart and soul of Sunshine, and the rock of all of them.

"I tried calling you," she murmured, turning into him for a hug.

"I was in surgery. I called you back—you didn't get my message?"

"No." She pulled out her cell, which now showed one missed call. "Must have been in the shower."

"It's okay." They were out of view from the people that were waiting on him, and he smiled into her eyes. "We have news."

"About . . . ?"

Dell turned her toward the hallway, where Adam was coming out of his office. Leaner than Dell, Adam was built more like one of those cage fighters, tough and edgy and hard—except for that face.

An angel's face. Her angel. Dark disheveled hair, strong features, and like Dell, a devastating smile when he chose to use it.

The man with Adam had the same badass smile—as she already knew all too well. She watched Brady walk toward them and had to acknowledge their odd attraction as something low in her belly quivered. She kept herself cool on the outside, but on the inside she was thinking that a half hour ago he'd kissed her till she purred.

"Remember when Adam and I lived in that foster home on Outback Road?" Dell asked her quietly.

"Yes. With the man who eventually left you the money to buy this land."

"Sol Anders," Dell said. "He took on Adam and me, but he had another kid first."

Lilah hadn't known them then, but Dell had told her about the other boy. He'd been a few years older than Adam and he'd graduated early and gone off to the military.

Brady, Of course. She'd heard his name before, but she'd just not connected it to her gorgeous stranger. And it wasn't as if Brady had visited—he hadn't, not once in the past few years since she'd been close friends with Dell and Adam. "The missing foster brother."

"Not missing," Dell said. "He was Special Forces, then working out of the country. We've been trying to get him to come see our operation for a long time. Now he's finally here."

Brady hadn't yet spoken; he was just now getting close enough to them to do so, but she felt the weight of his assessing gaze. And in fact, all three men were looking at her. There was so much freaking testosterone in the room that she could scarcely breathe. Brady had the same tough, sharp always-aware-of-his-surroundings demeanor as Adam and Dell, and the three of them together—good Lord.

Three magnificent peas in a pod.

She'd never really understood what had kept Brady away all this time. Neither Dell nor Adam had ever said. Guys, she'd long ago discovered, weren't exactly forthcoming with emotions and details.

As she stood there absorbing that shock, Adam shifted close to greet her with his usual—a tug on her hair. "Hey, Trouble."

"Hey." She couldn't object to the nickname. She'd earned it. Hell, she'd earned it this morning alone.

Adam ran his hand down her arm to her hand, which he squeezed, then gestured to the man whose truck she'd hit, the man who was so yummy he'd reminded her hormones that they could still indeed do a heck of a tap dance. "Lilah," Adam said. "This is—"

"Brady Miller," she murmured.

Brady's mouth curved in a slight ironic smile, his eyes lit with the same. He bowed his head slightly in her direction. "Lilah."

Dell divided a surprised look between them. "You two know each other?"

Brady lifted a brow in Lilah's direction, clearly giving her the floor.

Great. She hated having the floor. "Well, it's a funny story, actually." She managed a weak smile. "We, um"— she lifted a shoulder—"had a little run-in this morning."

Brady was hands in pockets, rolled back on his heels. He was obviously enjoying himself, the bastard, and damn if something deep within her didn't react to all that annoying charisma and male confidence.

"You had a little run-in," Dell repeated, and shook his head. "What does that mean exactly?"

"It means . . ." *Crap.* "Okay, so it's more like I ran into him."

"Explain," Adam said. No words were ever wasted when Adam spoke.

"Literally," she said. "I ran into him. As in, I hit his truck with my Jeep."

Brady's mouth twitched, though his eyes remained sharp.

But not as sharp as those on the two men that Lilah thought of as her brothers as they took in both Lilah and Brady, more specifically Brady and the way he was looking at her.

Which was a little bit how a tiger might eye his prey after a long, cold, hungry winter.

Oh good Lord. She definitely hadn't put on enough deodorant for this. And even more unsettling? Just this morning she'd have sworn she was completely happy and settled with her life. Sure she was overworked and stressed and about an inch from financial disaster at all times, and yeah, she'd been battling that vague sense of loneliness, but compared to lots of people she had things good.

So she couldn't explain this new restlessness.

But then her gaze locked with Brady and she had to revise. She could explain.

It was all his fault.

# Four

Brady had been to every continent. He could speak three languages enough to get by and could understand a handful more. Over the years he'd amassed a whole host of skills—some he was proud of, some not so much. He'd seen a lot of shit. Hell, he'd done a lot of shit.

So he knew when to back off and let a situation take its course.

This was one of those times.

The reason he was here was complicated, and went back years, to old ties he hadn't even realized he still had. He'd been given up by his too-young, drug-dependent mother when he'd been five to a distant uncle not all that keen on kids. By the time he'd gotten to his teens, he'd been down-graded to group foster homes. He'd been a puny, scrawny runt, and an easy mark.

Until he'd landed at Sol Anders's.

Sol had been a badass cowboy and a large-animal vet. With him, Brady had been given two things he'd never had before—acceptance and an outlet for his anger. There'd been a gym in Sol's basement, specifically a punching bag, and Sol had encouraged Brady to make good use of it.

Later, two more "lost boys" had come along to be under Sol's care. They'd all lived together for two years before Brady graduated high school a year early and went into the army.

Adam and Dell.

By the time Sol died in a freak riding accident a few years later—on a wild mustang in Montana while gathering a herd for the government—Brady had been a pro at survival and winning his fights. He went on to serve multiple tours with the army, which is where he'd learned to fly anything with an engine, working in some college in between.

All with Sol's solid memory guiding him.

He'd been well aware that Sol had left some money, that he'd divided it among the three lost boys; himself, Adam, and Dell. But Brady had refused to take his share. He hadn't needed it. So he'd signed it over to Dell and Adam and had continued with his wanderlust lifestyle while they'd bought this land and built the animal center. Made a life for themselves.

They'd put Brady's name on the deed to the land, which he hadn't known. And now they were in the black this year and wanted Brady to be a part of it.

Brady didn't have the same wants. He didn't have a need for either a place to call home or the money Dell and Adam felt they owed him.

They'd known that and had come at him with a dangling carrot, something he'd found he couldn't quite resist—a helicopter that needed restoring and the chance to, for however briefly, fly in the good old safe USA.

It was nice what they'd done to honor their brief history together from a million years ago, one that had involved stolen candy, pilfered porn, and many late nights sneaking out on their bikes . . . But there was no doubt in Brady's mind that Lilah's history with them went far deeper.

So he let the drama unfold, fascinated in spite of himself.

"Is that why you walked over here instead of driving?" Adam asked Lilah, voice low so that the patients and their owners, just around the corner waiting to see Dell, couldn't hear. "Because you had an accident?"

Adam's voice was curt and gruff. And though not as obviously dark-skinned and dark-eyed as Dell, he was dark in persona and could be as intimidating as hell.

Except Lilah didn't seem intimidated.

At all.

"It's a half mile," she said. "Good exercise."

"Uh-huh. Except you hate exercise."

"Maybe my jeans are tight and I needed to burn the calories," she said. "And to be honest, it wasn't an accident so much as a little oops. It could have happened to anyone."

Brady choked out a cough, and she sent him a dark look before turning back to Adam. "And maybe we can review my stupidity later because I'm really busy today."

One corner of Adam's mouth turned up. "Really? We can discuss your stupidity later? Do you promise? Because normally you hate discussing your stupidity."

Lilah shoved him with the ease of two people extremely comfortable with each other, and extremely familiar.

Brady studied them both for hints of sexual tension, wondering if they were lovers as well as friends.

Lilah shoved Adam again. Adam didn't budge. Instead he caught her up, wrapped an arm around her neck and hauled her in close, rubbing his knuckles against her head until she swore at him and slugged him in the gut.

Nope, Brady decided. Definitely not lovers. This was definitely a brother–sister relationship.

"*Pendejo,*" Lilah muttered, attempting to fix the hair Adam had ruffled.

Dumbass. She'd just called Adam, six feet of solid muscle, a dumbass.

"It's the only bad word she knows," Adam said, side-stepping another shove. "Probably time to learn something new, Trouble."

Lilah straightened her shoulders and gave a little toss of her head, like she couldn't be bothered with details. "Listen, while this is ever so much fun, I have two puppies, a piglet, two cats, a lamb, and a duck boarding today. I need to get back to it. Where's the rescue dog?"

"Pen three," Dell said. "Male, grown, neutered, mutt. Heads up—he was abandoned in a warehouse and, as far as we can tell, hit by a car."

Brady watched the undisguised emotions chase each other across Lilah's face. Horror, sorrow, determination. "Injuries?" she asked.

"Herniated diaphragm," Dell said. "And yes, I operated. Fixed him right up."

All the worry drained from her and she smiled sweetly at Dell, heart in her eyes. "How bad's the monetary damage?"

"Pro bono for you as always, sweetness. He's already feeling much better and is ready to go when you are. His meds are with him. Oh, and be careful, he's a little skittish and anxious, especially with men. You should probably warn Cruz."

Adam reruffled the hair she'd just fixed. "Meet me out front with him in five and I'll give you a ride back. We'll go look at your Jeep."

Sighing, she gave up on her hair and strode past both Dell and Adam. As she came up even with Brady, her eyes went a little guarded.

She'd showered and changed. Her long brown hair was wet and wavy past her shoulders, held off her face by the sunglasses she'd pushed to the top of her head. The work clothes were gone, and the body he'd only caught a hint of before was much more visible now in snug, hip-hugging jeans and a knit T-shirt that revealed a set of curves hot enough to sizzle.

Lilah Young cleaned up good.

Without a word, she walked by him as well, giving him a quick hint of the scent of her hair.

Coconut. She smelled like a piña colada, and it was making him thirsty.

And hungry.

Or maybe that was just her. Maybe she was making him hungry.

Hips swaying, she moved past the receptionist desk, exchanged a smile with the mid-twentysomething woman behind the counter, and then disappeared into the back without another glance. Which was okay, because Brady was probably doing enough looking for the both of them. But hell, she had a very fine ass. He met Adam's dark gaze—a fairly clear tell-me-you-are-not-looking-at-her-ass kind of gaze.

"She get hurt today?" Adam asked. His voice was low, casual even, but Brady wasn't fooled.

Adam wasn't happy.

It didn't take a genius to figure out who he was unhappy with, and it wasn't the Easter Bunny. "No," Brady said. "And I'm fine—thanks for asking. Look, it was just as she said, a fender bender. I wasn't even in the truck at the time. It was out front of 7-Eleven."

Dell shook his head at Adam. "She's pushing it too hard again."

Pushing it too hard? What did that mean?

"Adam," the woman at the receptionist desk called out. "There's a woman on line one who saw your picture in the *Coeur d'Alene Chronicle*."

"So?" Adam asked.

"So she says you're hot and wants to know if you're single. She says she's like one of your golden retrievers, cute and trainable."

Dell grinned.

Adam's left eye twitched.

"That's Jade at the desk," Dell told Brady. "She's in charge of things, and when I say in charge, I mean In Charge."

From behind her desk, the coolly beautiful Jade raised a brow, not amused.

Dell, looking amused enough for the both of them, went on. "You want to stay on her good side. She's the sharpest of all of us, but she never learned how to chill."

"Sitting right here, you know," Jade said.

Dell grinned outright. "So I should just come right out and say you're anal and uptight then?"

Jade turned her back on him, nose in the air. It went with the runway clothes and crazy-ass heels she had on.

Adam shook his head. "Man, you're going to pay for that. You know you are. She'll double-book you from now until hell freezes over, or switch the sugar and salt again, or something equally evil."

Dell wasn't looking too concerned as he turned to Brady. "So, what do you think of the place?"

"It's a pretty sweet setup," Brady said. "Between the animal care and the breeding and training, you're meeting a lot of needs here."

"And the helicopter," Dell said. "Adam showed you the helicopter."

"Yeah." Adam had also told him that up until six months ago, there'd been a pet groomer here as well. The company had leased one of the smaller buildings, but they'd gone belly-up, breaking the lease without paying out. Apparently a month ago Dell and Adam had finally received back payment in the form of a Bell Soloy 47 helicopter. It had been delivered from Smitty's, the small-craft airport directly across the meadow from the center, and was sitting in the yard like an eyesore.

Brady had taken a good long look at it, feeling a stir of interest he hadn't wanted to acknowledge. The Bell 47 was a legendary and pioneer flying adventure. The thing needed some serious work before it would be fly-worthy, but Adam and Dell had been looking for a way to further expand their business. They were fairly isolated out here in Sunshine, and Dell was sometimes spending entire days on the road to get to some of the patients that couldn't come to him, so they'd thought that maybe the helicopter could actually be of use.

If it ran.

And if they had a pilot.

Which was where Brady came in. The Bell 47 was the bait, of course. Dell had used it ruthlessly, knowing damn well Brady wouldn't be able to resist, that he'd want the challenge of fixing it up until it sang, that he'd want to fly it.

He'd been right. "It's a beauty," he admitted.

"Can you fix it?" Dell asked.

"Yes." He could fix pretty much anything, but the Bell he could do in his sleep.

"Can you fly it?"

"Yes." He could also fly anything and started to say so when a tingle of awareness raced down the back of his neck. He turned as Lilah came back through, holding a dark brown shaggy dog in her arms.

The dog was scrawny to the point of being painfully lean, with dull eyes and an expression that said he no longer cared what happened to him.

"How long do you think to get it running?" Dell asked, still talking about the helicopter.

Brady pretended to think about that while watching Lilah hug her rescue dog.

"Good boy," she was murmuring softly, rubbing her jaw to the top of his head.

The dog hesitated, then gave her a hesitant little lick on the chin.

"Aw, that's a really good boy," she said again, nuzzling him close.

And once again Brady found himself jealous of a four-legged creature.

"I was hoping you'd stay a month," Dell said.

"A month? Why?"

"I figured that would be enough time to decide if having a pilot and the helicopter on staff is worth the expense."

Lilah lifted her face from the dog and leveled those mossy green eyes on Brady.

A month . . . He had several assignments within the next couple of weeks.

"Come on," Dell said. "It'd be great to have you."

A fucking month. In one place. He glanced at Lilah and felt something within him ache. Don't do it . . . But the truth was he was due a break, and no one, least of all the company he flew for, would begrudge him taking one.

And he sure as hell could do worse than the Coeur d'Alene mountains in summer.

He made the mistake of looking at Lilah again. If he let the sexual tension shimmering between them choose, he knew exactly what his answer would be—but he never let his dick rule. He put what he needed ahead of what he wanted.

Always. "Look, thanks for the offer. But I'm going to get a room for the night. I have some calls to make before I can commit to anything."

"Take the upstairs loft," Dell said. "It's Adam's, but he's not staying there right now." He swiveled a look in his brother's direction and smirked. "Not since he was stalked by one of his crazy-ass exes."

Adam's expression didn't change, but he slid his eyes to Dell in a go-there-and-die look.

"Cameron," Dell said. "Pretty little thing, too. Only there was a . . . misunderstanding. She thought they were exclusive, except Adam here doesn't really know the meaning of the word. So Cameron broke in one night and tried to convince him she was his one and only. With handcuffs. Adam walked away from her after that. Actually, he ran away like a little girl, but he doesn't like to talk about it."

"She had a fucking taser," Adam said tightly. "You always leave that part out."

"No, we understand," Dell said, nodding. "She's terrifying. All five feet two inches of her. It's been six months," he
said. "And he still twitches at the sight of a stacked blonde.
It's probably plenty safe enough for you to stay there. Plus
you can handle yourself."

"Hey, I could have handled myself just fine without the
taser," Adam said. "And you're an asshole. Come on, Lilah,
let's look at your Jeep."

With one last indecipherable look at Brady, Lilah and
her dog left with Adam.

Five minutes later when Dell had finished fielding
a phone call from a worried pet owner, he accompanied
Brady outside to get his duffel bag from his truck before
showing him the loft. It ran the entire length of the upper
floor of the center. The slanted ceiling gave the wide open
space a warm feel, certainly warmer than anywhere Brady
had stayed in recent memory. Hell, any place that didn't
have dirt floors would be a step up from where he'd stayed
in recent memory.

"The heater doesn't work for shit up here," Dell said,
nodding to the stack of wood beside a large fireplace.
"Takes that in the winter to heat the place."

Which wouldn't be Brady's problem. By winter, he'd be
in some third-world country dreaming about being cold
enough to need a fireplace. He walked to the far wall, which
was nearly all windows. He looked out into the meadow
behind the center, rich and lush with growth.

"This was my favorite part of the place when I lived
here," Dell said.

"Did you get chased out of here by a crazy ex, too?"

"No." Dell grinned. "I bought a house in town last year.
Probably I shouldn't bait Adam like that but Christ, he's so
easy."

"What happened to him? I don't remember him being
so . . ."

"Surly? Rude? Pissy? He forgot to take his Midol." But Dell's smile faded and he lifted a shoulder. "He had a rescue go bad."

"Bad?"

"Shit intel, lost half his crew, and he blames himself. Which is stupid because it wasn't his fault, but you try telling him that. He likes guilt. Anyway, after he got out of the Guards, he started working with the rescue dogs, training and breeding. He's still not quite back on the people train."

"PTSD?"

"Oh yeah," Dell said. "But don't let him hear you say that."

"And you help by, what, poking at him?"

"It's my brotherly duty."

Brady opened one of the windowpanes, and seeing there was no screen, he gave in and pulled his camera from his bag, snapping a few shots right then and there. His usual subject of choice was faces, but this land drew him.

It always had.

Off to the side, Adam and Lilah came into view. Adam had an arm slung around Lilah's shoulders, and though he wasn't smiling, she was. And laughing, too, her smile open and easy and unguarded as she set the rescue dog down, probably for a pit stop.

Brady snapped a few shots of them before turning away for reasons he didn't understand, or care to.

Dell was watching him. "You and Adam are a lot alike these days."

"I'm not suffering from anything."

"Except an inability to connect."

Brady snorted. "Look at you, not letting your psych degree go to waste."

Dell smiled. "It was only my minor."

Brady turned back to the window.

"We're updating the center's website, which has really taken off. Appointments, self-help with animals, training—

it's all going on there. Adam took pictures of our clients, both the owners and the animals. People love to see themselves on the site. Or they would, except Adam has this tendency to cut heads off. Think you could do better?"

Brady sighed. "Dell—"

"I just thought while you're here . . ."

Fuck. "Yeah. I can take pictures that include heads."

"I was hoping you'd say that."

There were framed pictures on the windowsill. Adam in full search-and-rescue gear surrounded by four beautiful golden retrievers, all wearing red rescue totes. Lilah and a guy he didn't recognize, both seated on a tailgate of a truck mugging for the camera. Dell on a horse. "You're happy here," Brady said.

"Very. Maybe you'll feel the same."

Brady shook his head. "Why does it matter so much to you?"

"Sol gave us this land. All of us. But Adam and I have gotten all the benefits."

"You guys built this place. It's yours."

"You know, once we meant something to each other."

Surprised by the vehemence in Dell's voice, Brady looked at him. "Yes."

At that, Del seemed to relax marginally. "We came from nothing—less than nothing—the three of us. And we forged a family. Your family, you stubborn ass, whether you like it or not."

Brady's eyes locked on the last picture. A lone man, head shaved, built like a tree trunk, staring into the camera with fierce intensity, and just looking at him made Brady's chest ache like hell. Sol. "I know," he said very quietly.

Besides him, Dell let out a breath. "I was beginning to wonder if I was going to have to kick your ass to remind you."

Brady let out a rare smile. Because it was true that Dell had kicked Brady's ass, exactly once. Of course Brady had been drunk as a skunk at the time and already down for the count. They'd been teenagers, and once Sol had gotten hold of them, they'd all been down for the count because Sol had made them drink the rest of the stolen vodka, watching in stoic silence as each of them had puked up their guts. Probably not a condoned method of parenting, but it'd worked.

Brady had never overindulged again.

"I could have taken you even without the vodka," Dell said, reading Brady's mind.

"Hey, whatever helps you sleep at night."

They both laughed softly, the tension gone. "When the Bell came into our possession," Dell said, "I knew we had you."

Brady blew out a breath. What the hell. No use denying that. He was here in the States with nowhere else pressing to be, and it was a sweet old chopper. "Yeah."

"You going to stick, then?"

Chances were he'd stick all right. He'd stick out like a sore thumb. But he was used to that. And what the hell. He watched as below Lilah carefully picked back up her precious bundle, loving him up as she did so.

He wouldn't mind being loved up by those arms, that was for damn sure. "For a month," he heard himself say. "Just a month."

# Five

Lilah took Toby back to the kennels. Actually, she had no idea what the dog's name was since he hadn't come with a collar, but he was an adorable mass of tangled fluff and looked like a Toby to her. He was also in desperate need of a bath, but getting him cleaned up turned out to be tricky since he told her he was deathly afraid of water.

Loudly.

She sweet-talked him into calming down and carefully soaped him up, working around the stitches from his surgery, and ended up wearing more of the soap than he did. Keeping up a steady stream of soft cooing and baby talk seemed to soothe his concerns quite a bit.

"There," she murmured. "Doesn't that feel better, to be clean?" Giving him a final rinse, she wrapped him in a towel.

He watched her solemnly from the most adorable, soul-searching eyes she'd ever seen, then very carefully licked her face.

"My second kiss of the day," she said.

"And the first?" Cruz asked, coming into the back, leading Lulu the lamb to her pen.

"Not telling," Lilah said.

Lulu stretched her neck and tried to take a nip out of Cruz's tush, and Lilah burst out laughing.

"That's okay," Cruz told the lamb. "All the ladies want to bite my ass. You can't help yourself."

Lilah rolled her eyes. "You leaving for your gig?"

"Yes. Unless you want to take a bite out of my ass. No?" he asked, grinning when Lilah just gave him a shove to the door. "Okay, but you're missing out. I taste better than the jelly filling you have on your right boob."

Lilah looked down. Strawberry jelly, from her toast. "Balls!"

"Balls?"

She sighed. "I can't afford to say 'Goddammit.' I'm out of cash for the swear jar. And stop looking at my boob!"

He fished a five out of his pocket and slapped it into her hand for her swear jar. "Even though I don't like to hear a woman talk disparagingly about my second favorite body part," he said on a laugh as he left.

Alone, Lilah began the afternoon routine of cleaning out cages, changing blankets, changing water bowls, and starting laundry. She fed everyone and administered any medicines required. Then she cleaned and disinfected the entire kennel.

After that, she dealt with all the animal pickups and drop-offs for the day, which they had scheduled for certain hours only to make the running of the place go a little smoother. Then she took their overnight guests—all dogs today, plus Abigail—for one last walk before tucking everyone in for the night.

With that done, she faced her desk. She was behind in the paperwork and needed to type up their monthly newsletter and file, not to mention a little thing called study.

It used to stress her out how much endless work there

always seemed to be, but it piled up in the best of times and she'd learned to let some of the little stuff go.

She gave Toby an extra treat, and while he wolfed it down, she went to her computer and pulled up the database of people in town who were willing to foster animals and had already been thoroughly checked out and approved. She ran through the list, calling potential candidates and hitting bingo on the third try. A woman named Shelly who worked at the rec center had lost her dog to a coyote earlier in the year. Lilah didn't know Shelly personally, just in passing, but she was relieved to find her so ecstatic about Toby. Shelly said she could get him first thing in the morning if Lilah wouldn't mind meeting her in town since the roads out to the kennels were still bad from the rains and Shelly only had a VW Beetle. They arranged to meet at the bakery, which worked for Lilah. Two birds with one stone and all that.

She'd have to eat a bag of carrots tonight to make up for the donuts she'd consume in the morning but it would be worth it.

With that accomplished, Lilah broke her own rules by taking Toby home with her, letting him sleep on a soft blanket next to her bed.

Sadie hopped up onto the mattress to look disdainfully down at the rumpled, tired dog.

"You were a stray, too," Lilah reminded her.

Sadie gave her a banal stare.

"Stop. It's just for the night. And you will not smack him around."

Sadie lifted her nose in the air, turned in a circle, and daintily sat with her back to Toby, as if to drive the point home that he wasn't even worth watching.

Sighing, Lilah pulled open her books to study, but she had trouble concentrating. Her mind was on the new strays. Toby, of course, but also the six foot, blue-eyed, badass stray who'd kissed like heaven on earth.

* * *

The next morning started at the usual crack of dawn. Sadie mewled a protest at the blare of the alarm. Not Toby. He was much perkier than he'd been the night before, even seeming to smile at Lilah as he padded with her into the small bathroom. He lay quietly on the rug while she showered—cherry blossom soap today—and yelped along with her as the hot water gave way to cold.

Lilah dressed and headed outside, the dog so close on her heels that he ran into her when she stopped short.

Early as it was, someone had been up earlier than her because her Jeep was in her yard waiting for her, a note taped to the windshield:

> *Hey Trouble—Note that the brake is not the skinny one on the right but the fat pedal on the left.*

Adam humor. Lilah sighed and looked the Jeep over. The front end was still dented in pretty good, but it'd been hammered out a bit, and best of all, the engine started.

She and Toby turned away from the Jeep and headed inside the kennels, where Lilah made her way through her morning routine: feeding, watering, walking, cleaning . . . From seven to nine was drop-off/pickup time. This was when clients could drop off their animals for the day or pick up from the night before. They had another two-hour stretch at the end of the day for the same thing. At nine thirty, she put a sign on the door saying she'd be back at ten and told all the animals she'd return. Time to bring Toby to Shelly.

Lilah bribed Toby into the Jeep with his antibiotics wrapped in a piece of cheese, which he took with a sweet lick, and then they took off. Ten minutes later they stood outside the town bakery. "We can't go in," she told Toby. "I didn't eat any carrots last night."

Toby looked sad. She couldn't blame him. But she'd

promised herself to eat healthier and she meant it. "Of course, we could buy, say, a bran muffin. Or . . . carrot cake." Yeah, that was brilliant. Cake and veggies, all in one. "Let's do it," she said, and Toby's ears perked up. Clearly, he agreed wholeheartedly.

"Plus," Lilah said, "it's cold, right? It'll be much warmer inside. And Dee allows dogs—she even has a canister where she has doggie treats. You'll see."

Toby nodded. He was on board. So Lilah opened the door. They were immediately blasted by the heated oven air and the scent of fresh sugary goodness and coffee. Her stomach growled. "Let's get in line," she said. "For carrot cake."

The bakery was set up buffet style, meaning customers grabbed a tray for themselves and then had to walk by the open displays of all the goods in order to get to the cash register.

Cruel, cruel setup.

Lilah grabbed a tray, and oh look at that, two old-fashioned chocolate-glazed donuts somehow landed on it. "I don't know, must be fate," she told Toby, who followed closely on her heels, the leash slack and unnecessary.

The guy in front of her turned around and smiled. "Thought you didn't believe in fate."

Nick McFarlan, who ran the hardware store down the street. Lilah and Nick had gone together on and off through high school and had gone to prom together. He'd been her first kiss, her first boyfriend, her first everything.

Until they'd gone their separate ways for college, breaking up to experience new things. Lilah had done that all right, only it hadn't exactly been as positive as she'd hoped for. When Nick had returned home after college, he had wanted to pick up right where they'd left off. But Lilah had been too raw and devastated over two unexpected things—her grandma's death and a bad relationship experience while she'd been away.

So they'd fallen into a sort of friendship zone instead. Nick, buying two dozen donuts for his customers, smiled. "You're looking good," he said softly.

She laughed. "I'm wearing Carhartts."

"I have fantasies about those Carhartts."

"Really?"

"Okay, I have fantasies about what you might be wearing beneath them." He leaned in playfully as if to peek for himself.

"Stop it."

He grinned. "Admit it, one of these days I'm going to wear you down."

She smiled, but the truth was he probably could. Like Cruz, he was good-looking, kind and familiar.

But she was tired, oh so very tired of familiar.

Dee smiled as she rang him up. "You can look beneath my Carhartts, Nick. Any time."

Game, he looked her over. She was ten years older than them but still trim and pretty. And wore a man-eater smile. "You're not wearing Carhartts," Nick said.

Dee leaned over the counter, eyes sultry and laughing. "For you, I'd buy some."

While Lilah waited for them to stop flirting, a jelly-filled donut fell onto her tray, all by itself, joining the two old-fashioned glazes. "Oh, look at that," she murmured to Toby. "Fruit." She started in on that one first and moaned in sheer bliss. "God, so much better than carrots."

"You're going to start a riot."

At the low, familiar voice in her ear, she went still, then slowly turned to face Brady.

He was halfway through his own donut—a chocolate-frosted by the looks of it. And good Lord, talk about starting a riot. He was wearing army flight cargoes today and a soft-washed long-sleeved polo that was form-fitted to his toned body.

"Hey," she said.

"Hey back, Crash."

"Okay," she said. "I object to that—" But she was talking to air because he'd crouched in front of Toby, elbows braced on his thighs as he offered a hand for the dog to sniff. "How's he doing today?"

"Good." She kneeled down as well. "But he's really skittish, so you need to—"

Toby licked Brady's hand, then arched up to lick his chin as well.

"Go slow," Lilah finished on a sigh.

Toby was rewarded by Brady with a behind-the-ear scratching that had the little guy sliding to the floor in a boneless heap of pleasure.

"Ah, good boy," Brady praised, giving him an all over body rub that left Lilah yearning for the same.

Brady rose fluidly on his feet, and for a beat, she found herself eye to eye with his flat, zero-fat stomach. That he could even have a flat, zero-fat stomach with the way he ate really irritated the hell out of her.

And/or turned her on. She couldn't decide which. It was early yet.

A small smile curved his sexy mouth as he offered her a hand, telling her that he knew of her battle, and hell if that didn't settle it. Irritation.

He gestured to the choice on her tray. "Nice."

She winced, then realized he wasn't judging her but truly complimenting her choice of breakfast. "I almost got one of those," she admitted, gesturing to his chocolate-frosted. "But I didn't eat carrots last night."

Nodding as if this made perfect sense, he sank strong white teeth into his donut, licking chocolate frosting off his upper lip. "Mmm . . ."

Her mouth watered. "I'll give you a piece of mine for a piece of yours."

His eyes darkened and he immediately broke off a large part of his donut and offered it to her. She did the same and felt his warm breath brush over her fingers before he sank his teeth into her jelly-filled.

Eyes on hers, he smiled as he chewed and swallowed. "Yeah, that's good, too. Hey!" He pulled his tray back and looked at the second chunk she'd quickly snagged from his donut.

"Sorry," she said with an easy grin. She wasn't sorry. At all. And she might have laughed at the look on his face as he studied what was left, but she was up next at the cash register. She gently nudged Toby forward, as just ahead, Nick picked up his bag and turned to her.

"Hey, I saw your Jeep. I meant to ask what happened."

"A little fender bender," she said, extremely aware of Brady behind her.

Brady coughed and said, "Bullshit," softly in her ear at the same time.

Lilah gave him a little nudge with her hip, knocking him out of her personal space bubble. He might kiss like heaven, and maybe he had great taste in food, but he was far too cocky.

Nick divided a look between them, then settled on Lilah. "I'm sensing a story here."

"No. No stories, good or otherwise, and it wasn't my fault." She paused and sighed. "Okay, it was totally my fault."

"She has a parking problem," Brady said.

Nick laughed. "She has a lot of 'parking' problems."

Great. Lilah loved Nick, but he had a big mouth. "My foot slipped," she said. "No big deal."

"Uh-huh. Remember our senior year when your foot 'slipped' and you drove off the bridge in your granny's SUV?" Nick asked.

Both men were smiling now, and Lilah took a moment for a deep breath. "We're not discussing this." Digging through her purse for her wallet, she turned to Dee.

From over her shoulder a ten appeared. "For both of us," Brady said.

Dee shot Lilah a brows-up look.

Lilah ignored the unspoken question. "Thanks," she said to Brady. "I'll owe you."

"Donuts," he clarified. "Not carrots."

Dee smiled. "So, who's the cutie?"

Lilah very carefully didn't look at Brady "Brady Miller. He's come to visit Adam and Dell."

Dee cackled. In fact she laughed so hard, she ended up doubled over. "Honey, I meant the dog."

"Oh." Lilah grimaced as her face heated and tried to pretend that Brady wasn't right behind her, looking far too amused.

"You're right, though," Dee said, sizing up Brady. "He's a real cutie, too."

Lilah sighed. "The dog," she said firmly, "is a rescue. He's going to a good home." And finally, as she said this, she saw Shelly pull up out front. Which made her realize she had only a few minutes left with Toby.

She was well aware that the whole point to running the humane society was to place animals in loving homes. She knew this, but her gut didn't always get it, and both it and her heart squeezed hard as she looked down at Toby waiting patiently at her feet, so quiet and accepting of whatever fate came his way. Dammit. Every one. She mourned every single one. "I have to go."

Dee cocked her head, then looked to the door as Shelly entered the bakery. "Aw, honey," she murmured, covering Lilah's hand with her own, her voice holding so much sympathy that Lilah's throat closed. "Never gets easier for you, does it?"

"What?" Brady asked, looking into Lilah's eyes with a frown. "What doesn't get easier? You stay up all night studying again?"

"Studying?" Dee asked in surprise. "Studying what?"

Lilah sighed. Her studies weren't classified information, but neither had she told anyone other than Dell and Adam.

And Brady—by accident. Literally. It was just that she'd quit college and come home with her tail between her legs. This time if something happened, she'd rather be a two-time failure in private. "Nothing," she said, grabbing a bottle of water to offset the donut calories. She fumbled through the bottom of her purse for loose change.

"Oh, don't worry about it." Dee patted her hand. "It's on the house since I know you're about to get your heart broken." She smiled sweetly over Lilah's head at Brady. "I adopted my own sweet Lexie from her last year. She cried for a week. Lilah, not Lexie."

"I did not," Lilah said. She'd cried for two weeks. She knew exactly how ridiculous that was, just as she knew how silly she was being over dreading handing Toby off. She'd only had him one night, and he was going to a woman who really wanted him.

"She still comes and visits," Dee told Brady.

Lilah felt the weight of Brady's gaze as he studied her thoughtfully, but she couldn't concentrate on that with Shelly waving at her. She was midforties, with wavy brown hair piled on top of her head and a friendly, kind face. She wore jeans and a rec center sweatshirt, perfect for a day with kids at the rec center and for being a new doggy mama.

Lilah grabbed the donuts Dee had bagged, murmured "let's go" to Toby, and walked blindly toward Shelly. The two of them moved outside for some privacy. Lilah gave Shelly both her bag of donuts—she'd lost her appetite— and an introduction to Toby. In five minutes Shelly and Toby were fast friends, walking off together into the sunset.

Okay, it was morning, and the sun was nowhere close to setting, but to Lilah it felt like an ending nevertheless. She swiped at her eyes. "Suck it up," she whispered fiercely to herself. "It's all good, no matter how hard it is."

"I'm going to refrain from saying 'That's what she said' since you seem to be having a moment."

Whirling around, she glared at Brady, who was leaning against the front wall of the building. "Why do you keep sneaking up on me?"

Instead of answering, he handed her a bag.

Opening it, she found two additional old-fashioned chocolate glazes. "Since you handed yours off. Thought you could use them," he said with a shrug.

"I gave them away so I wouldn't eat all three. I was saving myself."

"Okay." He tried to take the bag back, but she slapped his hand and hugged the bag to her chest.

He appeared to fight a smile, but his voice was serious. "Are you okay?"

"Yes. Though I'd be a hell of a lot better if you hadn't told the whole world that I have a parking problem."

"I didn't tell the whole world. Just what's his name. Your friendly ex."

She blew out a sigh. "Nick. And how do you know he's an ex?"

"It's either that, or he's a prospect. Which would explain the hungry look on his face."

"Ex," she admitted. "And he looked hungry because he was. For donuts."

"And for you as well." Stepping into her personal space bubble as he had a habit of doing, Brady cupped her face and tilted it up to his, running his thumb under her eye, catching a tear she'd missed. "You don't look like you're okay," he said quietly.

She sent him another glare just for the heck of it and tried to turn away, but he held her still.

And close.

And Lord, he was deadly up close. "What?" she asked, sounding testy. Because she was.

He backed her closer to the building, under the eaves and away from the window, giving them a little bit of privacy. "You look like you need . . ." His eyes darkened a little and his thumb brushed over her bottom lip now, making it tingle and tremble open.

"What? I need what?"

"This." Holding her gaze for as long as possible, he leaned in and lightly brushed her mouth with his warm, firm one.

She heard a sound, a whimper really, and realized it was her. He was right. She needed this. Bad. Fisting his shirt to hold him close, she heard the sound again, horrifyingly, embarrassingly needy.

"Shh," he whispered soothingly, and then kissed her once more, not lightly this time.

She promptly forgot everything, including the fact that they were standing on the sidewalk in broad daylight, with cars going by and people moving in and out of the bakery. It all faded away behind the wild pounding of her heart.

With a hand on the nape of her neck, Brady deepened the kiss, his other hand gliding down to the small of her back to hold her against him.

On board with that, she loosened her hands from his shirt and slid them up his chest and around his neck, pressing as close as she could to his hard, warm body.

When they were both breathless, he pressed his lips to her throat and murmured something she couldn't quite catch because her blood was still roaring through her veins. "What?" she murmured.

He rocked her against him. "No idea what I'm going to do with you."

She didn't know what he was going to do with her either, but she hoped it was good. She might have asked him to speak slowly and in great detail but she became aware that her hands had migrated and were now perched precariously low on what felt like perfect eight-pack abs.

Two inches south and she'd have hit the jackpot.

She glanced down and revised. One inch. He hadn't moved so she tipped her head back up and found his eyes on hers, dark and scorching. "We seem to have a little chemistry," she whispered.

His lips curved slightly in acknowledgment.

"I should go," she said slowly, but her mind wasn't on the words. Instead it was thinking, *One more inch!* "Really. You're going to need to back off a little, because I need to—"

He lifted his hands, indicating that he wasn't holding her in any way and she felt the blush on her face. Gathering her dignity, she forced herself to back away and turned to the Jeep.

"Lilah."

She kept her back to him and closed her eyes. "Yeah?"

When he didn't say anything, she glanced back.

"Why do you give the animals away if you want to keep them?"

"Because that's what I do," she said, surprised. "It's my job."

He came up behind her, putting his hand on hers on the Jeep handle, preventing her from opening the door. "And what's up with the studying all night and not telling anyone?"

"That's . . . private."

"A secret?"

"Sort of." She paused. "Okay, yes, I told you a secret. I was frazzled and had just hit your truck, and you were holding the babies in the box for me, and . . ."

And she'd been thinking he looked so cute holding them, too, looking all helpful and tough at the same time.

Oh, and that he had a nice ass, and that she hadn't been with a man in a long time. Too long.

And that he wasn't a fixture in this town, which made him both dangerous and safe . . . "I was momentarily distracted," she admitted. "And it slipped out. But now that you've reminded me of it, you do owe me a secret in return. Make it a good one. I could use a distraction."

"I don't do secrets."

Okay, then. Good to know. Drawing a deep breath, she pushed his hand out of her way and he let her. She opened the Jeep's driver door and climbed in, taking just one more last quick glance. But only one because more than that with him tended to render her incapable of reason. "Thanks for the donuts," she said. "Twice."

He nodded but didn't otherwise move. She blew out a sigh and eyed the truck parked in front of her. "You should probably go first. I'm even more distracted today than yesterday. And as you know, I tend to do stupid things when distracted."

"Something to remember," he said lightly.

## Six

The next evening, after Dell had seen all his patients, he closed up shop and set Brady up for a website photo shoot. He showed Brady into one of the exam rooms and patted the exam table. "I was thinking we could have a series of pictures of 'patients' in various rooms, as if maybe animals led this place, you know?"

"That's good," Brady said, nodding. "Funny. Warm. Makes the place seem welcome and readily inviting. None of you?"

"Nah," Dell said. "I like the idea of just the animals. You can put one in Jade's reading glasses behind her desk. One with my stethoscope sitting on this table, maybe."

Brady had spent the day cataloging all that was wrong with the Bell 47, in a hurry to get that renovation on track. He'd spent the hours alone with his own thoughts, and they hadn't always been good ones. At least ten times he'd started to go in search of Adam and Dell to tell them he didn't want to stay for another twenty-nine days. He couldn't handle the thinking.

But he hadn't.

Now all he wanted to do was grab a shower and hit the sack, but he'd promised to take these pictures. He'd been dreading this, knowing the only time he liked being behind the camera was on his own terms. It was, after all, a creative release for him, not a chore. But he found himself liking Dell's ideas for the pictures and felt an energetic creative surge. "Yeah," he said. "We can do that. But are you going to materialize your patients? Because you sent them all home."

"I've got that handled," Dell said, just as the sounds of a wild stampede sounded from down the hall.

Brady poked his head out of the examination room in time to see Lilah appear, both hands occupied with myriad leashes. In one hand she had one, two, three dogs. No. Two dogs and a lamb. In her other hand she held Abigail's leash. And Brady couldn't help it—he felt the smile crack his face.

"I've got two cats and a bunny available as well," she called out, blowing a few strands of hair from her eyes. "Where do you want us?"

Brady didn't give a shit about where the animals went, but he knew exactly where he wanted her.

Beneath him, panting his name.

A little unsettled at that thought, he shoved a hand through his hair and shrugged at Dell. "You're the director."

"Um," Dell said, looking guilty as he pulled his keys out of his pocket. "Actually, you are. I've got a date."

"What?"

"Now don't let the lamb scare you. Lulu's really very sweet. Just don't let her get her nose in the family jewels, man. She's been known to take an unexpected bite."

It wasn't Lulu he was afraid of, and something of that must have shown on his face.

Dell studied him a moment, brow drawn. "I can trust you with her, right?"

"The lamb? Sure."

When Dell only looked at him, Brady glanced at Lilah

as she moved toward them and slowly shook his head. "Definitely not."

"Christ," Dell muttered, and swiped a hand down his face. "I'm going to hope to God you're kidding." And with that, he met Lilah halfway, kissed her cheek, shot one last long warning glance in Brady's direction, and was gone.

Lilah came to a stop before Brady. "What was that?"

"Nothing."

"You told him you couldn't be trusted with me."

Brady arched a brow. "So if you overheard, why did you ask?"

"Because I wanted to see what you would say. What kind of an answer was that?"

"What did you want me to say?" Brady asked her.

"Not that."

He shrugged. "It was the truth."

She stared up at him, looking a little flummoxed at that. "Oh," she breathed.

Yeah, oh. Just being near her like this—she smelled like mangoes tonight—drained some of the tension in him, in spite of himself. No matter what she thought, she was a sight for sore eyes, that was for damn sure. She wore snug, hip-hugging jeans and a lacy white T-shirt that was sheer enough to reveal the white cami beneath it and a faint hint of an equally white bra.

Which he found ridiculously, inexplicably hot. The past few nights he'd fantasized about Lilah. He'd told himself that he was an ass, but his self seemed completely unconcerned.

The lamb—Lulu, he presumed—stepped forward and tried to shove her face into his crotch, but duly warned by Dell, Brady backed up.

"Don't be afraid. She's sweet."

At Lilah's words, Lulu appeared to smile, pulling back her lips to show her teeth, which didn't look sweet to Brady.

"She just wants to catch your scent," Lilah assured him.

Pushing aside images of dropping to his knees and pressing his face to Lilah's crotch to catch her scent, he grabbed the dogs' leashes from Lilah. Given the unstableness of his brain tonight, it was best to get this over with.

Two hours later, he got the last shot of the night, a cat sitting on Jade's desk daintily washing her face with the computer opened on the schedule behind her.

Lilah gathered up all the animals while Brady slipped his camera back into its case. "Think you have everything you need?"

He knew he didn't. Not even close. She looked up from wrapping a leash around her wrist, caught his expression, and went still. "Are you going to kiss me again?"

"Yeah," he said, surprising himself as he moved in. With two dogs, a duck, a lamb, and a cat between them, he cupped her face and kissed her. A brush of his lips to hers, once, twice. Unable to pull away without more, he settled in against her mouth, their lips the only points of their body touching. He'd meant it to be short and sweet, but she made a sound that went straight through him and the kiss deepened, a hot, intense tangle of tongues that ended abruptly when one of the dogs at their feet barked.

She let out a shaky breath and backed to the door. "I don't know what that means."

He did. It meant he was fucked. "It means good night."

She nodded and turned away but not before he caught the quick flash of disappointment and hurt.

"Lilah—"

But she was gone.

For two days Lilah worked and avoided going to Belle Haven, and for two days all she thought about was Brady. She knew from Adam that Brady had started uploading pics for their website and brochures. She knew from Jade that he was also working on the Bell, and apparently upping foot traffic to the center because he was looking good while doing it.

A part of Lilah had wanted to go see but she'd been busy. Busy thinking about her growing restlessness and what she needed. She was pretty sure that what she needed was Brady, but she wasn't sure he was on board with the program.

"You okay?" Cruz asked after they worked the midday shift together.

"Yeah. Why?"

"We've had three customers mention the new guy"— Cruz put air quotes around *new guy*—"and you've gotten a look on your face each and every time." He gave her an exaggerated look of dazed lust, complete with dopey eyes and tongue hanging out.

"I never look like that," she said, and shoved him. They were in the back, organizing outside playtime. They had two of the dogs separated from the others because they were elderly and liked sedate, quiet playtime, which they'd just had. They were now lying happily on the floor at Lilah's feet, cooling down, and she took a moment to hug · each of them.

"You do so get that look. When it's been a while since you got laid."

"Bite me, Cruz."

"I'd love to bite you," he said as they escorted the older dogs back to their area and took out their three other guests; Lulu and two rambunctious dogs. "But been there, done that. And you bit back, remember?"

She laughed and, not for the first time, felt grateful that they'd realized that they were so much better together like this, bicker-buddies. It'd have been awful if they couldn't make this work because she cared about him so very much and knew the feeling was mutual. "Kissing and telling, Cruz?"

"Biting and telling."

They took the rest of the animals outside for supervised

playtime in the sunshine and fresh air. Later, when they were back inside, Cruz administered meds and Lilah moved to the kitchen to do the dishes and general cleaning. Afterward, she worked on paperwork until it was pickup and drop-off time.

Celia came in for Lulu. Celia Ayala had been Lilah's grandma Estelle's frenemy and bridge partner for fifty years—until Estelle had committed the ultimate faux pas and gone to the Big Bridge Game in the sky. Alone.

Lilah accepted Celia's check and wrote up a receipt.

Celia was the approximate size and shape of an Oompa-Loompa, and thanks to the new tanning salon in town, she had the same skin tone as one, too. "Can you book me for next Thursday, dear? Oh, and also tell me about the new sexy hunk working at Belle Haven. What's his name?"

"Brady," Lilah said without thinking, making Celia grin. "What?"

"I hear you're seeing him."

"What? No. No. I'm not, I only—" *Kiss him every chance I get . . .* "No," she said again weakly.

"Someone told me you'd been seen in his truck."

Lilah sighed. "I hit it. I was tired and—"

"You work too hard. Listen, dear. Your grandmother—bless her ornery soul—agreed with me on one thing."

"Are you sure? Because I never knew you two to agree on anything."

Celia waggled a finger. "We agreed on this. You only get one life. So you need to find the right man. Do you understand what I'm saying?"

"Do you?"

"Listen to you," Celia chided. "You have a mouth on you, just like Estelle did."

Lilah thought about her beloved grandma, who for all intents and purposes had been her mom, her dad, her everything, and smiled even though her chest felt too tight. "You miss her."

"She drove me crazy." Celia sighed. "But yes, I miss her. She was my last friend. The rest are all dead. Since I'm planning on living forever, it's going to be lonely. Now stop changing the subject. I'm old, not stupid. We all know how much you gave up to care for her in the end, but she's gone, Lilah. It's your turn to live."

"I am."

"Then stop wasting time talking to old ladies. Go back to kissing the hunk."

Lilah stared at her. "How did you know?"

"Well, honey, if you want to keep a man a secret, you don't kiss him out in front of the bakery on Main."

Later, Lilah was in the middle of an online lecture for her animal biology class when she got a call from Dell.

"Got a check for you," he said. "For last week when you boarded those two beagles for us."

Belle Haven didn't keep overnight guests; they paid the kennels to do that for them. "My favorite kind of call," she said.

"And here I thought just hearing my voice was your favorite kind of call."

"That, too."

"Oh no, it's too late. You've given yourself away. You only want the money."

"Yes, it's ridiculous how fond of eating I've become."

Dell was silent for a beat. "You were supposed to tell me if you need help."

And wasn't that just the problem. She hated needing help. Always had. "I'm fine, I was kidding."

Mostly.

"I'll bring the check over with dinner," he said. "We'll talk."

Oh great. A talk. Where he'd try to butt in and she'd dance around her money problems. "No, I'll come to you. I have some files for you, anyway. And I'm busy for dinner."

She had a date with a very healthy, very green salad, followed by a little ice cream—or the whole pint, depending on how her studying went.

A few minutes later, Lilah walked to the center, eyeing the dark clouds drifting down from the peaks, turning into shreds of mist that gave substance to the raw wind. She zipped up her sweatshirt and picked up the pace. Either Mother Nature had forgotten it was summer, or she needed some Midol.

At Belle Haven, she went straight to the reception desk. Jade sat behind the counter working the phone and the computer at the same time with her usual calm, implacable efficiency, with a kitten sleeping in her lap. Behind her chair on the floor lay a 150-pound St. Bernard dog, snoring with shocking volume.

Jade had glorious strawberry blonde hair that she kept perfectly twisted on top of her head and sharp green eyes that didn't take shit from anyone. Her clothes looked straight out of a magazine, some sort of belted shirt dress, bangles up one arm, and shoes to die for. She'd moved to Sunshine a few years ago from Chicago so she could ski her way through the winters. She and Lilah had since become good friends, so Lilah knew the real story, that Jade's move hadn't so much been a desire to ski as it'd been a need for some space from a tough situation.

"Check it out," Jade whispered, nudging her chin in the direction of the windows.

Lilah's attention was first caught by the very full waiting room and the women whose noses were practically glued to the windows leading to the side yard. "What's going on?"

"That's what I'm trying to show you. It's our newest attraction." Jade pointed outside, off to the right where the Bell had been parked for weeks now, ever since it had been delivered from Smitty's airport across the meadow. From the hood the lower half of a male body stuck out. Scuffed work boots and long legs that led to—

"The best ass I've ever seen," Jade whispered.

It was true. Brady absolutely had the best ass ever seen. Lilah took a minute to admire it.

"Don't you think?" Jade asked.

"Well . . . he sure looks good in cargo pants," she said carefully. "All those pockets for his stuff."

"And you just know that not all of his . . . stuff is in his pockets." Jade slid her a look. "You kiss him again?"

"What?" Lilah started guiltily. How the hell did everyone know this? "I don't . . . I haven't . . ."

"Main Street, Lilah," Jade said patiently. "You might as well have sent a clip to YouTube yourself."

Oh, good grief. "Dell said there was a check . . . ?"

Jade laughed, but took mercy on her. "In his office."

Lilah made her way through the crowded reception area to the offices. Dell wasn't behind his big desk, but there was an envelope leaning up against his computer with her name on it. In it was the check for services rendered, plus three hundred bucks in cash. "Oh, hell no."

"Not enough?" he asked, coming into the room. He was wearing scrubs and a white lab coat, both emphasizing his tall, lean form in a favorable way. His charming smile only added to his appeal. It was the smile of a man who knew it rendered most females stupid.

"Don't you smile at me." She pulled out the three hundred dollar bills and slapped them down on his desk. "I don't take pity cash."

"Noted, but that's not what that is. It's a loan." Clearly seeing the ready denial on her face, he added softly, "We just want to help, Lilah."

Damn if that didn't melt her. "You can. By believing in me."

"I do."

She sighed and hugged him hard. "The kennels are doing better this year, really. I'm going to be fine."

Hopefully.

He held her a minute, cheek pressed to the top of her head as he let out a long breath, a good indicator that she was being a pain in his ass. With a sigh of her own, she patted his chest, took the check, and left him. She was back at the main counter saying good-bye to Jade when the front door opened.

Brady strode inside, moving with that easy economical grace that spoke of a lifetime of discipline and military training. His T-shirt was snug around his broad chest and biceps, loose over his flat abs. He was streaked with grease and looking hot enough to be on the cover of *Aviation* as he stopped in front of Jade's desk with a bundle in his hands. "Either of you know what the hell this is?"

Lilah took a look at the small brown dog, though its color might have been due more to the dirt and mud that was stuck to its tangled and matted fur. His floppy ears nearly covered his sweet soulful eyes. He sneezed once, hard, and then the ears did cover his eyes. With a violent shake of his head, they fell back into place.

"It was sitting in front of my truck," Brady said, frowning.

"It's a dog," Jade said.

Brady lifted the scrawny, clearly neglected dog up a little higher and inspected it. It licked his chin.

"Aw," Jade said. "He likes you."

Brady looked so horrified, Lilah laughed.

Brady turned his head and narrowed his razor-sharp blue eyes on her. Probably he wasn't used to being a source of amusement. Probably, mostly women just lay down at his feet and begged him to take them.

Not that she was even close to doing that. No siree. She had some pride. She did all of her begging in private.

"It looks hungry and thirsty," Brady said. "And maybe

he has a cold, I don't know. I thought I'd bring him inside, out of the sun."

Oh. Oh, damn. He cared.

Either she made a sound or he sensed her softening because he thrust the dog at her. "Here. I think it needs to be checked out by Dell."

The dog wore a midnight blue rhinestone encrusted collar, though most of the rhinestones were missing: TWINKLES.

"Cute," she said, but didn't take the dog. She couldn't have said why. She automatically gravitated to all animals, especially lost, hurting ones, but there was something so innately sweet about seeing the little thing in Brady's big, capable hands.

"Twinkles," Brady said with disgust. "It should be illegal to name a dog that."

"Twinkles is a perfectly fine name for a little girl dog."

Brady shifted the dog, rolling it easily over in his big hands, revealing his distinct boy parts.

"Oh," Lilah said. "Huh. Well, maybe he's named after someone."

"Not my problem. You're the humane society." He was still holding out the thing as if maybe the dog was a ticking time bomb. "So it's your job to take him, right?" He looked to Jade for confirmation of this.

"Yes," Jade said. "We do get abandoned animals dropped off here all the time. Since we're the biggest animal center in this part of the state, we get a lot of business from the outlying areas, so who knows where he could have come from. If there's no owner to call, we get them to Lilah here."

"Hopefully he has an owner nearby." But Lilah could tell by the look of the little guy that he'd been on his own for a while, and in her experience that meant there'd probably be no owner forthcoming. "I'll put up flyers and get it on the website."

Brady nodded, looking a little impatient that neither she

nor Jade had relieved him of his burden. "Here," he said again.

She couldn't explain even to herself why she did it. Temporary insanity owing to a severe lack of sugar. That, or a case of severe unfulfilled and overworked hormones, she decided as she turned the sign-in sheet toward him. Because how many times had he kissed her now? Three.

Three.

She felt like she was going to self-combust. And she'd even self-combusted in the shower that morning. "Dell's pretty busy today, but I'm sure Jade can squeeze you in to see him at some point. Does your dog need any vaccines?"

Brady scowled. "My dog? Is that supposed to be funny?"

Lilah smiled and stepped on Jade's foot when the receptionist opened her mouth to speak. "As I said, I'm sure Jade can work Twinkles in, but there's a bit of a wait at the moment."

Brady stared at her for a long moment. She'd bet that there'd been many who'd cowered beneath that look. And she might have, except that the pathetic little creature quaking in his big hands, the one her heart was dying to grab and snuggle, was looking up at him like he was salvation.

She recently felt the same way.

"You're the humane society," Brady said a little tightly.

"I am. And you know where my kennel is, if you decide to abandon the animal."

Brady glanced down at the dog's miserable face and his own took on a pained expression. "I didn't abandon it. Someone else did. Christ," he muttered when she just looked at him serenely. "Is this about me telling your ex you rear-ended my truck?"

"Cruz?" Jade asked, surprised.

"Cruz?" Brady slid a look at Lilah. "I was talking about Nick. How many exes do you have?"

"None of your business."

"Two," Jade told him. "She doesn't get out much since her grandma passed on."

"Really?" Lilah said to her, heavy on the disbelief. "You're going to go there?"

Jade lifted a shoulder. "Sorry. It's been a long day."

Brady gave Lilah a long look she couldn't begin to interpret to save her own life before turning to Jade. "Book me for the last appointment of the day. I'll be back." He glanced down at the dog. "He looks like he's healthy enough to make it until then." Clearly frustrated with the lot of them, he made his way back toward the door to leave, the dog tucked against his chest.

*The sexy cuteness*, Lilah thought. *Oh good Lord, the sexy cuteness . . .*

Jade was brows up. "What was that?" she whispered.

"Don't start. And why did you bring my grandma into it?"

"It slipped out. I'm telling you. I need a nap. But seriously, what was that, making him keep the stray? What are you up to?"

Lilah watched Brady stop just outside the door and stare down at the dog in his arms. "I don't know what you're talking about."

"Really? Because forgive me if I'm wrong," the receptionist said dryly, "but I was under the impression that you take in all the neglected, forgotten animals around here."

Lilah shrugged.

Jade's smile came slow and proud. "You wanted him to suffer. Nice. So what did he do to you exactly—besides kiss you into apparent insanity?"

Exactly? Lilah had no idea.

Except she did. She was horribly, devastatingly attracted to him, like moth to the flame attracted. Which technically wasn't his fault, but she felt that if she had to suffer, then so did he. "Does there have to be a reason?"

"To make a guy suffer? Absolutely not," Jade said with certainty.

That night Lilah was sitting at her table doing a balancing act with her bills when the knock came at her door.

"Mew," Sadie said, all soft and warm and cozy in Lilah's lap. The watchdog on the job.

"Have to get up," Lilah told her.

The cat dug her claws in just enough to have Lilah hissing in a breath, but before she could dislodge the cat, Adam let himself in. His big body filled up her kitchen as he dropped a large pizza box, a six-pack, and a bag on the table.

"Dinner," he said. "A meat supreme special and, in case you're feeling girlie, a salad."

She stared at the food, torn by the rumbling in her belly and the sick feeling that he was babysitting her. "I told Dell I was busy."

"Yeah, but I'm not the sucker he is."

This was true. Nothing got by Adam. Which is what worried her. "He told you that I didn't take the money."

Not answering, he handed her a bottle of Corona before getting another for himself. Then he opened the pizza box.

They ate in silence for a while, silence being Adam's favorite state of being. She tried going with that, but in the end she was just not in the mood. "So . . . you're worried about me," she said flatly.

Adam grabbed another slice of pizza.

"Let me guess—you lost the coin toss with Dell, which left you stuck with me. Only you don't know how to tell me this because you're a penis-carrying human and can't figure out how to communicate with a mere vagina."

He choked on a bite and reached for his beer.

She clapped him on his broad-as-a-mountain back, then ruffled his short, silky dark hair. "I'm okay, you know. Really." She looked at the last piece of pizza. She didn't need it. Problem was, it was calling her name.

"It's got the same amount of calories if you eat it now or after agonizing over it for another two minutes," Adam said.

Blowing out a breath, she snatched it before he could.

"And I didn't lose the coin toss," he said. "I won it. Loser had to talk to Brady."

That caught her interest. She licked cheese off her thumb. "About?"

His silence was answer enough.

"Oh, for God's sake!" she burst out. "Are you kidding me? Haven't you done enough to my sex life?"

He choked again and spilled beer down the front of him. "Fuck," he muttered, rising, then tripping over Sadie.

"Mew!"

He scooped up the three-legged cat and held her to his wide chest in apology as he grabbed the paper towels. "Want to run that by me again?"

"Sure. You're ruining my sex life!"

He carefully set Sadie back down. "I didn't realize you had a sex life."

"Exactly!" She rose, too, giving him, for good measure, a shove to the chest that didn't budge him one single inch. "You hover like an overprotective mama bear, scaring all the guys away except for the ones I don't want anymore. And I'm . . . Argh!" Turning away from him, she went to the sink and stared out into the night, gripping the edge of the tile so she didn't smack him again.

"You're lonely," he said, sounding surprised.

"What, you think only guys need regular orgasms? And before you get all sanctimonious, I wanted Brady well before I knew he was your foster brother."

"Jesus."

In the reflection of the glass in front of her, she watched as he pressed his fingers to his eyes and grimaced. He drew a deep breath and pointed to the table. "Sit."

"Why, because you asked so nicely?"

"Sit your ass down and I'll tell you about Brady."

She fought with her curiosity and lost. She sat.

Adam strode to the freezer, grabbed her always present ice cream, retrieved two spoons from a drawer, and sat next to her. "He was fifteen when we showed up at Sol's. I was thirteen, Dell was twelve. None of us had ever had a steady home."

She already knew this, about Dell and Adam at least. They were blood brothers. Their mother was Native American and lived on a reservation somewhere. She'd left only to give birth and had gone back to that world. Their father had taken the boys but then had died when they'd been young. Their mother, already moved on to another husband and family, had not wanted them back.

"Dell kept getting beat up at school," Adam said, staring at the beer in his fingers. "I kept getting suspended for fighting—badly, by the way. I had no idea what I was doing. Brady scared the shit out of us. He was silent. And tough as nails."

Lilah could imagine that without too much difficulty.

"Sol had a gym in his basement," Adam went on. He ran a finger over the bottle. "One day Brady took us down there. We were pretty sure that he was going to kill us and no one would ever find the bodies, but instead he taught us how to protect ourselves."

"He taught you how to fight?"

"Yeah. It took a good long while, too—we were pretty pathetic. About a month into this, we were out past curfew. I can't remember why. And a group of, I don't know, maybe five or six kids tried to jump us." He laughed softly but without much mirth. "Dell was feeling brave and swung the first punch. The guy ducked and Dell hit Brady by accident."

Lilah gasped. "Oh no."

"Brady had to fight the guys trying to jump us and keep Dell from hindering the process."

"Well?" she demanded when he didn't go on. "What happened?"

"We managed to come out on top but only because of Brady's skill at hand to hand."

"Did any of you get hurt?"

"Some. Not too badly." He rubbed his jaw as if remembering the old aches.

"So that's how you got so tough," she said, going with a teasing tone to lighten the mood.

But Adam didn't smile. Instead he hesitated. He never hesitated.

"Uh-oh," she said. "Is this where you tell me the three of you launched into a life of crime?"

"No, I was already well into my criminal career by then, all on my own." He rubbed a hand over his eyes, looking weary. "I already had two arrests for underage drinking and then I got caught trying to steal a car."

"Oh, Adam."

He shook the sympathy off. "I was young and stupid and angry. Brady helped steer me through the aftermath of that disaster on the condition that I straighten my shit out or he'd straighten me out himself. Painfully."

Lilah felt her heart turn over in its chest. "He cared about you, like a brother."

"At the time it felt more like a prison warden, but yeah. The point is, he always came through for us when we needed him."

"And you want to come through for him now?"

"Yeah. This land is one third his. And it's good to have him here."

"Where he's safe," she guessed. "For those few years he kept you safe, and you'd like to return the favor. Look at you trying to save us all."

He grimaced. "Jesus, don't make me out like a saint."

"No, a saint would have brought something good to top off my ice cream with." She smiled at him. "And I think it's sweet. Even if Brady, and me for that matter, don't like to accept help."

"No," he said quietly. "But you want him."

"Yes," she admitted, unwilling to lie. "Is that going to be a problem?"

He shrugged, his eyes dark and troubled. "Just . . . be careful. He's not the white-picket-fence type."

"I don't want a white picket fence." Yet. Because the truth was, she did want to meet the One and get married. Someday. But she'd waited this long, she could wait a little longer.

And in the meantime, there could be Brady. The pros far outweighed the cons. He wouldn't let Adam and Dell scare him off, and she didn't have anything to lose because they both knew the score up front. He was leaving. So there were no expectations and she could be free to enjoy herself.

A lot.

A corner of Adam's mouth quirked as he read her thought like a book. "Brady was tossed around more than we were. Something like four or five foster homes before Sol got him."

"Which makes it all the better that he has you guys and this place." And me . . .

Adam nodded. "Yes. He's had a lot of people in his life who didn't stick. So you should know . . . he doesn't tend to stick either."

"That's actually pretty funny coming from you." She hugged him. "Listen to me, okay? I'm not looking to make him stick. I'm just looking for some company."

"So you're okay being his one-night stand?"

"Not a one-night stand, no," she said. "I'll take a couple of nights. Or as long as it lasts. On our terms, his and mine. Not yours." She kissed his tense jaw. "Love you, though. Always will."

Adam just sighed and reached for the ice cream.

## Seven

Brady stood by the unlit fireplace and stared at the rug in front of it.

Or more accurately, the thing on the rug.

It was staring back at him. It was now midnight. An hour ago Brady had gone to sleep. Or tried to. The loft, being one room, allowed noise to carry, so when the dog had started crying and howling almost immediately, it was a shocking decibel level considering the pup was maybe seven pounds.

He'd tried everything. A blanket. A ticking clock from the mantel. Soft music from his own iPod. Okay, not soft, he didn't have soft, but hell, it was hard rock, the good stuff.

Every single time, the dog would appear to settle and Brady would crawl cautiously off to bed. He'd get comfortable and start to drift off.

And then the hell would begin all over again.

"They tell me that you're one hundred percent canine," Brady said, hands on hips. "But I'm thinking you're one hundred percent pussy."

The dog—Brady refused to think of it as Twinkles—let out a low whimper and rolled over, exposing its belly.

"Jesus." Brady sank to the couch in nothing but his knit boxers. "Come here, then."

Its sorrow apparently forgotten, the dog leapt up with enthusiasm and bounded over. He tried to jump up onto the couch, making it only about six inches off the ground before falling to his back on the floor.

Brady shook his head. "Failing is not an option, soldier. Try again."

Gamefully, the dog did just that, getting even less height this time before he once more hit the floor. With another sad whimper, he sat at Brady's feet, tail tentatively sweeping the floor.

Brady sighed and scooped a hand beneath his little concaved belly, lifting him up so that they were eye to eye. "Out of all the trucks in all the land, why mine?"

The dog wriggled joyfully. "Arf."

Brady blinked, then found himself grinning at the unexpected bark. It had been high-pitched and soprano, but hell it was better than a meow. "So you are a dog. You've got to work on the pitch, man. Can't have all the chick dogs thinking your boys never dropped." No need in telling him he probably wouldn't get to keep his boys.

"Arf!"

He'd created a monster. Brady laughed, then started to set the dog down, but he clung to his hand. Shaking his head, Brady set the thing on the couch next to him, where he immediately crawled into his lap.

Brady stared down at him and realized he was shivering. "You're nothing but a bag of bones." Pulling the dog against his chest, they had a little moment, and finally the dog stopped shivering. He licked Brady's chin.

"Listen," Brady said. "This is just temporary. Tomorrow we figure out what the hell Lilah's game is and she'll find you a home. She's good at it."

The dog didn't even blink, but in its chocolately eyes, Brady saw a hint of sadness. "Don't even try the puppy eyes, they don't work on me."

The dog blinked slowly.

Brady pointed at him. "Knock that off."

His answer was a soft whine.

"Look, I'm just passing through, that's it."

Not getting it, the dog set his head against Brady's chest and let out a shuddery sigh.

And Brady did the same. In his life, he'd taken responsibility for more people than he could count, but he'd steered clear of animals, never keeping one for himself. He'd not needed the extra burden. "If I were going to keep a dog," he said, "it would be a big one. Or at least one that could get up on the couch by himself."

He would have sworn censure filled the dog's dark gaze. "Hey, I'm just being honest here. You little things are yappers."

The little guy put his ears down, the picture of innocence.

And Brady had to laugh. "Right. Save it for someone you can manipulate, okay? Maybe the ladies." He thought of Jade and Lilah, both of whom had manipulated the hell out of him. "I deserve this," he muttered.

The dog cocked its head.

"Never mind. I'm so tired I'm talking to a dog." He got up, set the dog on the blanket, and then dropped like a stone onto the bed. He remained tense a moment, waiting, but he heard nothing and slowly relaxed.

Ahhh, sleep. He was halfway to paradise, lying on a warm beach with a beer in one hand and the silky coconut-scented skin of a woman under the other. And yeah, okay, maybe the woman looked a little like Lilah, right down to the mossy green eyes and deliciously curvy body, which was at the moment wearing nothing but the smallest of string bikinis . . .

And that's when he heard it, the one sound that could

bring him back from the beach and the sexy woman on it: "Arf!"

Fuck.

"Arf, arf, arf . . ."

The next morning, Brady came awake to a noise he didn't recognize and rolled off the bed, automatically reaching for his weapon.

When he realized he wasn't in combat, was in fact a million miles from any combat zone, he lay back down and scrubbed a hand over his face.

Then the sound came again.

What the hell?

He sat up and found the dog sitting in front of the kitchen sink, head deep in the trash he'd clearly hauled out from its place in the cupboard beneath. He was surrounded by a pizza box, an orange juice container, and two bottles of beer.

All empty.

"You are a menace to society," Brady said, and scrubbed a hand over his face. What had he gotten, maybe half an hour of sleep? Well used to sleep deprivation, he staggered out of bed thinking he might as well get on with what he'd agreed to do here.

Work on the Bell. "No more trash," he told the dog after he'd showered and dressed. "It'll make you sick." And with the little guy happy at his side, clearly not sick at all, they headed downstairs, stopping at Jade's desk. "Anyone come looking for him yet?"

Jade was one of those women who looked like she belonged in *Vogue*. Gorgeous but . . . different. Today she was wearing a sunshine yellow sundress that required sunglasses to look at her straight on. Her hair was piled on top of her head in a haphazard knot, held there by wooden tongue depressors. Her makeup was photo-ready. He nearly looked around to see if he'd stepped onto a movie set. "His name is Twinkles," she said.

He just looked at her.

Not particularly intimidated, her mouth twitched suspiciously.

He narrowed his eyes, and she let a very small smile free. "Lilah did her thing, putting out notices and flyers. We'll let you know."

"It's been two days."

"It has. Dell told me he examined him. He's about a year old, and other than slightly malnourished, he's healthy. Great news."

"Uh-huh. And you're certain Lilah's trying to find the owner," he said.

Jade smiled and patted his hand. "Lilah would never put a dog's well-being at risk for her own amusement."

"But she is amused."

"Oh, honey. There's no doubt."

It took Brady three days just to clean out the Bell 47. Not surprising, considering the chopper had suffered nearly three decades of neglect and abuse. It also needed airframe repairs, battery servicing, and a whole long list of engine and parts maintenance.

He enjoyed the work. In the army, he'd started out as a nobody, but well used to that he'd worked his ass off and through performance had earned a warrant officer slot, which had qualified him for flight training.

He'd never looked back. He loved being in the air, but when he couldn't be, his second love was this, taking apart and reassembling a chopper. As he worked, his new shadow stuck close, alternately snoozing in the sun or watching him with hero worship.

Belle Haven continued to do business around them. Del and Adam ran a tight ship, and it was a busy one. Adam, apparently the resident dog whisperer, was currently in the yard with three golden retrievers and their owners, teaching a class. Even from twenty-five yards away, Brady could tell it was more about training the wayward owners than the dogs.

When class ended, Adam ambled over.

"The dogs are pretty good listeners," Brady said, wiping his hands on a rag.

"It's not the dogs that need to listen."

"This one does." Brady nodded to the dog sleeping his day away in the sole sunspot as close to Brady as he could possibly get.

"What's his problem?" Adam asked.

"He won't sleep."

There was a moment of silence while Adam took in the dog doing just that. Well, not complete silence, since the mutt was snoring like a buzz saw.

"I mean at night," Brady said with a disbelieving shake of his head.

"What does he do instead of sleep?"

"Cries. Barks. Drives me up the fucking wall."

Adam's mouth hinted at a smile. "I'm going to tell you what I tell all of my clients. You're the one in need of training, not him."

"What are you talking about? I'd sleep all night just fine if he'd shut the hell up."

Adam let the smile escape. "Okay, man. Let me know when you're interested in being trained." He crouched and ruffled the dog's fur, and the little guy immediately rolled over on his back, exposing his belly for more.

Brady slid the dog a dark look, at least glad to see that his little belly was rounder now, no longer concave. "Traitor."

With a smirk, Adam rose. "So what's going on with you and Lilah?"

Dell had tried asking him this question days ago. Brady hadn't answered. Not because he wanted to be an ass, but because he honestly hadn't known. "Other than she saddled me with this thing?"

"Yeah. Other than that."

"Not sure."

"But something," Adam said.

Brady nodded. Yeah. There was definitely . . . something. And holy Christ, that something was explosive whenever they got too close.

"She's important to Dell and me."

"I know." He wondered if Adam was telling him to back the fuck off, and if it mattered. Could he back off? He honestly didn't know.

Adam was quiet a moment, just studying the Bell. "You're important to us, too," he finally said.

Brady let out a breath and nodded, feeling an unexpected tightening in his chest at that. There sure as hell weren't that many people who felt that way about him. He started to say something, he had no idea what really, when a truck pulled into the lot, interrupting him.

A leggy blonde hopped out of the truck wearing a business suit, the skirt as narrow as a pencil, emphasizing mile-long, perfectly toned legs. The high heels added an I'm Sophisticated and Expensive tone.

Turning to her truck, she reached back in and the red suit tightened across a world-class ass, wrenching a sound from Adam.

Brady looked at him but his face was carefully blank. Too blank. "Know her?"

"Yes," Adam said tightly.

The woman straightened and Brady saw that she was carrying a golden retriever puppy. She glanced over, drew herself up at the sight of Adam, then strode toward them, face cool and impassive.

Actually, Adam's expression was impassive. A battle-ready soldier.

The woman's face was set in stone. Angry, cold stone.

Brady figured she was one of those snooty bitches who was wound too tight. And going off the steam coming out of her ears, her hair was also wound too tight.

"Holly," Adam said with no inflection in his voice.

"Adam." There was plenty of inflection in her voice. Mostly temper. "Here." She thrust the puppy into Adam's arms. "She's defective."

Adam looked down at the puppy, who wriggled and licked his nose. A genuine light of affection came into his eyes. "Defective?"

"She's up all night crying."

At that, Brady was forced to rethink his opinion of her. She wasn't bitchy. She was exhausted.

He knew the feeling.

Adam gave Brady a brief look. "He's in a new place, Holly. He's scared." He thrust the puppy back into her arms, where it wriggled some more and licked her, too.

"I suppose you think this is funny," Holly said, attempting to stay lick-free.

"A little bit," Adam said evenly, not showing the smile that was in his voice.

Her mouth tightened. "My father's a domineering, annoying, meddling ass. And you. You're . . ." Breaking off, she shook her head. Turning on her heels, she strode off, long gorgeous legs churning up the distance while her puppy looked back over her shoulder at Adam, head bouncing.

"Big fan of yours?" Brady asked.

Adam didn't rise to the bait. He merely looked at the helicopter and then back into Brady's eyes. "You in for the month or not? I need to know whether to make plans."

"I said I'd do it. Make your plans."

With a nod, Adam was gone.

Brady went back to work for the rest of the day and then spent the night hours once again attempting to get the mutt to sleep.

But the damn dog was not interested in anything but driving Brady to the edge of sanity. At two in the morning, he was over it and reached for his cell phone to call Adam. "Fine," Brady grated to Adam's voice mail. "I'm waving the white flag. I need training."

At three A.M., Adam hadn't called back, and desperate, Brady tried Lilah, feeling completely justified at the late hour since she was the one who'd foisted the damn mutt on him in the first place. If he had to be up, she should, too.

He got her voice mail as well. "Come get him or I'm shipping him to Afghanistan," he said, and tossed his cell phone aside to flop to his back on the bed, listening to the damn dog cry.

Thing was, Brady was used to going on little sleep. He'd been trained for sleep deprivation in the military. But this wasn't an enemy thing. Hell, this wasn't even a logical thing.

It was one damn little dog getting the best of him. He'd tried everything short of strangling him, and finally somewhere near dawn, the mutt finally crashed. A grateful Brady fell into one of those dead slumbers that nothing short of a world-wide catastrophe could rise him from.

And yet he came suddenly awake what felt like a minute later to the sun poking him in the eyeballs. Sprawled facedown and spread-eagle on the bed, he cracked open one eye and blinked blearily at the clock.

Seven thirty.

Since the last time the dog had woken him up had been seven, he'd had exactly thirty minutes of sleep. "Fucking mutt."

"Aw. Is that any way to talk about your bedmate?"

"Jesus!" He pushed up on his arms and turned his head, his gaze landing on Lilah's. She stood at the foot of his bed in a pair of hip-hugging, ass-snugging jeans, a knit top, and a smile he couldn't quite read but was pretty sure was smug.

Then he realized there was a weight on his lower back, and that it was the dog.

Sleeping.

Brady dislodged it and rolled to his back. Grabbing his pillow, he shoved it behind him to lean back against the headboard.

The dog simply rolled onto its back and kept sleeping. The fucker.

Lilah's eyes were on Brady's bare chest. "Um."

Brady raised a brow and waited for her gaze to meet his.

When it did, she had two spots of color high on her cheeks. "Sorry, my phone was off last night, but I came over as soon as I got your message. Wanted to see if you were still alive."

Which he most definitely was. Alive. Very . . . alive. Some parts more than others.

Her gaze jerked back up to his eyes. "I thought you'd be . . . up."

They both knew just how *up* he was. "It was a rough night." He jabbed a finger in the direction of the dog, who was slowly coming awake and blinking innocently. "That thing kept me awake all night."

"What did you do to get him to go to sleep?"

"I told him to shut up."

She looked at him like he was an idiot. "Twinkles is a rescue. He needs love and affection."

"Sorry, fresh out of both." He sighed at her look of disappointment. He'd gone years and years, and to his recollection, he'd never once sighed. And yet he'd sighed more in the week he'd known her than he had in his entire life. "I gave him my blanket," he said. "I put a loud clock in that blanket to simulate the sound of a mother's heartbeat. But I'm starting to think he never had a mother, that he came from the devil himself."

"Did you try cuddling with him?"

"Huh?"

"Cuddle," she repeated. "You know, hold him close, snuggle, nestle . . . Like what you'd do if someone was with you in there . . ."

"The only someone allowed in my bed is a woman."

"Pretend he's a woman, then!"

Fascinated by her, he plumped his pillow some more and gave her a go-on gesture with his hand. "No, I don't know. Tell me what I'd do. In great detail."

She blew out a breath. "You're sick."

"Depends on your definition of sick."

"Just hug your dog!"

"Not my dog. The dog you foisted on me. Which begs the question: why?"

"Twinkles. His name is Twinkles," she grated, hands on hips now. "Not 'the dog' or 'it' or whatever else you've been calling the poor thing."

Probably best she didn't want to know what he'd called it earlier this morning around three thirty A.M.

And again at four thirty.

And five thirty.

"Haven't you ever had a dog?" she asked in exasperation.

"No. And I don't want this one. Fun's over, Lilah. You're taking him back."

She was just studying him speculatively. "Really? You've never had a dog?"

"Never."

She looked surprised for a beat, and then her expression softened. "So you don't know."

"Don't know what?"

"What having a pet can add to your life."

"Pain and suffering?"

She slanted him a pitying look and crossed her arms, which plumped up her breasts. "Unconditional love."

"Lilah, I travel all the time. I don't have time for unconditional love that comes with the responsibility of pet care."

"Or . . . you don't like attachments."

"Attachments are messy," he agreed. *She's chilly*, he thought, watching her nipples press against her white shirt. *Or maybe turned on.*

That made two of them . . .

"And messy can make you feel too much," she said. "Right?"

"Actually, at the moment I'm feeling plenty," he said softly.

Again her gaze flickered downward, past his chest to his lap, where the sheet was pooled. Two high spots of color appeared on her cheeks. "I should . . ."

"Go?"

"Yes." She lifted her chin. "Good-bye, Mr. No-Strings."

"Nice."

"Just calling it like I see it."

"Are you casting stones, Ms. Safety?"

Her brow furrowed. "What does that mean?"

"You let all your animals into your heart the same way you do the people."

"I don't—"

"And," he went on. "You do it for keeps. As far as I can tell, your friends have been your friends forever."

"So? That's a good thing."

"You also have two exes, both apparently still in your life."

"It's a small town. And actually, I have three exes, if you must know."

"Fine. Three. My point is that it's a comfort for you, having familiar people around you, and I get that. But I see it as a barrier to trying new things or stretching yourself. You live your life safe, Lilah."

He could tell he was back to pissing her off again. It was a specialty of his.

"Safe," she repeated in disbelief.

"Yeah. When was the last time you left this podunk town and saw the world?"

Something crossed her face at that, but she recovered quickly and narrowed her eyes. "I came to help, not be analyzed. Now do you want my help or not?"

"Yes."

"Okay, then." She scooped the dog off the bed. "This would be a lot better if we moved this to the kitchen. Or outside."

"Fine," he said. "I'll have to get dressed."

Her gaze once again slid to the sheet. "Don't tell me you're naked under there."

"Okay, I won't tell you."

She bit her lower lip as she hugged the dog close. The smart little shit licked her cheek and gave her the big, ol' puppy-dog eyes. "Aw," she murmured, and nuzzled him. "You're so sweet."

The dog craned his neck and sent Brady a knowing grin, the little shit. Brady must have made some sound of annoyance because Lilah turned back to him. "Look, it's a simple thing to make him feel safe and secure. It's a simple hug or a kind word. A quick cuddle. I mean, honestly, how hard is that?"

*Currently hard enough to pound nails*, he thought grimly.

She thrust the dog at him. "Practice while I'm here so I can see your technique."

"I'd rather practice with you."

She just looked at him, a tactic she'd learned from him, Goddammit. He snatched the dog then and, dangling him from his hands, brought them nose to nose.

"Not like that!" His sexy-as-hell teacher put a knee on his bed and leaned over him to press the dog to his chest. "Like that."

Her hair fell forward, dragging like fine silk over his shoulder and arm. Her breath was warm against his jaw as she held his hands on the dog. "Hug him."

He'd never been one to easily follow a command, even after all those years in the military, but he held the damn dog instead of doing what he wanted, which was to roll Lilah beneath him to show her cuddling. "Maybe we can call it something other than cuddling," he said.

"What, that threatens your manhood?"

Brady was wearing just a cotton sheet and a boner for the record books, so he was pretty fucking sure he was secure "in his manhood," but he decided to keep that to himself. More disconcerting, the dog had settled quietly on his chest, looking at him adoringly as his big puppy-dog eyes slowly . . . fluttered . . . shut.

The little shit was going to sleep. "You have got to be kidding me."

"See?" Lilah said. "It works."

"Yeah, now that I have to get up. I'm supposed to go running with Adam."

Their eyes connected, and as if she suddenly realized she'd gotten on his bed and was leaning over him, she hopped up and nearly fell to her ass.

"You okay?"

"I have to go," she said, whirling toward the door.

"Now who's chicken," he murmured.

"I have a lot to do."

Yeah, he was getting that. Maybe he should have opted for plan B which would have been pulling her down on the bed and cuddling her. They could both be naked by now. Yeah, he liked plan B. A lot.

"You're giving me mixed signals, Lilah."

She dropped her forehead to his door with an audible thunk. "I know! I'm sorry."

"When you settle on a decision, you'll let me know."

"My decision's made. It's courage I'm waiting on."

He didn't like the way that sat in his gut. "I scare you?"

Forehead still to the door, she let out a short laugh. "No. I scare me. And I should be scaring the hell out of you." She turned to him. "I'll tell Adam that you're coming—" She

broke off and grimaced. "I mean that you're getting up—"
She closed her eyes, her cheeks going pink.

Grinning, he set the sleeping dog next to him. When he made to toss back the covers to get out of bed, she squeaked and left, slamming his door.

He laughed—until he realized she hadn't taken the damn dog. By the time he got downstairs she was gone, and stayed gone. Which, he told himself several times throughout the following hours, was probably a good thing. A month was plenty of time for him, but he thought he knew her now, or at least he was starting to know her. And she gathered people in and kept them, not walking away after four weeks. Ever.

Yeah, she was the exact opposite from him in that respect, but he was drawn to her all the same, just as he was drawn to this small town. A novelty. A diversion. It would wear off, all of it.

Any minute now.


That night Brady stood in front of his bed staring down at the dog.

In return, the dog looked at the ceiling. At the floor. Anywhere but at Brady.

Finally Brady picked him up and dangled him nose to nose. "Here we are again. Bedtime."

The dog tried to lick him, but he wasn't holding it close enough. "And don't start with the eyes. We're going to sleep. Do you really need to"—*Jesus*—"cuddle?"

"Arf."

With a long-suffering sigh, Brady held him close and let himself be licked half to death. "There," he said, and carefully set the dog down on the blanket between the fireplace and the bed. "Stay. Sleep." Brady paused to inhale the delicious silence before getting into bed with a heartfelt groan. He was exhausted.

Three minutes later the whining started. "Christ on a stick!" He sat up, shoved his fingers through his hair and dropped his head to his knees. "I'm begging you. Shut up."

That didn't work either.

Throwing back the sheet, Brady dropped to the floor and the very nice pad of blankets he'd carefully folded, littered with stolen treasures. A shoe, a watch, a shirt—all Brady's.

The dog was a thief.

"We cuddled already. Don't tell me you need more. Come on, man, where's your self-respect?"

"Arf."

Shit. Brady crouched low and pulled the dog into his chest. The bundle wriggled with pleasure. Brady sighed, and beyond exhausted now, slowly lowered himself to the blankets.

Not bad.

"Arf!"

In the darkness, on the floor, Brady squeezed his eyes shut and tried to pretend he was back in Afghanistan, in the middle of a war zone, which was starting to seem like it might be easier.

"Arf!"

"I've been to places that look at you as a free meal," he warned softly in the dark. "Not my thing personally, but I'm willing to make an exception."

There wasn't another sound.

With a blissful, exhausted sigh, Brady began to drift off.

Only to come awake some time later. He lay there utterly still in the dark night, aware of the fact that something had woken him but not sure what. He was still on the floor, but there was no warm lump on his chest. Sitting up without a sound, he found the dog—in the middle of the fucking bed. How he'd gotten up there was a mystery, possibly by using the chest at the foot of the bed as a stepping stool.

But that's not what had woken him. Pulling on his jeans,

Brady grabbed the gun he'd stowed in the nightstand, moving soundlessly through the loft.

Then he heard it again, a crash from downstairs in the center that was completely closed up for the night. Thinking of the drugs that were kept there, he headed grimly toward the door, intending to protect what was Dell and Adam's with whatever force was necessary. He turned to tell the dog to stay, but he hadn't so much as taken a break in his snoring. Shaking his head, Brady moved out.

Downstairs, the open reception area was dark and empty, but the first examination room was lit, and sounds of a struggle were coming from within. Moving quietly along the shadows of the wall, Brady stepped into the open doorway, gun drawn.

"Don't move," he said.

But he was the one to go still.

In the room, arms full with an injured dog on the examination table, was Lilah.

The dog was snarling and trying to bite her, and as she wrestled with him, she spared Brady a quick glance.

"How's this for too safe?" she asked.

# Eight

Lilah took in the sight of Brady, gun in his right hand, the safety flipped off, and his hands braced in a shooter's stance and thought, *Holy shit*. That was her sole thought. *Holy shit*. She might have even murmured it in shock, in sheer appreciation for the magnificent male form standing there so utterly completely, fantastically . . . dangerous. She couldn't help it. In the overhead light, his nearly naked body gleamed muscular, lethal, and entirely too sexy. "You going to shoot me or help me?" she asked, as if her heart wasn't lodged in her throat, thundering so fast there were no pauses in between the beats.

"Fuck," he whispered under his breath and lowered the gun, thumbing the safety back on. The sound of it clicked loudly in the very still, very tense air as he tucked the gun into the back of his jeans before stepping close to lend her a hand.

Lilah let out a breath and shook it off. He seemed impossibly large and unyielding as he reached up and adjusted the overhead light so she could better see what she was doing, which she appreciated. "Thanks."

He nodded, looking a little worn, a little weary, and a whole lot rough around the edges.

When he was tired, as he clearly was now, his features were wary, as if he knew he was on autopilot and simply trusting his instincts. It did something to her, looking at him like this, almost . . . no. Vulnerable was not the right word.

Accessible.

"I'm sorry," she said quietly. "I should have let you know I was here."

He said nothing. Probably still working through his adrenaline rush.

She sure as hell was. And it was to her shame that she hadn't thought of this. Of him. She should have thought about the fact that he'd be upstairs sleeping, but the truth was that she broke in all the time with Dell's and Adam's blessing, and it hadn't occurred to her to wonder what his mental condition might be at being stirred in the middle of the night. He was ex-military but clearly not so ex. He certainly hadn't lost any of his skills.

Startling him had been bad.

He recovered far faster than she, but then again, she had her hands full. And still, all she could think was that she surely looked like crap in her baggy sweats, and he looked . . .

Hot.

God, so very very hot.

Tearing her gaze off him, she put her mind to the task at hand. She had Lucky's head tucked beneath her arm and was struggling with holding the rest of the seventy-pound animal still. She hadn't wanted to muzzle her and didn't, but now, it seemed, that might have been a mistake.

Lucky was in Lilah's care for two days while her owner was on a business trip. As had happened twice before, a porcupine had broken into the kennels through the cellar, come up the stairs to the main level, and ended up in the room where Lucky had been crated for the night. Lucky had played Houdini and gotten out, and dog and porcupine had done the tango.

Now Lucky was sporting ten quills, Lilah was up in the middle of the night playing doctor, and she'd nearly gotten shot by the sexiest, most gorgeous night prowler she'd ever seen.

Those loose Levi's of his were threatening to slip down his lean hips, and the lack of shirt was deeply distracting. Smooth tanned skin sliding over muscle, perfectly flat, ridged abs building up to a powerful triangle of chest, shoulders, and arms. His eyes, so sharp when he'd first appeared, were going back to a sleepy look. His hair was mussed as if he'd been tossing and turning. Then he made it worse by shoving his fingers through the silky strands, and when he was done with that, he came close and took over the task of holding Lucky down for her with strong, firm hands and arms.

And sweet baby Jesus, those arms. That whole body. It was completely functional, nothing wasted, no excess, and she couldn't look away from it. It was enough to make her walk into a wall if she'd been stupid enough to attempt walking and looking at him at the same time. "You going to say anything?" she finally asked.

He slid her a long look. "I was finally sleeping."

She laughed and he brooded. "It's not funny. You have me living with the devil's spawn. So nothing personal, but what can I do to help you here so you'll get the hell out?"

"Just holding her like that is great. I'm having a tough time here."

"You would have managed. You're good with animals."

"Yes," she agreed, thinking she'd rather be good with men right about now. In particular, a big, badass, silent, edgy, dangerous man who carried a gun in the waistband of his jeans and had a body so cut it made her want to run her tongue over every indention and then some. "And you're good with . . . well, just about everything," she said. "Well, except cuddling."

He flashed her a look that was so innately male, as if she'd just questioned his Guy Card or something. It should have been annoying, but instead it made her nipples contract in greedy anticipation. She busied herself with parting Lucky's fur to get a better look at the first quill.

Brady grabbed the spotlight above the table and better aimed it for her as she poured vinegar over Lucky's punctured skin. Lucky whined and Lilah did her best to soothe her before glancing at Brady. "Thanks," she said gratefully.

He leaned close to see what she was doing, and that's when she realized he smelled amazing.

Warm and sexy and . . . amazing.

Lucky was growling low in her throat, showing her teeth, worrying Lilah. The dog was older, around nine, and usually sweeter than molasses, which is where Lilah's decision not to muzzle her had come in. A mistake.

Brady came in from behind Lucky's sharp teeth and clasped the dog's head in his big hands, holding her still. "Why the vinegar?"

"It loosens up the quills. It's why I broke in to do this here. I couldn't find any white vinegar at home." Leaning over Lucky, Lilah snipped the first quill at about the halfway mark.

The dog whined and Brady stroked her face in sympathy. "You're cutting them to let out some of the air," he guessed.

"Yes." She forced her attention back to Lucky, using pliers to get a good grip on the quill as close to the dog's flesh as possible, and pulled.

The quill slid out.

Lucky cried.

Still stroking the trembling dog, Brady bent low to murmur to her softly.

"Another talent of yours?" she asked. "Soothing the scared female?"

He smiled, and she had the most ridiculous urge to pretend to be terrified so he'd hold her and murmur in that voice and hold her close, too. And maybe do other things . . . "You do this a lot on your travels?"

Brady's eyes were still amused, suggesting maybe he knew where her thoughts had gone. "Assist a sexy woman in the middle of the night with a dog? Almost never." He shifted, turning so he could more comfortably hold Lucky for her, and Lilah went very still.

Brady's back was broad and smooth and gorgeous . . . except for his side, where a long, jagged scar ran from his armpit down to his ribs. It was a few shades lighter than his normal skin tone, signaling that it was at least a few years old. There were other scars as well, but nothing as major as that one long imperfection.

Lifting his head, his gaze met hers without hesitation or resignation.

Her fingers itched to touch it, to soothe him, which would be a little bit like trying to soothe a wild, untamed mountain cat. "What happened?" she asked as casually as she could, pouring vinegar over the next quill, then snipping it with scissors as she had the first.

He remained quiet and she figured he had no intention of answering. "I suppose," she finally said, "it's one of those you-could-tell-me-but-you'd-have-to-kill-me things, right?"

His mouth quirked but he held his silence. He was good at that.

"I heard you spent some time in Afghanistan," she said softly, working out the next quill.

"I flew medical choppers."

"And in Iraq?"

"Same thing. I was good at the hot spots."

She poured the vinegar and then snipped the quill halfway as she thought about Brady out there on the front line, right in the thick of things, bringing people in and out on a daily basis, constantly in more danger than she could possibly imagine. "Does it still hurt?" she asked as she pulled out the quill.

"No."

"How—"

"A machete." His voice was easy enough, but she heard the steel undertone—he was done talking about this.

She could understand that. "I'm guessing you've seen parts of the world that would seem like another planet to me compared to this place," she said softly after yet another quiet moment.

He let out a low sound of agreement.

"You must think I'm pretty naïve and sheltered."

"No."

"But you do think I live safe."

He didn't answer, and lifting her gaze, she met his, which was sharp yet warm. It seemed impossible that he could be both, but he was.

Just outside the exam room door, the rest of the center was dark, filled with shadows. Not in the exam room, which felt . . . close. Intimate.

"You're right," she said. "I do live safe. I grew up in this one-horse town with my grandma and good friends, and it's always been a comfortable fit for me. And very safe."

"It suits you."

"It didn't always," she said wryly. "By the time I graduated high school, I was chomping at the bit to get out of town and find the real world."

He smiled, interested. "So did you?"

"I went to UNLV. University of Las Vegas."

He choked out a laugh. "About as different from here as you could get."

"You could say so," she agreed, and yet again wielded

the pliers on poor Lucky. "I was a little out of my element." Like a babe in the woods. Which had been the whole point.

"Is this the part where you tell me you made your tuition by becoming a stripper?" he asked hopefully.

"No," she said on a laugh.

"A showgirl?"

"No!"

He looked her over. "I know. You became a phone sex operator."

"Stop." She rolled her shoulders, the smile fading because the truth was worse.

His expression turned serious. Reaching up, he stroked a loose strand of hair off her jaw. "Something happened to you."

There was concern in his eyes, and a protectiveness that shouldn't mean anything to her.

But it did. "No. Not like you're thinking. It's really just a very boring old story."

"You're in luck, then. I love boring old stories."

"No you don't," she said on a laugh. "You hardly talk at all unless I'm bugging the hell out of you with questions."

"True," he said stroking poor Lucky to keep her calm. "But I like to listen to you."

Her heart tumbled and she sighed, again moved by him when she shouldn't be. She supposed she could tell him a little more. "I got accepted on a scholarship into the animal science program."

"To become a vet?"

"I wasn't sure. Mostly I just wanted out to see what I was missing. Nobody wanted me to go to Vegas. They all wanted me to go to Idaho State, so of course I did the opposite."

"And hit the city of big lights."

"Yeah, I followed the scholarship, I really had no choice—I needed the money." She hadn't been able to keep it, unfortunately. Among other things, her grandma had gotten sick, and she'd ended up coming back and forth too much. Her grades had slipped and she lost her scholarship.

Okay, so it hadn't all been because of her grandma's failing health, but that part of the story wasn't in the short version, nor was it up to be shared. "Vegas was a culture shock," she allowed, and smiled a little at herself, at the good memories she could summon. "But for a time, I loved it." At least at first. "My roommate was a local girl, and she was determined to help me experience everything I'd missed by growing up in a small ranch town."

Lilah had been extremely determined to get out and live. Never look back.

Well, okay she'd planned to look back a little. After all, there were her friends here, and her grandma, but in those years, she'd been an idealist, thinking her grandma—and everything else here—would remain the same, locked in time, safe in the capsule that was Sunshine.

Which hadn't happened.

"I was going to make something of myself," she said, adjusting the overhead light to the other side of Lucky's nose and continued to work. "I was going to be the first Young in my entire family to get a college degree and do something with my life."

Which she'd pretty much blown on all counts.

"So what happened?" he asked quietly when she stopped talking.

She shrugged.

Cocking his head, he studied her for a long moment. "You're leaving out the juicy stuff."

Yes. Yes, she was. On purpose, because she was pretty sure she couldn't tell the story without losing it and she wasn't ready for that. There were quills to remove. "Maybe it's your turn to tell me juicy stuff. Why did you come to Sunshine?"

He didn't say anything to that. Shock.

"Oh come on, that's easy enough."

"You already know why I came," he said.

"Because Dell badgered you. Yeah, yeah. But you don't seem like the kind of guy to be . . . badger-able."

His eyes slid her way. "You think there's some deep, dark reason?"

She didn't know what she thought—he was an enigma. And also, sin on a stick. "You owe me a secret," she reminded him.

That got her nothing but a little smile.

"Come on," she said. "There's got to be something you can tell me."

Apparently not.

"You and the guys grew up rough," she said. "I know that much. Then you went in the army, which was obviously a different kind of rough altogether, and now you roam at will because you never learned to settle down in one spot."

Annoyance flickered across his features. "Adam and Dell can't keep their mouths shut."

"I think it's more that they don't see us as a good fit."

"They're right," he said.

"They have no idea. And I'm not looking for a damn ring, Brady. Any more than you're looking to give one."

He studied her. "What are you looking for?"

She shrugged. "A fun and easy relationship with someone who gets me," she said without hesitation.

He took the vinegar and poured it over the last quill.

She cut the quill close to the skin and pulled it out while he soothed Lucky, calming her with his quiet voice, assuring her that her trial was over and she'd been very brave. When the dog settled, Brady lifted his head. "I'm a short-term bet at best."

"Maybe I wasn't considering you for my fun, easy relationship. I mean, let's face it, you're not exactly easy."

He laughed softly, wryly. "Yeah." He met her gaze. "But we both know that there's no one else here in town right for you."

Her breath caught. He did want her. "No?"

"No." He put Lucky down, where she immediately twisted into a pretzel to try to inspect the damage.

Lilah was resisting the urge to check for damage as well, within herself. That he'd so accurately read her was startling. "I am content," she told him. "At least for the most part. I like my life, quiet and simple as it is. I like being anchored." She met his gaze. "Maybe you can't understand that because you've never done the anchor thing."

"Sunshine is really your anchor?"

"The people in it, yes. My grandma. She raised me. She died two years ago after a cancer battle, but until then we were a unit." Her voice had gone a little husky. That whole awful time in her life—losing her grandma, her college funding, and then Tyler—was still very hard to talk about. "Dell and Adam are my unit," she said. "My friend and business partner, Cruz, is in that unit."

"Everyone you know is in your unit." He flashed a small smile. "It's who you are. What happened to your parents?"

"My mom lives in France with her boyfriend." Squatting low, she rubbed Lucky. "She didn't take much to motherhood."

"And your dad?"

"Not around." She knew her voice was flat when it came to her father, but he deserved no less. He'd walked away before her mother had.

"So let me see if I get this right," he said. "For the most part, people stay in your life until they leave or die?"

She stared up at him, not sure she liked the fact that he'd analyzed her so accurately. "Yes." Was there any other way? And why did he make it sound like it was so unfathomable? "What about you?"

"Until coming here, I was the only one in my life." He shrugged. "Easier that way."

"Talk about safe."

He choked out a laugh. "You think my life is safe?"

"Maybe not physically, no. But emotionally? Yes. Yes, I do." She paused, watching him touch a finger to his own palm and wince. Rising, she took his hand between hers. "You got poked by a quill."

"It's okay."

"No, but it will be." With no idea what was coming over her, she pressed her lips to the rough calluses of his palm. *Take that, too safe life.*

He went very still. "What was that for?"

"To make it better." She lifted her head, closed the space between them and kissed one corner of his mouth.

"And that?" he asked, his voice lower now, and husky.

"Same." She kissed the other side of his mouth. "Is it working?"

"Getting there." He slid his arms around her, hauled her in tight against him and took over, kissing her long and wet and deep, and by the time he lifted his head, she was shaken to the core.

"And now?" she managed.

"Much better." He was reaching for her again just as a thump sounded above them.

"What was that?" she asked.

He was already moving up the stairs. "Stay here."

She and Lucky followed him, so close on his heels that she nearly plowed into the back of him when he stopped short in the center of the loft. Her hands slid up his back for balance, encountering warm skin, smooth, sleek muscle.

"Shit," Brady said.

"I'm sorry, I—" She yanked her fingers back, but he shook his head. "The damn dog."

Peering around his broad shoulder, she caught sight of

Twinkles devouring the trash and having a good old time while he was at it.

At Lilah's feet, Lucky whined. She wanted some trash, too.

"He's already eaten more than his own weight today," Brady said in disgust. "Nice job on the staying put thing, by the way."

"Me or him?" she asked.

"Both."

Lilah ignored the bad temper in his voice and went to her knees to hug Twinkles close. "Oh, you are one very bad little boy."

"Yes, and you can spank me later," Brady grumbled. "When are you going to admit you've had your fun and take him to the kennels?"

"Aw. A big, tough guy like you, afraid of one teeny tiny dog." She set Twinkles on the blanket on the floor, which he'd clearly been using as a bed. Lucky joined him. They sniffed each other's hind ends and settled together.

"That's not one teeny tiny dog," Brady said, staring at Twinkles. "That's the devil in disguise. And besides, I'm way more afraid of you."

She smiled. "You are not."

"Terrified. You'd better hold me."

She burst out laughing at that, and gave him a shove instead, her hands against his hard chest.

Damn, he felt good.

He shook his head when she continued to grin at him. She couldn't help it, she couldn't stop.

"What?" he asked.

"Nothing."

He shook his head. "With you, Lilah, it's always something."

Yeah, actually. It was. "You were right before. I'm restless and no one else in town is able to help me."

"No?"

"No." Stepping into him, she kissed him. She kissed him like she meant business, and by the time she pulled back, neither of them were breathing so steadily. "I hope you're ready for this," she said, because she'd consulted with the part of her brain in charge of making rash and stupid decisions, and it'd been unanimous.

"Lilah—"

"Shh," she said. "Don't be afraid. I'll be gentle."

## Nine

Brady didn't say anything, but his eyes were aroused and darkened with something else as well. He took Twinkles from Lilah's arms and set him on his blanket in front of the fireplace. He snapped his fingers and Lucky joined Twinkles, the two of them sitting perfectly still and at rest, ready for their next order.

"You're good," she said, and turned to the bed, where if the tossed bedding was any indication, Brady had been restlessly sleeping, if at all.

"And you're drowning in these sweats," he said, coming up behind her. "You must be hot."

Yes. Yes, she was.

Hot.

God, so hot.

She'd been sleeping in just a lacy tank and matching panties, but when Lucky had gotten hurt, she'd thrown on an old pair of sweats, both the top and bottoms several sizes too big. Obviously she hadn't planned on a seduction, but that's exactly what she wanted. A seduction. A night filled with passion and desire.

Brady was the man for the job, she knew it. He made her yearn and burn, he made her want. And then there was the added bonus of each of them knowing exactly what this was, and what it wasn't. When the expiration date was up and he left Sunshine, she'd watch him walk away with a smile on her face.

"I want you," he said, and stroked a finger over her shoulder, evoking a shiver. "I usually put what I need ahead of what I want, but with you the line blurs." He slipped an arm around her waist, dipping his head to press his mouth against her jaw.

She had to clear her throat to speak. "I want you, too." And needed him. Lord, how she needed him.

He ran his talented mouth up the side of her neck. His hand was low on her belly, the very tips of his fingers playing just beneath the elastic of the sweats, gliding lightly back and forth on her bare skin. "Be sure. This is unlike you, and a bad idea to boot."

"It feels like a great idea," she managed.

A low laugh escaped him, disturbing the hair at her temple.

"Christ, Lilah." His other hand pushed her hair out of his way and then his mouth was on the nape of her neck, his teeth scraping over her, making her shiver. "Tell me no."

"Yes." She clutched the arm bracing her against him, already halfway to the "great" part of "great idea." She could feel the heat of him, the strength, and it aroused her, making her shiver.

"Are you cold?" he asked against her skin.

"No. Hot." She wanted—needed—his hand to move, either north or south.

Preferably south.

"Please," she finally whispered, only to break off with a moan when his fingers trailed up her belly, along the zipper of the sweatshirt and then back, the rasp of metal on metal filling the room as he slid the zipper down. "This needs to go," he said, and urged it off her shoulders.

The camisole beneath was white silk, a little sheer, and barely contained her breasts, which were spilling out over the top.

From over her shoulder, Brady took in the sight and groaned. His hand skimmed up her belly again, his thumb tracing the heavy underside of a breast for a moment before he nudged the spaghetti straps to her elbows, pressing his mouth to her shoulder. "Pretty," he said in a voice gone so low in timbre as to be almost inaudible.

"My underwear matches."

With a rough growl, he nipped at her shoulder and palmed her breast, grinding his erection into her bottom.

Lost in pleasure, her eyes drifted shut and she let her head fall back to his chest. "I've pictured this with you. Hope you live up to the fantasy," she teased, then practically purred when his thumb rasped over her hardened nipple.

"You let me know." He turned her to face him and she slid her hands up his chest and over his scruffy jaw, feeling the roughness beneath her fingertips. It was arousing and intimate.

His eyes were dark and heated and on her. Unwavering. Fierce. Protective.

He was beautiful. Everything about him was beautiful. "It's been a long time for me," she admitted. "But I'm pretty sure I remember what comes next." She played with the top button on his Levi's, the backs of her fingers brushing against the smooth, taut skin of his abs, which were washboard ridged and hard.

"Lilah." His fingers speared into her hair, holding her head in his big palms as he searched her gaze for God knew what. "How long is a long time?"

"Long. But I hear it's just like getting on a bike."

"Yeah," he said, his words hot along her skin as his lips

grazed her earlobe. "It's just like getting on a bike." He untied her sweat bottoms, causing a rush of heat to slide south.

As did her sweats.

They slid south right off her hips and onto the floor.

He took in the white boy-cut panties that indeed matched the cami and palmed her ass, which increased her heart rate and made her already hardened nipples tighten even further. "What comes next, Lilah?"

That slowed her down a second. "You mean . . . you don't know?"

His soft chuckle raised goose bumps on her skin. "This is your show. You call the shots."

The thought of doing just that, in effect bossing this big, tough edgy man around in bed gave her a rush only a millimeter below an orgasm. She pulled back enough to look into his eyes to make sure he wasn't just teasing. "Really? I'm in charge?"

His smile was slow and sure, and so hot she'd have sworn it singed the hair right off her skin. Yeah. She was in charge if that's what she wanted. "You shouldn't give someone that much power," she whispered. "What if I take advantage?"

He slid a muscled thigh between hers. "You going to take advantage of me, Lilah?"

His tone suggested that would be okay with him, very okay. His hands were on the wall on either side of her head, his body pressed tight to hers.

And he was hard. Everywhere. "Yes," she decided. "I'm going to take advantage of you."

"Just remember," he said hotly against her ear. "It's my turn next, and turnabout is fair play."

Oh boy. "M—maybe we should start easy."

He laughed softly and kissed her with such gentleness that her heart quivered. "Easy works. Tell me what you want."

"I'd rather show than tell." She let her cami slip to her hips.

"Mmm." Dipping his head, he ran his tongue across her nipple. "Show is nice. But I really like tell. Tell me what's next, Lilah."

"Fewer clothes—God," she burst out when he sucked her into his mouth, "don't stop."

His hand pushed her cami down, and her panties with it, then slid between her legs. "Don't stop what?"

She fisted her hands in his hair and pulled his mouth back to hers. "Don't stop kissing me."

"Where? Where do you want me to kiss you, Lilah?"

She shivered at the thought of where she wanted his mouth, but he pulled free to look at her, waiting for her answer. "Everywhere," she managed.

"Should I use my tongue?"

"Yes." Her eyes closed as his fingers stroked her wet flesh. Tipping her head back, she cried out and arched into him when he slid a finger into her. It was all she could do to remain standing. "I'm—"

"Hot," he said, his thumb softly outlining her wet folds. "Hot, and very, very wet." His lips were moving against her breast, and when he sucked on her nipple, holding it between his tongue and the roof of his mouth, her hips ground helplessly against him.

"Easy," he reminded her, pulling back to blow on her nipple.

A shiver wracked her. And she couldn't catch her breath. It felt like her blood had turned to liquid fire in her veins, and all she could think about was touching him, wrapping her fingers around him and making him as crazy as he was making her. She reached for the remaining buttons on his Levi's, feeling his abs clench as she ripped open the jeans.

He was commando, and . . . big.

Lifting her head, she looked into his eyes, which were dilated and darkened, burning with desire.

"Are we stopping?" he asked.

"No." She bit her lower lip. "But it's not exactly like getting back on a bike."

"It's better."

She let out a breath. "I was really hoping you'd say that." She shoved the jeans down his legs.

Hauling her back upright, he kissed her hard and deep. They kicked their fallen clothes away while his mouth continued to claim her, rough and wild and erotic.

"Inside me," she whispered. "Oh please. Please, get inside me." She backed him to the bed and shoved him onto it. He arched his brow, but stretched out on his back.

Gloriously naked.

Gloriously aroused.

"Come here," he said, and gave her a finger crook.

Forgetting that she was supposed to be the one with the orders, she crawled up the bed and straddled him, moaning in delight at the feel of him beneath her, at the way his hands slid over her hips, cupping her ass, grinding her against him.

"Do I need a condom?" he asked, and she went still, her mouth falling open.

How could she have so thoughtfully lost herself as to forget birth control?

A wry smile touched his mouth. "You don't have one?"

"No! Don't you?"

"No."

With a half laugh, half sob, she collapsed over him and dropped her head to his shoulder. "I can't believe it."

"I know where there are some stashed, does that count?"

She lifted her head. "What?"

"In the nightstand drawer," he said with a jerk of his head, not taking his hands off her.

Leaning over him, she opened the drawer and found a stack of condoms. Probably Adam's. "That was mean," she told him, sucking in a breath when, hands tightening on her hips, he surged up and ran his tongue over a nipple. When he sucked her into his hot mouth with a strong pull, she decided to forgive him.

He reached for the condom in her fingers and tore it open. She took it back and rolled it slowly down his length, so slowly that he went from cocky and teasing, to swearing roughly, to begging for her to get to it.

She was still smiling smugly about that when she lifted up and slowly let just the tip of him inside her.

But it all backfired on her when the feel of him stretching her was enough to render her a panting idiot. She arched in an attempt to draw him in deeper but he held her firmly in place, his fingers digging into her hips.

"More," she demanded.

"Thought you'd never ask." He rolled her beneath him and pinned her to the mattress beneath his welcome weight, sliding all the way home.

"I thought I was in charge," she managed to say, her hands gliding up the hard muscles of his biceps.

"My turn."

The timbre of his voice when he was aroused was like a caress as he began to move in exactly the right rhythm to drive her out of her mind. Combined with his talented mouth on hers, and a clever calloused thumb oh so unerringly stroking her at ground zero, she was a goner, and she burst into orgasm with a startled cry.

"Again," he demanded while she was still trying to put herself back together.

"I know it's your turn and all," she panted. "But you should know . . . I don't take direction as well as you do." He thrust deeper now, harder, pulling back each time until he was just barely inside of her, making her clutch at him. It was torment, it was ecstasy, the feel of his hard body taking her on a ride like she'd never experienced before. "Brady . . ."

"I know." Pushing up to his knees, he dragged her up with him so that she was straddling his lap. The new angle had him touching a spot that she hadn't even known she had, and she arched back, crying out, lost in the sensations, lost in him.

Sliding his hand into her hair, he lifted her to him, staring deeply into her eyes. His mouth came down on hers, hot and demanding, pretty much just like the man himself. His hands were still holding her, completely controlling their movements, which should have been annoying. Instead, it turned her on, big-time. Her breasts were crushed to his chest, her nipples hard and aching, sending bolts of pleasure to her core every time he moved against her. His breath was hot on her neck, his teeth scraping along her throat, his muscles flexing as his hips rolled into hers.

"Open your eyes." His voice caressed her as surely as his work-roughened hands did. "Open your eyes and come with me."

And as he moved within her, she did just that. She opened her eyes, locked them on his, and her world exploded. Gripping her hips, he thrust hard inside her, finding his own long, silent release.

They kissed through the aftermath, rough and deep as they both came down from the high. Then he gentled the connection, softly touching his mouth to hers, moving it along her jaw to her forehead, where he lingered.

They collapsed together into the mattress, Lilah's bones were . . . gone. Just gone. "Okay, that was so much better than getting on a bike," she told him, still trembling.

He pulled her in tighter, holding her close, sharing his body heat, which he had plenty of. His mouth curved into a faint smile as he reached for the quilt as well, pulling it over them.

"I mean holy smokes . . ." she began, her breathing still irregular.

"I wasn't going for holy smokes, I was going for what felt good."

"Well, you nailed both. Can you imagine if there hadn't been a condom?"

"You'd have seen a grown man cry."

She laughed and he kissed her again, then rolled off the bed and vanished into the bathroom.

"So," she said when he came back out, watching his very fine ass as he strode to the pile of their discarded clothing "you weren't kidding about the cuddle thing."

He pulled on his jeans even though he was still semi-hard. He managed two buttons and gave up, leaving the pants riding indecently low on his hips. It gave him a dangerous, edgy look to go with the fact that he was clearly ready for another round.

So was she.

She patted the mattress.

His gaze slid slowly over her, and her body reacted like his hands touched her everywhere his eyes traveled.

He walked back to the bed until his knees bumped the mattress. "Again?" he asked, voice thrillingly rough.

"Yes, please." She cupped him gently through the jeans. "Who gets to be in charge this time?"

With a slight smile curving his lips, he shucked the pants and got in bed, his body relaxing into hers. Sprawling over the top of her, he entwined their fingers and lifted their joined hands to either side of her face, kissing her softly. "What am I going to do with you?"

"You've asked that question before."

"Still don't have the answer."

"Neither do I, but I have several ideas."

His soft laugh disturbed the hair at her temple as he pressed his lips there. "I was thinking you might."

## Ten

He woke up alone. Lilah had rocked his world once, twice . . . he leaned over the bed to count empty condom wrappers . . . three times, and then she'd . . .

Walked off before dawn.

That was usually his role. "My own fault," he told the mutt, who was sitting on his chest. "I was easy."

"Arf," the dog said in complete agreement, and licked Brady's chin.

"You're one to judge," Brady said in disgust. "If someone even thinks about petting you, you drop and expose your kibble and bits. No soldier worth his salt does that. You're like a damn dog."

"Arf."

"Okay, good point," he said, shaking his head. "You are a dog. And so, apparently, am I." He lay there staring at the ceiling for a moment more, replaying the night before. He'd loved watching Lilah's animated face. As someone who'd forced himself to keep every emotion in check for the better part of his entire life, he found it endlessly fascinating.

He found her endlessly fascinating. He'd not been able to get enough of her, not of her body writhing beneath his, not of her soft sighs, her scent, her taste . . . And then there'd been the way she'd begged him for release when he'd had his mouth between her thighs—

Great. And now he was hard.

Again.

Still.

It was becoming a perpetual problem.

"Arf."

"You're a pain in my ass, you know that?" Brady rolled out of bed, showered, pulled on some clothes, and prowled around in the kitchen. He'd bought the bare minimum from the grocery store, which included the required frozen breakfast wraps. He tossed three on a plate and nuked them.

He'd have made a few for Lilah, too, except, oh yeah, she'd left.

Christ and she'd been right to do so. One night, that's all she'd wanted. Hell, one night was all he wanted as well.

So why wasn't he still grinning like a guy who'd gotten his rocks off three times?

Because he was brooding about her doing to him what he'd done to women his whole life. Which settled it. He really needed to have his head examined. A beautiful, passionate woman had had her merry way with him—and vice versa—and she'd left before dawn rather than face the awkward morning after, and he was bitching about it. "I need mental help."

"Arf."

"No comments from the peanut gallery."

The dog eyed Brady's plate and licked his chops, making Brady laugh. In the military, there'd been two kinds of people—the quick and the hungry. Brady had been the quick. "No. It's bad for you."

Although the thing did appear to have a stomach of iron. Brady ate for a minute while the dog watched him, tail thumping hopefully on the floor every time Brady looked at him. "What is it with all of you here in Sunshine anyway? You're all eternal optimists."

Another whine, and with a shake of his head, Brady shared half a Hot Pocket. "Fucking softie," he muttered to himself. "Let's go."

Grabbing his camera and the leash, they walked. The meadow between Belle Haven and Lilah's place was lined with stands of cedar, tamarack, and fir and had been calling to him for days. The dog darted around the tree trunks, eyes bright, barking happily at absolutely everything as Brady took pictures.

It was one of those glorious mornings that made him grateful to be alive, the sky such a pure blue it almost hurt to look at it, a single cotton puff of a cloud floating lazily by. The night had been chilly, but the sun made its lazy appearance, and steam rose off the rocks and treetops. The bear grass was in bloom, each plant producing a cluster of creamy white tufts atop a stalk. The stalks were as tall as five feet, but even at that impressive height they were not sturdy enough to stand tall to the breeze.

And certainly not sturdy enough to stand up to the dog, who bounded with sheer exuberance through them to get to the lake. The water was a sheet of glass, a shade of blue beyond description. It was spring fed and loaded with native trout. Yesterday morning he'd seen a bighorn sheep and a mountain lamb grazing at the edge, but all was quiet this morning—no doubt in thanks to the mutt sniffing and pouncing on anything that moved, including his own tail.

"You're going to be bear bait if you don't cool it," Brady warned him.

But the dog's joy of the morning couldn't be contained, and Brady found himself smiling when the mutt accidentally roused a pissed-off possum and came high-tailing it back, eyes wide with terror as he hid behind Brady's legs.

Pulling the camera away from his face, Brady eyed the

silly dog and shook his head. "That was all you, soldier. Don't write checks your ass can't cash."

After recovering, the dog headed back to the lake's edge and drank.

"That water's tainted," Brady said. "Now you're going to fall in love with the first girl to give you a sweet smile and some tail."

Totally unconcerned, the dog panted happily.

"It's true. She's going to crook her little paw at you and you're going to roll over and expose that belly."

When he said roll over, the dog plopped to the ground and rolled over.

Brady stared at him. "Let me get this straight. You can't stop barking to save your own life, but you can roll over?"

"Who'd believe that I've found Brady Miller, ex–army ranger and all around badass, talking to a dog . . ."

Brady had already heard the footsteps coming up behind him and placed them as Adam's, so he hadn't turned. Rule number one in survival—always know who's coming up behind you.

"It's the first sign that you're becoming human, you know," Adam said, coming up alongside him. "Talking to your dog."

Brady lowered the camera and squatted to rub said dog's belly. "You think I'm not human?"

"I think you think you're not." Adam hunkered down too and looked at the dog with a smirk. "He's got you trained, I see."

Brady shrugged. Useless to try to deny the truth.

"Lilah told me she broke into the center last night."

Brady was used to the quick subject change when it came to Adam. Adam didn't waste words. "She did."

"You see her?"

Actually, Brady had seen a whole hell of a lot of her, but he kept that little tidbit to himself. He could hold his own against Adam and had, but he was feeling mellow and didn't want to go there. "Yeah, I saw her."

Adam looked at him for a long moment. He couldn't have any idea that Brady had slept with Lilah, not unless Lilah had told him, which Brady highly doubted. They were tight, united by this place that was home to them like no other. They'd grown roots.

Brady wouldn't know a damn root if it wrapped itself around his ankle and tugged, and they all knew it. He waited for Adam to warn him off Lilah, but he didn't.

"How's the Bell coming?" Adam asked instead.

"It's nearly there. You ready to be rid of me?"

"You said you'd stick around for a month. You've got more than half of that left. I'm looking to book some air time."

"Give me another week. You'll have your helicopter." As for his promise to stick for a month, he'd already said he would and he never broke his word. He turned to look into the woods, because someone was coming. Maybe a mob of someones given the noise.

Both he and Adam watched as Lilah came into view a minute later with about ten leashes and a dog on each of them. She was wearing short shorts, a snug T-shirt, those hard-on-inducing work boots, and a look on her face that rendered Brady stupid as she came to a stop right before him.

"You look amazing," he murmured before his mouth could reconnect to his brain.

She smiled the smile of a woman who'd had more than a few orgasms the night before. "So do you."

"Hello," Adam said, irritated. "I'm standing right here."

"You look amazing, too," Brady said, not taking his eyes off Lilah.

"Fuck." Adam shoved his hands in his pockets. "This is just fucking awkward."

"Then maybe we could have a minute?" Lilah asked him.

Adam looked pained. "Christ. Okay."

Her low laugh filled the morning air. "I meant with Brady."

"Fuck," Adam said again, clearly not liking Lilah's response, and with a long, level look at Brady, he strode off.

Brady watched his dog sniff at the asses of all the other dogs. And Jesus, when the hell had he started to think of the dog as his? "Last night," he started, and then ended up trailing off because he didn't know what to say.

She was just looking at him, smiling sweetly. Glowing.

He took that in and thought that she was the most beautiful thing he'd ever seen. "Should we talk about it?"

"Why?"

He scratched his head, and she laughed. "Aw, look at you," she said very gently. "Fine. If you need to talk about it, by all means go ahead."

"I—" He shook his head, baffled. "But you asked Adam to leave."

"Maybe I wanted to kiss you hello in private." She went up on tiptoe and did just that, with all the dogs entangled around their legs, kissing him until they were both breathless. Brady felt dizzy from the lack of blood in his head, combined with the unusual emotion called concern. He hoped to God she remembered he was temporary. "Lilah—"

"It's okay, Brady." She secured all the leashes in one hand and patted him on the arm like he was one of the dogs at her feet. "Don't worry. I'm not going to ask you to go steady." She kissed his jaw this time. "I meant what I said," she whispered against him. "I always do. This is light and easy, remember? You're in the clear, so you can breathe now."

Shit. She was right, he wasn't breathing. He drew in some air. "You really are different, you know that?"

"Uh-huh." She flashed a smile so contagious that he

found himself giving her one of his own. "You seemed to like those differences last night," she said, still grinning.

He had. Christ, he so had.

"And besides, we're not really all that different. Although I think I'm a little more . . ."

"What?"

"Optimistic." She nudged him with her shoulder. "You're Eeyore."

He blinked. "You think I'm Eeyore?"

"You tell me. I take my empty glass and try to fill it up with what happiness I can find. Friends, family, my work . . . And then there's you."

He raised a brow. "Me."

She nudged him again, looking playful and damn sexy while she was at it. It was the short shorts with the boots, he decided. Or everything. It was everything.

"You take that empty glass," she said, happily analyzing him. "And you wonder what the heck to do with it. You don't need the glass, you don't have time for the glass. Hell, you'll just drink from a spigot if you get thirsty. And in any case, there's probably another one up the road if that one runs out, so—"

"Are we still speaking English?" he asked.

Laughing, she kissed him again, blowing brain cells left and right when she touched her tongue to his. Before he could gather her close, she'd danced back with the dogs and gone on her merry way, leaving him staring after her wondering why he felt like he'd just been run over by a Mack truck.

*Because you got laid by a woman who wants nothing more than sex from you, and you want . . .*

Jesus.

He didn't even know how to put words to what he wanted.

# Eleven

I can tell that you think you know what you're doing," Dell told Lilah a few days later. "But you don't."

They were in her office at the kennels, where she'd just come in from the drugstore, having bought herself a present.

Condoms.

Dell, who'd looked into the brown bag thinking she had something to eat, had gotten an unhappy surprise.

"I know what I'm doing," she said, and hoped that was true.

"It's just a crush," Dell said.

"Yeah. So? You crush on anything with two legs."

He winced. "Not anything."

"Brady's a good guy," she said. "Or you wouldn't have invited him here."

"He's a great guy." Dell snagged her last candy bar from her not-so-secret stash in her bottom drawer. "But—"

"No. Nothing good ever comes after a but, Dell. I hate all buts." Except for Brady's. He had one really great butt.

"But," Dell repeated patiently, ignoring her annoyed snort, "he has one foot out the door."

"I know. It's the very definition of a crush, Dell. It's got an expiration date. At least we both know it." Coming around her desk, she hugged him tight and ushered him to the door. "I'm going to be okay, and so is Brady."

When he was gone, Lilah opened a different drawer with her real junk-food stash and dove into some cookies, and then a bag of chocolate kisses, promising herself that to-night she'd eat broccoli. Maybe.

She hadn't been kidding—she was crushing on Brady. In fact, if she closed her eyes, she could still feel him deep inside of her. She could see the fiercely intense pleasure on his face when he'd climaxed.

She got aroused just thinking about it.

She'd worn him out, which had been a source of pride. He'd fallen asleep in her arms and she'd listened to the beat of his heart meshing with hers. She'd watched him sleep, his long, thick lashes resting on his cheekbones, loving how for once he was completely relaxed, completely unaware of his surroundings.

He was beautiful, and in that moment, he'd been hers. And perhaps because she liked that thought a little too much, she'd slipped out of his arms and out of his bed.

They'd seen each other over the past few days; him working on the Bell, her going back and forth between the center and the kennels, but they'd been too busy to talk.

She eyed her overcrowded desk and sighed. She and Cruz switched off months being in charge of the paperwork that they both hated: the receivables, the payables, the cal-endar, the promotion and publicity work that had to be done to keep new business flowing. Switching off kept them sane, but more important, it kept them from killing each other. But she wished it were Cruz's turn now.

Or that her life was light and carefree enough that she

could say screw it to the work and go seek her pleasure. Her phone rang, interrupting the thought.

"I'm starving," Jade said. "And I need to get out of here before I kill any penis-carrying humans. Lunch?"

"Yes, if it has broccoli in it."

"You eat something bad again? You need some self-control, Lilah. What did you get into?"

Lilah sighed. "Everything."

"Be there in ten."

Brady surfaced after two hours inside the engine compartment of the Bell 47 and realized Twinkles wasn't in his usual sunspot. He walked around the Bell, the building, searching the entire area, but couldn't find him. Gut tight, he entered Belle Haven and found Dell behind the receptionist's desk looking hassled.

"Can't figure out her stupid system," Dell complained. "The woman runs this place tighter than a frigging ship, but no one else knows a damn thing—"

"The dog," Brady said. "You see him?"

Dell lifted his head, eyes dazed. "Man, I've seen fifty today alone. Maybe a hundred million and fifty."

Brady shook his head. "My dog. Twinkles," he corrected, saying the name out loud for the first time with a grimace. "He was outside with me while I was working and now he's gone. Have you seen him?"

Dell had gone brows up when Brady said "my dog," but without another word, he came out from behind Jade's desk. "Let's look outside."

"I did."

But Dell went outside anyway and started walking the areas that Brady already had, calling for the dog.

Brady did the same, moving around the building. He was at the horse pens, half afraid to look inside in case he found a squished dog, when he heard Dell yelling for him. He ran toward Dell's voice and ended up once again in front of the Bell 47.

"In here," Dell called out from inside the chopper.

Twinkles was on the pilot seat.

Which he'd chewed to shreds.

When he saw Brady, he thumped his tail happily and gave one loud "arf!"

"Are you kidding me?" Brady asked him, not wanting to analyze the relief making his legs weak. "You can't jump up onto the couch or get up on the bed without using the chest as a ladder, but you can get onto that chair and chew the hell out of it?"

Twinkles hopped down and sat on his left boot, gazing up at him adoringly.

"Cute," Dell said.

"Not cute. He just ate five hundred bucks' worth of leather."

"Shouldn't have let him be alone in here," Dell pointed out.

"Let him? I don't 'let' him do anything. He's utterly untrainable."

Dell grinned. "You know what Adam would say, right? He'd say it's you, that you're untrainable. And why are you always so on edge about the little guy, anyway? He's a dog. A damn good one, too." He ruffled Twinkles's head fondly. "You just have to be the boss of him, that's all. Be firm." He put a finger in Twinkles's face. "No more chewing."

Twinkles slid to the floor and exposed his belly to be scratched.

Brady shook his head.

"Oh, like you wouldn't do the same if you could." Dell crouched down and obligingly scratched Twinkles's belly.

"And why hasn't Lilah found him a home yet?" Brady wanted to know, staring grimly at the destroyed seat.

"Probably because she's having fun messing with you."

Dell let out a laugh at the look on Brady's face. "Guess you don't find this as funny as I do."

"Not so much, no. Though why I care when it's your dime, I have no idea."

Still chuckling, Dell pulled out his cell phone, speed-dialed a number, and put the phone on speaker. A woman answered with a professionally irritated tone: "What do you need now?"

"Jade," Dell said.

"Nope, it's the Easter Bunny. And your keys are on your desk."

Dell shook his head. "Now darlin', I don't always call you just because I've lost my keys."

"I'm sorry, you're right. You wallet's on your desk, too. As for your little black book, you're on your own with that one, Dr. Flirt. I'm at lunch."

Dell sighed. "What did we say about you and the whole power-play thing?"

"That it's good for your ego to have at least one woman in your life that you can't flash a smile at and have them drop their panties?"

Dell grinned. "I really like it when you say 'panties.' And for the record, I knew where my keys and wallet were."

"No you didn't."

"Okay, I didn't, but that's not why I'm calling. Can you bring burgers and fries for me and Brady? Oh, and Adam, too, or he'll bitch like a little girl."

"You mean 'Jade, will you pretty please bring us burgers and fries?'"

"Yes," Dell said, nodding. "That. And Cokes." He looked at Brady, who nodded. "And don't forget the ketchup."

"You forgot the nice words."

"Oh, I'm sorry," Dell said. "You look fantastic today, I especially love the attitude and sarcasm you're wearing."

Jade's voice went saccharine sweet. "So some low-fat chicken salads, no dressing, and ice water to go, then?"

"Fine," Dell said, and sighed. "Can we please have burgers and fries?"

"You forgot the 'Thank you, Goddess Jade,' but we'll work on that. Later, boss."

Brady looked at him. "How is food going to help with the dumbass dog and the shredded pilot seat?"

"I can't think on an empty stomach."

As promised, a week later, Brady had worked his ass off and had the Bell 47 ready to fly. He'd had it towed over to Smitty's, where it now sat on the tarmac. He'd just filed his virgin flight plan when Lilah appeared, a soft just-for-him smile on her mouth. If he'd been Twinkles, he'd have rolled over and exposed his belly. Instead, he brushed his hands off on his jeans and watched her walk toward him.

Just sex . . .

That's what she'd been looking for. Fun and easy. So he had no idea what the fuck was wrong with him that it had been bugging him for days.

Maybe because it felt like more. Which meant he was screwed.

"How's your baby today?" she asked.

"My baby?"

She ran a hand over the helicopter. "You think I don't see that even a big tough guy like you could have a weakness?"

"More than one," he murmured.

That seemed to fluster her, and liking that he could do that, he reached for her hand, intertwining his fingers with hers, bringing her hand to his mouth to kiss the palm. "You are my weakness, Lilah. The prettiest one I've ever had."

She bit her lower lip and stared up at him, definitely dazed. Call him sick, but he liked that, too. He'd been watching her twist the men in her life around her little pinkie for two weeks now—Dell, Adam, hell half the guys in Sunshine—and not a single one of them flustered her.

But he did.

He knew she thought he was tough, but the truth was, he thought the same about her. She handled her world and all it threw at her, no complaints, no whining.

And yet she didn't know how to take a compliment. It was adorable and charming, a devastating combination he discovered.

"I'm surprised you tolerate any weakness in yourself," she said.

"I usually don't."

She stared up at him, eyes sparkling with a heat and something more, something he couldn't even begin to pretend to read.

He ran a finger over her jaw and then slid his hand into her hair, which felt like silk over his skin. Tightening his grip, he drew her in a little closer.

She came willingly, her mouth opening a little in anticipation of a kiss.

Keeping eye contact, he gave her what she wanted, what he wanted, and brushed his lips over hers. "I've thought about leaving here in spite of my promise to stay the month," he said quietly. "Every day, I've thought about it."

"Hmm. Maybe you don't want to walk away from me," she teased, and nipped his bottom lip.

Holding eye contact, he nipped hers back. "I could leave. Don't ever doubt that, Lilah. Discipline runs deep."

Her smile faded and she tried to pull away from him, but he held tight. "But," he said, hating the quick flash of pain his words had put in her eyes, "I'm not going anywhere. Not yet."

She looked at him for a long beat. "You're a hard man, Brady Miller."

"In more ways than one."

Her gaze flickered to his button fly, and she let out a

shaky laugh and dropped her forehead to his chest. "Why do I like you again?"

"Because I'm about to give you the ride of your life. Get in." He hitched his head toward the chopper. "We're going out."

For a week Lilah had hoped to hear those words. Or at least the out part. Not the up part. She didn't love the up part.

Brady scooped Twinkles into his arms. "I'm going to run him over to Dell, be right back."

She was just stunned enough to still be standing there in the same spot three minutes later when he came back. "Let him drive Jade and Dell crazy for the afternoon." He moved to the door of the Bell. Turning back, he realized she hadn't come any closer and stopped. "Come on, get in."

Nope, not coming on or getting in. "Yeah. No, thanks."

"Is there a problem?"

Uh-huh. A big one. She didn't like to fly. In fact, it was safe to say she hated to fly. "You want me to go up with you."

"Yes."

Her stomach quivered, and she shook her head.

He looked at her carefully. "You're not on shift now, right? Cruz is there?"

"Yes. Look, did you mean out as in . . . a date? You're taking me out on a date in a helicopter?" Just saying it made her want to curl in a ball of both terror and excitement.

"Yeah. I want to test things out. We'll fly into Boise, have a nice dinner, and come back—" He broke off and cocked his head. "You're afraid."

"Don't be ridiculous." She wasn't afraid of anything. Well, except maybe admitting she was afraid. "It's that I can't just take off. I have stuff I have to do. Thanks for asking, though," she added politely, and turned away. She wondered how fast she could run back to the kennels . . .

"Lilah."

Damn. "Yes?"

"It's just dinner."

And a flight to get there. "Boise is hours away, Brady."

"Not by chopper."

Holding her breath, she turned back. "Another time, okay?" With a smile that hopefully didn't give her away, she started moving, forcing herself to walk not run.

"Which terrifies you more," he called to her. "Going up in the Bell or going out on a date with me?"

Ah, hell. She pivoted to face him. He looked good, so damn good. She wanted to lick him from head to toe. "Look at me," she said, gesturing to her work clothes of Carhartts pants, a long-sleeved tee layered with a short-sleeved one, both covered in animal hair. "I can't go out like this, there's no way."

"Why not?"

"Why not?" She spread her arms. "Because I'm a mess."

"So go home, grab some girlie clothes or whatever you need, and let's go."

"Girlie clothes?" she asked with a choked laugh. "Where am I supposed to get them, the feed store?"

"Hell, Lilah." He rubbed his jaw, looking sorry he asked. "Wear a potato sack for all I care—it's just dinner. And anyway, I like you how you look."

Crap. Crap that shouldn't melt her right down to a puddle of goo. "Fine. I need ten minutes."

"No problem."

She stared at him for a beat, then whirled and ran home to stare at her closet. In spite of complaining that she had no girlie clothes, she had plenty. He'd just knocked her off her axis is all. She wriggled into a denim skirt and knit top. She shoved her feet into cute boots and thought she looked a little bit like a country bumkin trying to play dress up. If he laughed at her, she'd slug him, she decided and ran back, half hoping he'd left. But nope, he was there, waiting.

He smiled at the boots.

"If you laugh at me, I—"

"I'm not laughing at you," he said, rising to his full height with easy grace, and he was right. That was definitely not laughter in his eyes, but something that nearly singed her skin.

"You look beautiful," he said with such simplistic candor that it rendered her speechless.

"You shouldn't do that," she finally managed. "You shouldn't use sweet words like that. Act like my company means something to you. Like you want—" She cut herself off from saying "more." "Not if you want me to remember what this is between us." And what it isn't.

He looked at her for a long moment. "Nothing was set in stone," he said softly, and boarded the chopper.

# Twelve

eft standing alone, Lilah looked upward. Blue sky, not a single cloud. Of all the times not to have a summer storm on the horizon.

There was a very slight breeze but definitely not the monsoon she could use right about now.

*Do it*, she told herself. *Get on, or you'll regret it.* So with that little pep talk out of the way, she took a deep breath and boarded. *Oh God.* She white-knuckled herself into the seat next to Brady, ignoring him watching her. "Let's get this over with," she said.

"You do realize it's supposed to be fun," he said, handing her a headset so that they could communicate over the noise while in the air.

She decided there wasn't a polite response to that so she went the route of Thumper's mother and said nothing at all.

He laughed, the sound soft and sexy, and reached over to squeeze her hand with his. "Don't worry," he said, flipping switches on the instrument panel in front of him. "I've seen a guy do this once or twice."

"Oh God." She closed her eyes.

"Are you going to look at all?"

It was weird, hearing him both in her headset and also outside of it. Brady, in stereo. "I don't know yet."

She felt more than saw him shake his head. "Here we go," he warned a minute later.

The roar of the engine, the rotation of the blades, the sheer terror of the sensation of going straight up into the air had her gripping the arms of her seat so tight her fingers went numb. She forced herself to breathe, but nothing could make her look as her stomach landed in her toes at that weightless feeling as they got air.

"You breathing over there?" he asked.

"Yes." *Barely.* "And don't talk to me. Fly the helicopter!"

"I can do both. Open your eyes."

"You're awfully demanding."

"Yes, and as I recall, you like that. Now, Lilah."

She sighed and opened her eyes, finding that they were very high off the ground. She'd had no idea how it would feel, but it looked as though there were nothing directly below her. All she could see was straight through the glass, which meant everything in front and around her. She gulped at the mix of vulnerability and excitement and studied her pilot.

His sunglasses were silver mirrored frames and gave nothing of his thoughts away. Though piloting a helicopter appeared to take all his limbs—both his hands and his feet were occupied—he was completely in control, aware of everything going on around them: the sky, the instruments, the ground, her. Her eyes were drawn time and time again to those hands, those long fingers moving precisely and surely, in perfect control, just like when they'd been in his bed and he'd handled her much in the same way he was handling instruments . . .

Turning his head, he met her gaze, the very corners of his mouth barely tilting up. "You okay?"

*No.* "Yes." He was far too sexy. She needed a distraction for herself. "If you don't have a home base anywhere," she said, "where do you keep all your stuff?"

He went brows up. "Where did that question come from?"

"It was either that or 'Are we there yet?'"

That got her an almost smile. "I don't tend to keep much stuff."

"Why not?"

"Is that your favorite question, 'why'?"

"Yes. Right after 'Are the donuts two for one today?'"

He laughed. "The why is simple. My life hasn't really been my own for years now. When and if that changes, I'll figure out where 'home base' is."

"But why isn't your life your own?"

The chopper dipped and she gasped and grabbed the armrests on either side of her hips. "What was that?"

"A pocket of air." Utterly unconcerned, he made an adjustment to the instruments. "I'll take us up a bit higher for a smoother ride."

Oh God. They were going even higher. *Be Amelia Earhart*, she told herself, but it didn't work. Maybe because things hadn't ended so well for Amelia. Choosing not to think on that too deeply, she pulled out her cell phone.

"You won't have reception up here," he said. "Nor would anyone be able to hear you."

"I need to text everyone my good-byes."

A big hand settled over hers. "In the seat behind you, grab my bag."

When she'd done that, he reached over and pulled out his camera. He flicked off the lens cover and turned it on. Then he set it to auto mode.

The moron-proof button.

"Go for it," he said.

She stared at him. "You want me to take your picture?"

"I want you to take pictures of whatever you want."

The Canon was digital and obviously expensive. She

brought it carefully up to her face and looked through the lens at the admittedly amazing view. "Is this a distraction technique?"

"Yes."

She laughed and let it work. After a few minutes, she turned the camera on him.

He was dressed in his usual cargo pants, the pockets filled with his essentials. Probably all sorts of tools, and a variety of weapons, and maybe the secrets of his world.

Last week, when she'd been at the loft and gotten him out of those pants, she'd seen the pile of things from his pockets on the dresser. Money, a credit card, his driver's license, and a wicked-looking pocketknife was as far as she'd gotten before she'd realized he'd been watching her.

She'd braced for his annoyance at her snooping, but it turned out that her curiosity about him had amused him.

"Just ask," he'd said in that low, easy voice of his. "Ask whatever you want to know."

"And you'll answer?"

He'd just smiled at her.

At the time, she'd blown out a breath and chickened out. Now she looked at his perfectly fitted cargo pants and wondered if one of today's essentials included a condom.

She had three in her purse now. Her new emergency stash, in the same pocket as her gummy bears—also an emergency stash. Just ask . . . "Do you ever get lonely? Up here in the air?"

"Lonely for what?"

"Friends. Family."

"I'm not always in the air," he pointed out. "And anyway, there are cell phones. E-mail. Visiting . . ."

"But you don't. Visit."

"I haven't made a habit of it, no."

"So you're saying that you're a creature of habit? You stick with routine?"

That got a bark of laughter from him. "That's new," he

murmured to himself, or so it seemed. "Creature of habit. Routine. Never been accused of either before."

"What about women?"

He glanced over at her. "What about them?"

"Haven't you ever wanted to change your life for a woman?"

"No."

A little shiver of disappointment went through her. "You've never been in love?"

"I've been in lust," he said with a small, private smile. "More than once."

She rolled her eyes as beside her he let out a breath. "The truthful answer is no," he said quietly. "I've never been in love."

They fell silent, and Lilah thought that was that.

"But you," he finally said. "You, Lilah, scare the hell out of me."

"Why?" she whispered.

He met her gaze and held it. "Because I could fall for you, Lilah. Hard and deep and never want to come back up."

She could scarcely breathe. "What's wrong with that?"

"We'd drown." And with that, he went back to his quiet flying zone.


Brady found himself smiling in sheer pleasure at the gorgeous day sprawled out in front of them, hundreds of miles in every direction, a maze of mountains and valleys that included a national forest.

Not a town or a paved road was visible. There was something about the high-pitched whine and whistle of a chopper, coupled with that sweet aroma of burning jet fuel that was more intoxicating than anything he'd ever experienced.

The wild northern Idaho wilderness was as untamed as it had been in the early 1800s when Lewis and Clark came through. He could see the crests of the ridges of the Bitterroots and beyond. The countless lakes and rivers and a glacier-scoured basin more formidable and rockier than just about anywhere on earth caught his breath in a way he hadn't expected.

If he ever wished to claim a home base, it would be here, the first place to make him feel wanted. He glanced over at his passenger.

And the most recent place to make him feel wanted . . .

Unlike him, Lilah wasn't smiling in sheer pleasure. They'd hit some turbulence and she was gripping the arms of the seat like she was expecting to go down any second and the armrests would save her. He'd asked her several times if she was okay, and he started to ask again. "Lilah? Are you—"

"Don't," she said through her teeth. "Don't ask me if I'm okay because I don't know. And we need to land soon, or I swear I'll stick you with the three kittens that were found at the river yesterday."

He landed soon.

She handled that with only a quietly repeated mantra that went something like "We're okay, we're okay." He was both proud and amused by her attempt at bravery. She was still sitting there, muscles clenched tight, eyes closed, when he opened her seat belt for her. "Good news," he said. "We're in one piece."

She cracked open an eye, took a peek, and then a deep breath. "We made it."

He felt his heart squeeze even as he laughed. "Lilah. Lilah, look at me."

She turned her head and met his gaze, face still pale.

He shoved his sunglasses to the top of his head so she could get a good look at him. "Two things. One, if there'd been even a sliver of a doubt about this thing being anything less than one hundred percent air-worthy, I'd never have brought you with me."

She stared at him, then nodded, even giving him a small,

trusting smile. "You're right. I knew that. What's the second thing?"

He paused. "There's a problem with one of the gauges."

"Oh God. Okay." She nodded. "We'll just rent a car and drive home."

Leaning close, he ran a thumb over her pale cheek. "We can fly without it. I just don't want to. I'll get a replacement from this airport's maintenance department and have it fixed in no time."

"In no time," she repeated, clearly realizing that that meant she was indeed still taking the chopper back. "That's . . . great."

Because she was still shaking like a leaf, he leaned in and kissed her softly. "Come on, Amelia. You look like you need your feet firmly on the ground. Let's go eat."

She nodded but didn't move.

"Want me to fly us to the restaurant?"

"Ha. And no." She rose, wobbled, and pointed at him. "Not a word."

He was good at not saying a word and, with an arm slung around her shoulders, led them across the tarmac and inside the airport.

The maintenance department informed them that they were backed up and needed an hour to locate the part Brady needed. Instead of waiting, Brady got them a cab and they headed to town. At an outdoor café, they ate fresh salmon and drank beer delivered in a metal bucket, all while being serenaded by a trio of birds sitting on a branch of a tree. Afterward they window-shopped as the sun set, walking down the main drag past a few galleries and artsy shops with the other tourists. Actually, Lilah shopped, and Brady just watched her. It was quickly becoming a favorite pastime.

"None of this interests you," she said after a block.

"Not much of a shopper," he admitted.

"Me neither. It's hard to be a shopper when you're perpetually broke—Oh," she exclaimed with a gasp, and stopped in front of a shop called the Pharmacy. Only it was unlike any pharmacy Brady had ever been in. Instead of medicine and various sundries, there was lace and silk. It was a lingerie shop, and there was tons of it, all displayed and surrounded by . . . fluff. That was the only word he could think of. There were boas and feathers, lotions and soaps. Lilah was standing there taking it all in when his cell phone rang. It was work. "I'm sorry. I need to take this," he told her.

"No worries," she murmured, still enthralled by the window display. "Take your time."

Brady stepped a few feet away to talk. "Miller."

"Got a job," came the familiar voice of Tony, his boss. "How soon can you be in Somalia?" he boomed.

Tony always boomed. Probably because he'd lost fifty percent of his hearing in the Gulf War, not that he'd ever admit the handicap.

Brady's gaze tracked to Lilah, still nose up to the glass. "Not anytime soon."

"What does that mean? You said you needed a couple of weeks and it's been a couple of weeks."

"It means I'm skipping this one," Brady said. "Assign someone else."

"But you've never skipped a job."

No. No, he hadn't. He'd never had a reason to. And he didn't now, except . . .

Lilah was looking at a silk teddy set. Spaghetti-strapped cami and a tiny thong, both in a pale blue that would make her gorgeous skin shimmer. She turned her head, found him watching her, and blushed gorgeously.

He didn't want to go.

"What the hell's up?" Tony asked loudly enough that Brady winced and pulled the phone from his ear. "You said you needed personal leave," Tony said. "Nothing special, you said."

"Yes. And I'm taking a full month off." That had been his promise to Dell and Adam, and he'd honor it. "I let the office know."

"Yeah, you said you were in Idaho. What the fuck's in Idaho?"

Brady let out a breath. "It's personal—"

"Ah, Christ. You're not going off the deep end and buying a ranch out in the middle of nowhere to raise cattle, are you? You belong in the air, man."

"Two more weeks," Brady said through his teeth. "I'll be back in two weeks."

"But not now?"

"No. Not now."

"It's a woman. No, what am I saying, not even a woman keeps you grounded. It's two women, right?"

Brady shut his phone and slid it in his pocket, giving Lilah a knowing shake of his head. "You can stop pretending not to eavesdrop now."

"You turned down a job."

"I just postponed it, that's all."

"Why?"

Well, wasn't that just the million-dollar question. His cell phone rang again. The Boise airport maintenance department. When he was done with that call, he shut his phone and rubbed a hand over his jaw. "I've got good news and bad news."

"Good news first," she decided, not looking sure she wanted either.

"Yeah, there isn't really good news."

Her eyes narrowed. "Then why did you ask?"

"Because normal people always want the bad news first."

"Just tell me!"

"The part I need for the Bell 47 won't be in until the morning."

Her mouth fell open. "How were you possibly going to make that good news?"

Brady pulled out his rarely used Visa. "With a nice hotel, including a hot tub for all those sore muscles?"

"How do you know I have sore muscles?"

"Because you had them clenched tight the entire flight. You're sore."

She looked him over speculatively, and he wished he knew what the hell she was thinking. But for all that she usually wore her heart on her sleeve for the whole world to see, she was keeping this one close to the vest. Finally she pulled out her cell phone. "Cruz," she said into it. "Remember that time I covered for you when you took Marie to Vegas for the weekend on the spot? Yeah, well, I'm calling in the marker. I'll be back some time tomorrow . . . No, you don't get to ask why. Use your imagination. Feed Sadie." She slid the phone into her pocket and looked at Brady. "What kind of a reputation do you have that this guy seriously thinks you'd sleep with two women at the same time?"

"Heard that, did you?"

"It wasn't hard, he talks pretty darn loud."

"He just couldn't imagine what would possibly be keeping me, that's all."

"Uh-huh. So tell me the truth," she said. "Was this all a plan to get lucky tonight?"

"If I'd been trying to get lucky, I wouldn't have terrified you first with the flight."

She thought about that. "Good point," she decided, and looked at the phone when it rang again, letting out a moan. "Why, Adam, what a shock," she said when she answered. "Tell Cruz he's a tattletale. We're just stuck waiting for a part, not running off to get married. Talk to you tomorrow." She shoved her phone back into her pocket and blew out a breath. "About this hotel . . ."

"Yeah?"

"I don't want you to spend a lot of money."

He knew the only thing she hated more than flying was being a burden to someone. "I don't care about the money."

"Hmm. Brady?"

"Yeah?"

"Two women?"

He sighed, and gently squeezed her fingers. "Let it go."

Half an hour later, Brady had reserved a two-bedroom suite in a boutique hotel that the restaurant had recommended. It had a lush lobby, done up in luxurious Old West–style with leather and dark, rich woods. They managed to buy some toiletries for the night in one of the shops before going upstairs.

When Brady escorted Lilah to their floor, she narrowed her eyes at him. "Penthouse? How's the penthouse being thrifty?"

He shrugged, then took her to the wide windows, where she gaped at the skyline view of Boise.

"Oh my God," she said for the tenth time as they walked through the opulent place. "What did you do?"

"My money," he reminded her.

"But it must have cost a fortune."

He opened the door to her room, nudged her inside, and then when she whirled to face him, mouth open—no doubt to bitch him out some more—he gently shut the door in her face.

And went to his bedroom. He had to, or he'd have taken her right there, and he couldn't do that. If they were going to sleep together again, it had to be her choice, not circumstance, but a real choice. He was flipping through one hundred and fifty channels on the TV when there was a quiet knock at his door. He opened it to Lilah.

"Hi," she said softly.

"Hi."

Putting her hands on his stomach to push him out of the way, she walked in.

Okaaaay. He leaned back against the door to study her.

It was that or grab her and toss her to the bed. Since his fingers were itching to do just that, he jammed them into his pockets.

"Hi," she said.

He smiled. "You already said that."

She nodded. "Right. Listen, I forgot to mention one more thing that I'm afraid of besides flying."

"What's that?"

"I'm afraid to sleep alone in a hotel room. Suite. Mausoleum. Whatever." She looked around the big fancy room. "Although yours doesn't look as scary as mine."

He arched a brow. They had the exact same rooms.

She returned his look with a guileless little smile. "So I was hoping you wouldn't mind letting me in," she said.

He was beginning to think he would let her in anywhere, at any time, and in any place she wanted. His chopper, his hotel room, his life.

His fucking heart . . .

# Thirteen

Lilah would have laid money down on Brady having her naked by now, but he was still standing all the way across the room, leaning back against the hotel room door just looking at her.

Silent.

He could be endlessly silent, she'd discovered. Miserly with words until she wanted to tear her hair out. Luckily she'd also learned that he was the opposite with his actions, instead being generous and infinitely giving, and it was those things she was interested in at the moment.

She wanted his hands on her. His mouth.

Everything.

"Is there a problem?" she finally asked him, unable to hold the silence.

"I don't know yet."

That had her raising a brow.

"You came here to jump my bones," he said.

That startled a laugh out of her. "Yes. Yes, I believe I did." He still didn't move, and she cocked her head. "And look at you standing over there like a virgin on her wedding night."

He didn't react. He was good at that, too, at making her come right out and say exactly what was on her mind. No games, not for Brady. "We had dinner first," she said, teasing. "Do you need more romancing?"

"Shit, Lilah." He shoved his fingers through his short hair, making it stand straight up in spikes. He should have looked ridiculous, but he didn't.

He looked hot and frustrated.

And hot.

He was staring her down, his dark blue eyes unreadable in the ambient hotel room lighting. She held his gaze, trying to outlast him, trying to convince him that she was totally cool and one hundred percent in charge of this situation, which of course she wasn't.

Not even close.

"We need to talk," he finally said.

Oh crap. The most dreaded three words in the English language. "Don't tell me. You're married."

"What? No."

"Engaged?"

"Jesus. No."

Hmm. She was starting to feel a little better about this talking thing. "Are you in a relationship?"

He shot her a look of pure alpha male annoyance, and she felt her nipples go hard. Goodness, he was a force.

"You know I'm not," he said. "Nor do I want to be."

"Great." She shrugged out of her top, leaving her in a tiger-striped demi-bra. She'd ordered it online from Victoria's Secret with a coupon, and it made her boobs look perky.

He took one look at her and groaned. "You're not listening to me."

"Oh, I'm listening." She unzipped her skirt. "You don't want to be in a relationship. Which is perfect because what

I want doesn't involve much other than a condom, and I'm packing this time."

He was staring at the condom she'd pulled out of her pocket. "You just happened to have a condom in your pocket?"

"Three. You are welcome."

"You going to come any closer? Because I have to tell you, that whole smoldering, brooding thing you have going on is actually doing it for me." She grinned. "You could just watch if you'd rather."

He choked out a laugh.

"Or sit on your hands if you're absolutely determined not to be a part of this."

That did it. He shoved away from the door and slowly stalked her with the confidence of a big wildcat at the top of his food chain, crowding into her space, pushing her back until her legs hit the big, fluffy, elegant, fancy bed behind her.

"Sit on my hands?" he repeated in a voice so gruff she felt herself go damp. Suddenly the room was feeling waaay too small and she wondered if maybe she'd poked the tiger a little too hard. "If you must," she whispered.

"Do your panties match your bra?" he asked, dipping his head to breathe the words in her ear, his hands going to her hips as if he intended to look for himself.

At the quick subject change, she blinked. "Yes."

"Are they wet?"

Before she could answer, he pushed her skirt down. As she'd already learned, once he was in control, he showed no mercy, and now was no different. He dropped to his knees, his hands sliding down the backs of her thighs to open them wider. "Yeah," he said when he had her legs the way he wanted them, his voice holding more than a hint of naughty accusation. "Wet."

"I . . ."

His hands skimmed up her inner thighs, meeting in the middle, where his thumbs brushed over her center, making her gasp.

At the sound, he surged to his feet, sliding his big hands up her now quivering body. She rocked into his touch as his mouth trailed along her jawline, nuzzling into her ear. "Look at me."

With effort, she lifted her head.

"I love your eyes," he said. "They glow when you're turned on. They're glowing like emeralds now."

No man had ever said anything like that to her before, ever. And that was the thing with Brady. He was cool and distant. Tough and edgy. Smart as hell and braver than any man she'd ever known. Testosterone and danger oozed from his every pore.

Even in bed, as she had good reason to know.

But he didn't hold back. Not in life, and certainly not in bed, where if he felt like it, he could linger until she lost her mind as he touched and kissed and nibbled and licked . . .

And sometimes, when it counted, he had words, too.

She slid her fingers into his hair and pulled until his mouth was on hers. He immediately opened for her, the kiss hard and fierce, and when they broke apart, they were both breathing hard.

"More," he demanded, and then stroked a hand across the curve of her belly. His fingers were roughened from hard physical labor, bringing delicious shivers to her body as he tugged the straps of her bra off her shoulders. He kissed the plump of each breast before unhooking the bra and tossing it over his shoulder. Leaning in, he flicked his tongue over a nipple and slid a hand into her panties, unerringly finding her happy spot.

When she cried out, he dragged the silk down her legs, leaving her exposed to his hot gaze. It was dark outside, but he had the lamps on and she knew he could see everything he wanted.

"You're overdressed," she whispered.

Muscles flexed as he reached behind him and tore his shirt off over his head. It went flying in the same direction as her bra and panties had, and she moaned at the mouth-watering view of him, all those perfect sinewy lines . . .

The metallic slide of his zipper sounded shockingly loud in the room and then his pants were gone, but before she could get a good look he'd dropped to his knees again, his hands back on her inner thighs. She felt his breath stir against her.

"I've been hungry for this all week, Lilah," he said, and separated her folds with his thumbs to put his mouth on her.

A sound escaped her, a wordless cry that she couldn't have held in to save her life as he worked her over with a delicate precision that spoke of how much her pleasure meant to him. Her hands were still in his hair—she couldn't help but hold on when he found her rhythm as if he knew her body better than she did.

She'd wanted the heat, she'd needed the escape, but she found more, so much more, and her orgasm hit hard and unexpected. When her legs gave out he wrapped his arms around her, effortlessly holding her up. Even after she stopped shuddering, he lingered, bringing her down gently before he rose to his feet. He tugged the bedspread off the bed, then tossed her on the mattress, crawling up her body, eyes glittering, muscles tense, his skin gleaming. He threaded his hands into her hair and tipped up her face, staring into her eyes as if he was trying to memorize her. She did the same, loving the way his gaze lit when he looked at her, the way his mouth twitched when she was amusing him in some way, how his voice sounded when he murmured her name. And then there was how his body felt against her own, how he made her feel.

Wanted.

Craved.

Safe.

She'd never experienced anything like how she felt surrounded by his arms. And still she needed more. She pushed, and he let her roll him beneath her, where she took her mouth on a tour over his pecs, across his abs, heading downward—

He reversed their positions again.

"Hey," she said.

He showed her the condom in his fingers, the one he'd snagged from her.

"Oh," she breathed. "I like how you think."

"Yeah?" He kneeled between her legs and rolled on the condom. "Then you're going to really like what comes next." He kissed her mouth, gliding up to graze his teeth along her jaw, then the sweet spot beneath her ear, the swirl of his tongue making her squirm with the memory of where else he was good with that tongue. As if he'd followed the train of her thoughts, he laughed softly and threaded his fingers in her hair, tilting her head so that he could hold her gaze as he slid inside her.

There was no space between them, nothing but pleasure. His hands slid down her back and over the cheeks of her ass, lifting her, changing the angle, making her moan helplessly at the sensation of him filling her so completely with nothing more than one sure push of his hips. She gasped and cried out at the same time, arching against him, rocking up as he started to move inside her.

"Lilah."

His eyes were fixed and unwavering on her. She lost her breath just looking at him, and she ground her hips to his, unable to control herself.

For once his own control seemed completely absent. Breathing heavy, face tight, he brought his mouth back to hers as he thrust deep, nipping her lip, sucking it into his mouth. "God, you feel good wrapped around me. So fucking good, Lilah."

Melting, she wrapped her arms closer around his broad

shoulders and stroked down his back, her hips rising to pull his body even tighter to hers.

The motion wrenched a very sexy, very male sound from him.

"You like?" she whispered.

"Love. I love."

She tried not to focus on his words, spoken in passion, about his physical pleasure. She tried not to hope that he was letting her in, letting himself fall.

But it didn't matter, her heart had its own agenda and his words made it ache. So she ground her hips into him once again, wrenching another groan from him. She throbbed in response, and the wave began to build within her as he kept moving, stroking hard, harder still, until she came with shuddering impact, crying out his name, arching up into him. He pressed himself even deeper, then stilled as he came with her, holding tight, keeping them connected.

They stayed that way, locked together, for a long time, each of them gasping for air, unable to say a word or move a muscle, shaking with the exertion and the aftershocks. Finally Brady rolled them to their sides. He had his arms around her, apparently just as content as she to prolong their connection. And as she drifted off, she realized that had been the most intimate experience she'd ever shared with a man.


Lilah came awake in slow degrees, aware only of being deliciously warm. Opening her eyes, she realized she was face-first in Brady's throat.

Mmm. A damn fine place to be.

She was also practically on top of him, a leg and an arm thrown over his body like he was her very own personal pillow.

And that wasn't all.

He had a grip on her, too, one hand cupping the back of her head, the other firmly on her ass.

His breathing was slow and deep and steady.

Unable to help herself, she pressed her lips to his throat and gently rubbed back and forth, knowing exactly when he came awake because his breathing changed. "Hey," she whispered. "Don't look now, but we're cuddling."

The hand on her ass tightened possessively, making her smile. "So whatcha doing?"

"Sleeping." His voice was morning rough and gravelly and sexy as hell. "But that's going to change quickly."

"I was hoping you'd feel that way." She gently bit the tendon where his neck met his shoulder, and in one smooth motion he rolled her beneath him.

"Let me guess." He lifted his head, his eyes and mouth soft in a way she hadn't seen from him before. "You don't want to waste our last condom."

"Well, that'd be a crime, right?" she whispered.

"Wrap your legs around me." Another command, uttered in that quiet but utterly authoritative voice of his, but since following his directives always brought her mind-blowing pleasure, she wrapped her legs around his waist and hummed her gratification. It was all she could manage because he was hard, deliciously hard and teasing them both. "Are we going to—"

"Oh yeah."

"And then again?" she murmured hopefully, sucking in a breath because his mouth was at her jaw working its way to that sweet spot beneath her ear, the one that, when he kissed it, made her want to offer him anything, anything he wanted . . .

"Greedy little thing," he accused.

He was right. When it came to him, to this, she was greedy. She was greedy as hell.

"Only one condom," he reminded her. "We used the other a few hours ago. We'll have to get creative."

Thank God. He was good at creative. Really, really good. They kissed and rocked up against each other for a few moments, the room quiet around them with the exception of her own heavy breathing and low moans, until she couldn't take the teasing any longer. "Brady."

He lifted his head and looked at her with lidded eyes. "Tell me."

"More," she said, making her own demands now. His big hands gripped her hips and tilted her in a way that pleased him, tugging a groan from deep in his throat. "Yes," she said. "More of that."

"Anything you want."

# Fourteen

It was midday by the time Brady replaced the gauge on the Bell and got them back in the air. For the return flight, he plied Lilah with a glass of wine first.

She denied that it helped, but he could tell by how relaxed she looked that it did—though that might have been from all the orgasms. Hard to tell.

She was quiet this time. Not so unusual for him, but absolutely unusual for her. Halfway home, she turned to him, nibbling on her lower lip.

He braced for the worst.

"About whatever it was that you wanted to talk to me about in your hotel room last night before I—before we . . ." She grimaced. "I didn't mean to interrupt you with wild sex."

That made him smile. "Yes, you did."

"Okay, true, I did. But I'll listen now to whatever you wanted to say."

He slid her a look.

She smiled at him, completely unrepentant, and he blew out a breath. "I wanted to warn you off of me," he told her.

"I like being on you."

He let out a low laugh. "Lilah."

"You like it, too."

"I love it," he admitted. "And you know what I mean."

"I appreciate the sentiment, but I'm a big girl, Brady. You're leaving soon. I haven't forgotten. I wanted this."

This won him another heart-stopping smile, which he told himself was the wine.

It was early evening when they landed. Lilah had checked in with Cruz several times, but she still headed right off to the kennels to make sure everything was okay. Brady went through his postflight maintenance, then walked across the meadow to Belle Haven.

Twinkles was lying beneath a tree out front looking glum, but he went bat-shit crazy when he saw Brady, wriggling, waggling, rolling in ecstasy when Brady stooped low to rub the dog down. He tried to remember the last time he'd come back from a trip and had this sort of reception but couldn't.

It was after closing time, and Dell and Adam were in the parking lot playing basketball like it was a war zone. Having clearly finished up at the kennels for the day, Cruz was playing, too, the three of them taking their game very seriously.

"Thank Christ," Adam muttered when he saw Brady. "It's these two idiots against me, and they don't know a foul from their own ass. We're skins."

Brady peeled off his shirt and joined the game.

In less than two minutes both Dell and Cruz were pissed. "You can play," Dell said to Brady in disgust. "When did you learn to play, because you were shit in high school."

It was true. He'd been shit at basketball in high school. "I played in the army every night with the guys in my unit. They were street players, hard core."

Adam grinned and passed the ball to him. Brady caught it, pivoted, and shot, making a very sweet three.

Dell swore viciously.

When the game ended, they were all sweating like hookers in a confessional, and Adam and Brady had won by two. He turned to grab his shirt and found Lilah standing there, his camera around her neck.

"I'm back," she said, and handed him his camera. "Nice game."

"Thanks." Brady watched her head off into the center. He took Twinkles and headed to the loft to shower, then checked in with work via e-mail to see if Tony was still pissed.

He was.

Brady closed the e-mail program and downloaded the pictures from his digital and realized he was in many of them.

Lilah had seen to that.

There was a photo of him flying the Bell, a look of concentration on his face as he spoke on his headset. Another of him glancing over at Lilah, eyes still serious, and then yet one more taken in the next instant, when he'd softened for her, a warm, caring smile in his eyes and on his mouth.

He would have sworn on his own life that he never looked at anyone like that, and yet here he sat staring at the proof.

Lilah had taken several pictures of the view, and they weren't half bad. There were also his shots from the restaurant, of Lilah. She was laughing in all of them, a silly, sweet little smile on her face, her eyes lit up with pure joy.

There was one of him at the table, clearly absorbed in watching Lilah. He had yet another small smile on his face, but that wasn't what caught him about that picture.

It was his eyes and the heat in them. The hunger.

The need.

A little shocked at the naked longing he'd displayed, he turned to the next group of pictures, which were of the basketball game, including a close-up of him sweaty and grinning from ear to ear as he came down from a layup.

The very last picture was him turning his head toward the camera—the exact moment he'd realized that Lilah was standing there watching. He was smiling with triumph right into the lens, looking more carefree than he could remember feeling.

He shut his computer just as Adam came up the stairs, suited up for a rescue, two of his dogs at his side. "Need a lift," he said.

"To?"

"There's a big search for a lost kid up in the Kaniksu National Forest. They need all the help they can get. You in?"

Yeah, he was in. An excuse to fly? Check. An adrenaline rush of a search and rescue? Check and check.

A reason to keep his brain from fixating on one Lilah Young? Check, check, and check.

They spent the next six hours straight in the mountains, providing assistance to the search. The kid was located, not by them personally but by a group of rescuers using dogs that Adam had trained last season, which was just as satisfying.

On the flight back, Adam looked over at Brady. "About Lilah."

"Christ. Again?"

"Just one thing. Don't play her, man. She . . . she's been hurt."

If the subject matter hadn't been so serious, Brady might have laughed. Because he was just beginning to realize the truth: for once he wasn't the one doing the playing.

Lilah woke up the next morning to Sadie bumping her little kitty nose into hers.

"Mew."

"It's not time," Lilah murmured. "The alarm hasn't gone off yet."

"Mew-mew-mew."

This was from the eight-week-old kitten trying to get around Sadie, the sole leftover from a rescue the week before. Lilah had placed both of the little guy's sisters but hadn't yet found him a home. He was black, with a white spot on top of his head that looked like a little cotton ball, and he liked to be the boss of his world, which is why Cruz had named him Boss.

Lilah pushed them both away and snuggled down into her covers. She was warm and comfy but not nearly as warm and comfy as she'd been in Brady's hotel bed, with his big, hot body as her personal furnace.

Just remembering the wild hotel sex heated her up pretty good. Sure, she had a small sneaky little feeling that maybe it hadn't been just wild sex, but that was hopefully the endorphins messing with her brain.

"*Mew*," Sadie insisted.

Dammit. "You have got to work on your aversion to the sandbox, missy." Staggering out of bed, Lilah pulled on a pair of sweats and opened the front door for the irritated cat, who was weaving in and out of her legs and threatening to topple them both over.

She caught Boss before he could escape with Sadie. "You're not old enough to run free, little man." She paused and stared down at her porch. "There's an army bag on my porch. Why is there an army duffel bag on my porch?"

Sadie didn't answer because she was already gone. Boss didn't answer because he was a man, after all, and didn't talk much.

Lilah sat on the top step in the early chilly morning, Boss in her lap and the bag at her feet. Adam had been National Guard, not army. She only knew one man who'd been army, and the thought of him bringing her something left a silly smile on her face.

Inside the duffel bag was yet another bag, this one a pretty frothy pink color, from the Pharmacy in Boise. It was filled with soaps and lotions and . . . the pretty blue lingerie she'd been drooling over in the window display. "He didn't," she said to Boss.

"Mew."

She laughed, even as her throat tightened. Heart melted clean away, she pulled out her phone and called Brady. "Morning, Santa."

He was silent.

"At least I hope you're my Secret Santa," she said. "I can't imagine Cruz or Nick picking out that thong—"

A growl sounded through the phone and she smiled. "Thank you," she said softly. "I love it, and the soaps and lotions, too. You shouldn't have."

"I like the way you always smell."

"That's the coconut and vanilla and stuff."

"It's you. You make me hungry, Lilah."

"You know," she murmured. "You don't have many words, but you seem to make the most of the ones you have."

"You going to wear that thong today?"

"You are such a guy."

"Guilty."

Their silence was comfortable, and she found herself smiling like an idiot, all alone on her porch.

"Wear it today, Lilah," he said softly, silkily.

And she knew she would do just that. "See you around, Brady."

"See you," he said, and she could hear the bad-boy smile in his voice.

She closed her phone. "I'm not falling for him," she told Boss, and pulled out a soap. She pressed her nose to it, inhaling the delicious scent. But she was.

Falling and falling hard.


That night she drove to Dell's house for their monthly poker night. Dell lived in town in a house he'd recently fixed up for himself. To Lilah's surprise, she found Brady already seated at the big round table. He was slouched in a chair, long legs stretched out in front of him, a ball cap low on his head hiding most of his gorgeous face except for his mouth.

Which had the sexiest scowl on it she'd ever seen.

Amused—and more—she plopped down beside him. "Heard about your day, Ace."

He slid her a dark look that made her nipples hard before he went back to his cards.

"I'm in," she said to Adam, who was dealing.

"Five-card draw." Adam shuffled the deck like a pro. "And he had more than a hell of a day," he said, tossing a look at Brady as he dealt, taking Lilah's ten bucks and handing her a stack of chips. "He went with Dell on rounds. They were unable to save Mr. Williams's dog after it got hit by a car, then got to the Cabreras' in time to watch their elderly cat die, and as a bonus, on the way home, they headed out to a ranch and had to euthanize a horse with a broken leg."

"It was just shit luck," Dell said, studying his cards, tapping the table to indicate he was holding. "No one's fault."

Brady tossed in some chips. "Raise you five."

"Fuck," Adam said conversationally, but put in his five.

Since she had nothing, Lilah folded.

Dell tossed in his five and shook his head. "Best part is his new nickname."

Lilah glanced at Brady, who was looking pained. "What is it?"

"Nothing," Brady said, and adjusted his hat even lower over his face.

"Dr. Death," Adam said, and flashed a rare grin.

"What?" Lilah burst out laughing. "Are you kidding me?"

The muscle in Brady's jaw bunched and Adam shook his head, still grinning. "Now no one wants him to go along on out-calls anymore, no matter how badly they need Dell."

Everyone but Brady cracked up. He just swore, with a

colorful assortment of four-letter words. Lilah wanted to jump him right then and there, but she controlled herself.

Or maybe not quite.

Brady turned his head and met her gaze. He studied her a moment, and though he remained scowling, his eyes heated. He saw right through her, she realized, not knowing whether to be embarrassed or aroused.

So she settled for both.

They played two more rounds before Dell looked at the grease streaked down Lilah's jeans. "Plumbing problems again?"

Her cabin had more problems than she could count, but she loved the old place ridiculously. For one thing, it was all she had of her grandma, and it was filled with precious memories that not even bad plumbing could erase.

For another, it was her only option, given that the money she made went back into the business or toward her tuition. "Nothing I can't handle."

"Lilah, you need to—"

"Change from brass to PVC. Yeah, I know." She hadn't budgeted for it this month. Or next month, for that matter. In fact, she wasn't budgeted for anything anytime soon. "I'm babying the plumbing along for now." Well aware of Brady studying her, she smiled. "Duct tape is a girl's best friend."

Adam shook his head.

Brady was still looking at her. Slowly his gaze dropped, taking in her clothes, probably wondering if she was wearing the lingerie. She gave him a secret smile. He didn't return it, but his gaze singed her skin.

Her cell phone buzzed with a forwarded call from the office line, the one she used for the humane society, and she picked it up to hear Mrs. Sandemeyer's voice.

"Someone did it again," the elderly woman said in her eighty-year-old quavery voice. She lived on the outskirts of town right off the highway. "Dumped a dog they don't want. I'll hold her for you, dear."

"Is the dog injured?"

"Not at all. And sweet as a lamb."

Lilah closed her phone and reluctantly folded her cards. "I'm out."

"But it's just getting good," Dell complained.

"Translation," Adam said. "He thinks he's about to kick our asses."

"I don't think it," Dell said. "I know it."

"Sorry." Lilah rose. "Much as I look forward to that ass-kicking, I have to go. Someone dumped a dog off the free-way again."

"Assholes," Dell said. "Be careful, Lil."

Brady stood up. "I'll go with you."

"No worries, I'll call Cruz if I run into trouble," Lilah said. "Finish playing."

"It's late."

"She has Cruz," Adam said softly. "It's his job."

Lilah patted Brady's arm, nearly hummed in pleasure at the hard, knotted sinew of his biceps, and smiled. "Adam's right. Stay for the ass-kicking."

His eyes met hers, dark and unreadable, and more than her nipples reacted. Her heart actually skipped a beat.

Stupid heart. Because he was leaving soon, she reminded herself, ignoring the little ping in her belly at that thought. She was going to have to give him up, but then again, she was used to giving things up.

She gave her animals up all the time.

She'd given her grandma up.

She'd given certain dreams up, and knew she'd give up more before it was all said and done.

And she'd give up Brady when the time came. She would. Even if the little ache in her heart reminded her that there would be a price.

She was halfway to Mrs. Sandemeyer's house when she got her second call of the night. This one from Cruz. "Babe," he said, voice solemn. "Problem."

"Well, it'll have to get in line," she said.

"There's a tourist looking for a three-legged cat that she lost a month ago."

Lilah's heart, already aching, full-out stopped at this news. "What?" she whispered.

"She's only just now seen the lost-and-found bulletins online. Lilah . . ."

"Sadie," she whispered.

"Yeah."

Seemed she had one more thing she had to give up, after all.

# Fifteen

B rady cleaned out both Dell and Adam at the poker table, which took his day from pure shit to pretty damn good, especially when Dell was reduced to whining.

By the time Brady and Twinkles got into his truck to drive back to the loft for the night, it was past midnight. Only he didn't go to the center.

Instead, he turned right. Onto Lilah's property. Twinkles got all perky as they passed the lake, but Brady kept driving. He didn't believe in the legend, but neither did he believe in tempting fate. "Don't want to risk you falling for the first dog you see."

The dog snorted because even he knew it was Brady who was afraid to take the risk. He pulled up Lilah's driveway and Twinkles looked confused. "Don't ask. I can't explain it."

Not even to himself. It wasn't as if he needed to see her—although having her naked and writhing beneath him again would be nice. "I just . . ."

Twinkles was listening, head cocked, and Brady let out

a breath. "I'm talking to a dog again." And worse, he really didn't know what he was doing here. He honest to God didn't. He sure as hell didn't want to talk. In fact, the only words he wanted to hear coming out of Lilah's mouth were his name, how much she liked what he was doing to her, and whether or not she wanted it harder.

The kennels were dark. But the cabin's kitchen was lit, so he and Twinkles headed that way and knocked on the front door.

Nothing.

He glanced back at Lilah's Jeep. She was most definitely here. Was she with someone? Whoever had helped her with the rescues? Cruz . . . ?

No, she'd still have answered the door. Or at least he sure as hell hoped so. He thought of all the reasons she'd be home alone with Cruz and not answer.

Finding that he didn't much like any of those reasons, he knocked again, harder now.

Still no answer. Reaching out, he tried the handle. It turned under his hand. She'd indeed been here, working on the kitchen sink. The lower cabinet was open, tools strewn around, and the pipes were wrapped in duct tape at the seams.

But the sexy plumber was nowhere to be seen, and the cabin was empty, including the bed.

He checked.

Stepping back outside, intending to touch the hood of her Jeep to see if it was warm, he heard a soft gasp for breath that made him frown. "Lilah?"

Nothing but the dark night.

But she was out here, he could feel her. He wasn't crazy about the fact that he was so in tune to her. It made him more than a little uneasy.

And vulnerable.

He didn't do vulnerable for anyone. But he heard the sound again and followed it into the woods. Just past the first group of trees, he came to the water he'd been determined to avoid at this time of night at all costs, only to find Lilah huddled down by it. She was sitting, arms wrapped around her bent legs, forehead to her knees.

Sobbing.

Twinkles bounded forward and ran a circle around her, then sat obediently at her feet, head cocked, eyes worried. "Arf."

Brady nudged the dog aside and squatted down in front of her.

"Go away," she said through her tears. "Please, just g-go."

He'd like to, Christ he really would, but the fact was that he could no more walk away from her than he could stop himself from breathing.

Or aching for her. "Are you hurt?"

Leaving her forehead against her knees, she shook her head.

He reached out to touch her, but she shoved at him. "Don't."

Fuck that. She was dirty again, more than she had been at poker, and between that and the dark, dark night sky, he couldn't get a good look at her. So he sat next to her and dragged her into his lap.

She fought for about two seconds then gave up and slumped against him, fisting his shirt in her hands as she quietly and thoroughly went to pieces.

He'd survived roadside bombings, dickhead officers with more stripes than courage, and once, being captured and tortured for two days when his chopper had gone down in enemy territory before being dragged out half alive by the good guys.

So this, holding a small sobbing woman, should be a piece of cake.

Instead it felt like someone had put a vise on his chest and cranked it impossibly tight.

While Lilah continued to let loose with the mysterious

waterworks, he ran his hands over her, making sure there was no physical injury. He was getting that it was something far deeper, but it was second nature for him to want to make sure. When he was positive she wasn't bleeding out and there were no broken bones, he just held her and let her get it all out, until she finally quieted down to the occasional hiccup. "Better?"

She tightened her grip on him, keeping her face buried in his tear-soaked shirt.

"Okay," he said. "Not quite yet."

They fell silent for a while. Which worked for him. Silence always worked for him. Around them, the night carried on. The water slapped at the rocks at the shore's edge. The crickets were going to town. Far in the distance came a howl of something, and then a beat later came a matching howl.

Lilah shivered.

Brady stroked a hand down her back and pressed his face into her hair. Coconut again, and something else, the combination both sweet and sexy. She was cold, her nose especially, which he knew because she had it pressed to the base of his throat. Her hands were tangled in the material of his shirt, her ass snug to his crotch. He was doing his damnedest not to fixate on that, but she was squirming a little.

He was aware that he shouldn't be turned on while holding an upset woman, and he gripped her hips to keep her still.

"Why are you here?" she finally whispered, voice hoarse.

The question of the day. "A friendly visit?"

"It's late for friendly. It's more like booty-call hour."

He tightened his grip on her booty and rubbed his jaw to hers. "Don't tease me."

She choked out a laugh—as he'd meant her to—and then there was more easy silence, which was his favorite kind. They continued to watch the night go by, and when her occasional shuddery inhales had dwindled away completely, he hugged her. "Tell me."

She sighed. "Sadie's mommy showed up."

"Does she have only three legs, too?"

She let out a mirthless laugh and rubbed her hands over her face. "Her human mommy. I had to give her back tonight, Brady."

Shit. He ran his hands up and down her back and neck, over her muscles which were rigid and tense. "So you reunited a family."

"Yes." She didn't say anything else, just sat there staring out at the water looking lost and sad. "Which I realize is the point. But . . ." She closed her eyes and fell quiet.

"You had this one awhile."

"Four weeks, three days."

The pain in her voice killed him. "You get attached. Emotionally."

She turned her head away from him, signifying he was an idiot. Which, of course, when it came to this stuff, he totally was. "I guess that's the brutal reality of your job, right? You care for them until you can reunite them with their family or find them a new family. I mean it sucks to let go, but doesn't it also make you feel good? A job well done?"

"Yes," she admitted. "But the letting-go thing. I have a hard time with that. Always have. I loved Sadie," she whispered. "So much."

He'd never felt so useless in his entire life. "But it's okay to let something go out of love," he said, trying logic and reason. "When you're being part of a solution, in making a situation better."

Lilah's eyes filled again, and he realized his mistake—there was no logic and reason for her right now.

"I hate letting them go," she whispered thickly.

"You'd rather keep them all?"

"Yes."

Well, if that didn't completely lay out their differences right there, he had no idea what could. "You have others still. Like that last wild kitten. Boss?" At her nod, he went on. "And you have all the others you care for, even if they're not technically yours, like the piglet. And that duck. And the lamb—"

Another tear escaped, running down her cheek. "Lilah," he said helplessly.

She choked out a laugh and dropped her head to his shoulder. Again he pulled her in, wrapping her in his arms, which by sheer luck seemed to be the right thing to do.

Letting out one shuddery sigh, she nuzzled in and he tightened his grip on the most confusing, baffling woman he'd ever met.

"Brady?" she asked, sounding waterlogged.

"Yeah?" He was still gob-smacked that logic hadn't worked but a hug had.

"About that booty call," she whispered, and it was his turn to choke out a laugh.

Lilah woke up with papers stuck to her face. She was in bed with her books and laptop.

She'd fallen asleep studying, again.

"Mew, mew, mew."

Boss, not Sadie, and her heart stuttered. Life went on . . . And Boss clearly felt that she'd slept long enough. He worked at climbing up the mountain that was her bed. It took him a while. He was tiny and new to his claws, but finally he stood triumphant on her chest.

She sighed and stroked him, and he began to rumble with his little baby purr. She'd pleased him.

She wished someone would stroke her until she purred.

Last night had been rough. Brady had brought her home, and though she'd attempted to pull him inside with her and let him distract her from her spectacularly bad night, he'd resisted. He'd tucked her into bed, kissed her long and thoroughly, then left.

Just as well, really. She'd been waaay too vulnerable, and given that being in bed with Brady tended to strip her down to a naked, raw, earthy emotional state such as she'd never felt before, she was grateful he'd been smarter than she.

Because last night? She would have fallen in love with him for sure.

So she'd forced a smile when he'd pulled free of the bone-melting kiss, playfully swatted him on his very fine ass, and watched him walk away.

And then, apparently, she'd studied until falling asleep. She dragged herself around the rest of the morning, finally stopping for a quick lunch break. Cruz had left the newspaper opened to page 2, which held a funny commentary about Dr. Death complete with a picture of Brady looking big, bad, and tough as hell standing in front of the Bell 47. Lilah grinned, tore out the picture, and taped it to the kennel's refrigerator, making Cruz shake his head.

Then she went back to work. With summer in full swing, people were in and out of town, many leaving their animals at the kennels. This was great for the bank account. Not so great for free time, not with midterms coming up, and Cruz readying to leave on vacation.

Three nights after having to give Sadie back to her owner, Lilah was in desperate need of a night's sleep that didn't include waking every hour to a ball of anxiety choking her. So she took two Tylenol PM and while waiting for them to kick in, sat at the table to study. Once again she fell asleep there and dreamed about a set of warm arms.

Brady's arms.

Mmmm . . . So nice of him to show up in her dreams. Smiling, she clung to him as he carried her off somewhere. Hopefully to an island. Maybe somewhere in the

South Pacific, where it would be just the two of them, a sandy beach, warm sun, and no responsibilities. She loved her life, but sometimes she dreamed about a day that didn't begin at the crack of dawn to clean pens and stalls. No dealing with the daily grind of running two businesses. No heartache . . .

She sighed in pleasure at the thought. "Just a day . . ."

The arms holding her tightened. "Shh, I've got you . . ."

She struggled to come out of the haze, but he nuzzled her hair. "Sleep," he commanded softly.

She woke up in the morning alone in her bed. Boss was standing on her, eyeing her accusatorily for having slept for so long. Her reading glasses were on her nightstand, her clothes on the chair in the corner of her tiny bedroom—

Wait a minute. Lifting the covers, she stared down at herself. She was in a big T-shirt and her panties—and nothing else.

She'd have recognized the T-shirt by the scent of Brady alone, and she brought the material up to her face for a big, delicious sniff of him.

God, she was a sap. A sap who smelled coffee. She followed the scent to her kitchen, a wave of sadness hitting her when there was no Sadie to trip over.

On the counter sat a large coffee, and next to it—be still her heart—two breakfast burritos. And a bright red shiny apple. For the first time in a few days, she smiled. "He's good," she said to Boss.

The kitten gave her a look that said, *Of course he's good, he's a man, isn't he?*

By the time Lilah showered and dressed, she was nearly late at opening the kennels, and her day got crazy from there. It wasn't until Cruz's shift in the afternoon that she managed to walk over to Belle Haven.

Brady was gone, having flown Dell up north for a complicated foal birthing, so Lilah stopped to talk to Jade at the reception desk. She had to laugh at the Dr. Death news-paper clipping taped to Jade's computer.

"Oh, you like?" Jade asked. "He's my beefcake of the week. Plus, it drives Dell nuts. He's been working for how many years, and he's never made page two in full color."

The waiting room was packed with patients waiting for Dell's return. There were dogs and cats and a ferret. Most were well behaved, but the same couldn't be said of a young boy around five, sitting on the floor with his army men, throwing a tantrum every time any of the animals looked at him.

His mother was sitting in a chair as far from him as pos-sible. Lorraine Talbot had been several years ahead of Lilah in school. She'd been prom queen, head cheerleader, and had never found much time for people outside her circle.

Lilah hadn't been in that circle.

Apparently neither was her own child.

Lorraine came in to Belle Haven often, mostly because she had a fat crush on Dell. It might have been the fact that he had "doctor" in front of his last name these days, as op-posed to their high school days when he'd just had "dweeb."

The front door opened and in walked Brady and Dell. They were both filthy from head to toe, covered in dirt and muck and God knew what else, looking weary and worn.

Dell turned to the waiting room and Lorraine immedi-ately leapt to her feet and gave him a finger wave and flirta-tious smile.

Dell nodded. Definitely muted from his usual wattage, which had nothing to do with exhaustion but the fact that he'd learned not to encourage her. The last time he'd smiled at her she'd come by every single day for two weeks.

"Sorry for the delay, guys," he said to the room at large. "I'll go get cleaned up and be right back." He went into his office, and Lorraine sat with a huff.

Brady's gaze tracked directly to Lilah, and a little frisson of anticipation danced down her spine. At the same moment, the ferret decided he was bored and leapt out of his owner's hands to playfully bump its head to Lorraine's son's leg.

The boy went berserk, tipping his head back and screaming bloody murder.

The ferret dove beneath his owner's chair, then peeked out, eyes bright, staring at the incredibly loud little human.

Brady was the closest to the kid. "Are you hurt?"

He only screamed louder. A few of the people waiting put fingers in their ears.

Brady craned his neck and eyed the waiting room, clearly trying to figure out who the boy belonged to.

Lorraine was filing her nails.

"Hey," Brady said to the boy. "Only people who are bleeding out get to scream like that. Are you bleeding out?"

The boy stopped screaming to stare at him wide-eyed and openmouthed.

"Are you?"

Probably having no idea what "bleeding out" even meant, the boy shook his head.

"Good." With a nod, Brady rose to his feet and headed toward the stairs but not before giving Lilah a look that had Jade fanning herself.

"Good Lord," Jade whispered. "Dr. Death is hot."

"*Hot,*" one of the women agreed from the first chair across the desk. "He makes me sweat in interesting places."

Every other woman in the room nodded.

"Did you see the look he sent you?" Jade asked Lilah. She gulped down some of her ice water. "If he ever looked at me like that, my panties would just go whoosh, up in flames."

Lilah could understand that. Her panties did the same. It did something to her to watch Brady deal with silly women who got too attached to every animal to cross their paths with the same aplomb he handled a screaming kid, even though he clearly wasn't sure what to make of any of it. Which didn't stop him from living his life the way he wanted to.

She admired that and thought maybe she could get better at doing the same.

Ten minutes later, he came back down the stairs wearing fresh clothes, hair still damp from his shower. He headed out the door, and she followed. "You brought me breakfast."

He looked at her, eyes warm and assessing. "You looked a quart low last night. Thought maybe you could use the pick-me-up."

"I was, and did," she said. "Why didn't you sleep with me?"

They'd crossed the yard and were heading toward Smitty's, where the Bell 47 was tied down.

"Sleeping with you is . . ." He hesitated.

"What?"

At the chopper, he turned to face her. At the confused, defensive look on her face, a faint smile crossed his lips. "Amazing." Then he shocked her by leaning in to kiss her.

When she sucked in an aroused breath, he slid his tongue against hers and melted all her bones. "And," he added, "confusing."

"Confusing. What's confusing?"

"You." He ran a hand over the chopper's steel body, making Lilah remember, vividly, what it felt like to have those hands stroking her.

"Okay," she said. "Now I'm confused."

He turned to face her. "You wanted fun and easy. A light relationship, with an expiration date."

"I did."

"So this is me, trying to give you what you want."

"Sometimes," she said slowly, "what a woman wants is complicated."

"No shit." He let out a breath. "I'm just trying like hell to be a good guy here and make sure no one gets hurt."

"Who's going to get hurt?" But she already knew the answer to that, of course.

She was going to get hurt.

He stroked a strand of hair from her temple, and then ran his finger over her jaw, across her lower lip until it trembled open for him.

And then he leaned in and kissed her again, with such heat and hunger and desire that she was clinging to him, shaking, by the time he pulled back. All she could do was blink up at him, realizing just how right he was to try to hold back. Because suddenly, or maybe not so suddenly at all, she was wanting a lot more than the easy fun she'd promised him.

She struggled to get a handle on herself. Was she so obvious in her feelings for him that he had to worry about her? Yeah. Yeah, she was. She didn't have his seasoned inscrutable mask to hide her emotions. "Maybe it's going to be you who gets hurt," she finally said. "I'm pretty damn unforgettable, you know."

"You are," he agreed so softly that she had to strain to hear him, and even then, she wasn't sure if he'd really said it or if she just wanted him to.

# Sixteen

Several mornings later, Brady drove into town. His plans included something hot for breakfast and caffeine, since he'd stayed up until all hours, restless.

Sleepless.

He and Twinkles had ended up going for a long drive, his mind free. No, that wasn't exactly true. His mind hadn't been free at all. He'd ended up sitting at the lake's edge, he and the dog, staring out at the supposedly magical waters. On his way home, the truck had taken him to Lilah's cabin.

Fucking truck.

Because there'd been a light on, he'd gotten out and knocked. When she hadn't answered, he'd looked into the window and seen her at her table, head down on her books, fast asleep.

Again.

He couldn't have altered what he'd done next even if he'd had to walk through an enemy camp to do it. Breaking in was no problem. Nor was being silent as he did so.

He'd been trained by the good ol' US of A.

For the second time that week, he'd carried Lilah to bed without waking her—and just how many times was she going to work herself into such exhaustion that he could even do that? Still, he savored the task and the silence of the night all around them for long moments before forcing himself to leave instead of climbing into bed with her.

He'd headed back out into the dark night from which he'd come, letting his eyes and ears search out anything that didn't belong. But this wasn't some third-world country, and he wasn't searching out some foreign operative. Unfortunately, old habits were hard to break, and at his core he was still a soldier.

But all had been as it should be, leaving him no choice but to go.

Now it was morning, and in the light of day he could only shake his head at himself. He was doing just that when a dented red Jeep pulled in behind him at 7-Eleven.

Familiar denim-clad legs and a set of scuffed boots appeared at his side.

Lilah shoved her sunglasses to the top of her head and grinned at him. "You'll notice I didn't rear-end you."

"I did notice." He looked down at the duck on the leash. "Abigail."

"Quack," Abigail said.

"Funny thing about last night," Lilah told Brady. "I fell asleep studying and woke up in bed. What do you think about that?"

"I think you need more sleep."

"I can sleep after midterms. I'm looking for breakfast. You?"

"Definitely." They walked into the convenience store together.

"Lilah Anne Young," the woman behind the register said. She was possibly a hundred years old, with an unlit cigarette hanging out of her mouth. "What did I tell you about that duck?"

Lilah smiled. "To cook her at three hundred and fifty for an hour and a half before eating?"

The woman cackled. "Yeah, and don't forget the pepper." She turned her sharp eye on Brady. "Morning, Dr. Death."

Lilah snickered and he sent her a quelling look that only made her snicker again. She had a bran muffin in her hand that he knew she would never eat and was looking over the drink choices when a guy walked up to her and slipped his arms around her waist as if she was his, whispering something in her ear.

Whatever he said made Lilah smile and lean back into him a minute before turning in his arms and giving him a hug that was warm and familiar and made Brady grind his back teeth together.

It was ten full seconds before the fucker took his hands off her, which Brady knew because he counted.

Lilah hadn't objected. Nope, she'd cupped the guy's face and grinned up into it. "When did you get back?"

"Late last night. Come on, I'll take you out for a real breakfast."

"Hey, Ian," the lady behind the counter called out. "Nice that you're back, but don't you be taking my paying customers elsewhere."

Brady decided it was a damn good time to come up behind Lilah, leaving just enough room for maybe a single sheet of paper to fit between them.

Ian took a long look at him, and from over Lilah's head, Brady looked right back.

Lilah craned her neck and gave Brady a what-the-hell-are-you-doing expression, but he ignored it.

"Ian," Lilah said with a little shake of her head, "this is Brady Miller. Brady, Ian runs an outfitter company out of Sunshine." Lilah turned back to Ian. "And sorry, no breakfast date today. I already have one." Again she looked at Brady, brows up, like yes, I'm still having breakfast with you even though you are a dumbass.

Fine. He was a dumbass. He could live with that.

"You want to explain that back there?" Lilah asked when they were outside on the sidewalk a few minutes later, with Abigail at their feet fussing with her feathers.

"Explain what?" he asked, leading her to one of the three small tables out front, where they sat to eat.

"The Neanderthal routine."

Ian came out of the store with a bag, stopping to squeeze Lilah's shoulder and give her another kiss on the cheek.

Brady considered his options. More Neanderthal-ness or play it cool. He went with cool because the poor bastard was clearly just another besotted fool. Probably another ex, which was baffling all in itself. For Brady, when things were over, they were over. He watched until Ian had walked away and shook his head.

"What," she said. "He's a friend."

"Another ex?"

She shook her head. "It never got that far."

Best thing he'd heard all morning. "And yet he's still in your orbit. You have us all just circling you, you realize that, right? Just hoping for a piece of you."

She stared at him, then laughed. "It's not like that."

"It's exactly like that. We're all pathetic." He playfully tugged a strand of her hair. "Willing to take any piece of you we can get."

"Yeah?" She cocked her head and studied him, amused. "Which piece would you want?"

Any piece you'd give me . . . "Guess."

Her smile went a little naughty. "Well, I do have a few pieces you especially like . . ."

There were more than few actually, but he shook his head. This time he wanted something she wasn't offering. Something he wasn't even sure he wanted to admit to yearning for.

A piece of her heart.

Just a little piece so that when he left and felt the pain of the separation, he'd know someone else felt it, too. "Dell's hinting around about me staying longer," he said out of the blue, and sipped his coffee to shut himself up.

She choked on hers. "Did you tell him that you don't do 'stay'?"

"I did."

Her smile slowly faded. "Don't tell me. Just thinking about it has you rushing out of here."

He took her hand. "Oddly enough, I don't feel much like rushing."

She nodded, face solemn now. "So . . . how much longer?"

He ran his thumb over her knuckles, scraped from her latest plumbing misadventure. "Eager to get rid of me, Lilah?"

She squeezed his fingers. "Maybe I just want to make sure you get that piece of me that you want."

*All of them,* he thought, revising her earlier statement. *I want all of your pieces.*

Several days later a situation came up about a hundred miles north. A pack of three dogs were making pests of themselves on a small ranch owned by an older couple who couldn't, or wouldn't, take over the responsibility of placing the animals. If Lilah didn't go get the dogs, they'd be euthanized.

She was just getting into her Jeep when her passenger door opened. Twinkles leapt into the back and then Brady folded his long body into the front seat next to her. He put on his seat belt and lowered his sunglasses over his eyes before he turned and looked at her.

She stared at him while Twinkles leaned forward and licked her ear in greeting. "What's up?"

Brady shrugged. "I thought about offering to fly you, but I didn't have any wine to ply you with."

"Why?"

"Because you fly better when you're wasted."

She rolled her eyes. "I mean, why are you here? In my Jeep?"

"Now see," he said all long-limbed grace and testosterone. "That hurts. Maybe I just want to hang out with you."

She stared at him. "Dell kicked you out of Belle Haven today." She laughed. "He did, didn't he, Dr. . . . Death?"

Brady swore and slouched in the seat, six feet of dark, brooding 'tude. "He said that they had some big rancher head honcho coming by today and that he and Adam couldn't afford to have him catch wind of the Dr. Death thing."

Lilah grinned. "Well, lucky for you, I'm not nearly so selective." She hit the gas and they took off. Brady was quiet but there was no denying he was nice company and even nicer to look at. Halfway there, she had to stop for fuel. Brady pumped the gas while she headed into the convenience store, coming out arms loaded. "Got us some goodies."

He took the bags from her and the driver's spot.

"You're a control freak," she said.

"I like to drive."

"Control. Freak."

He didn't bother denying that. He searched through the bag and gave a very male sound of satisfaction as he pulled out a loaded hot dog.

Lilah tossed Twinkles a doggie bone and pulled out the nachos for herself. "I know the way to your good side," she said to Brady.

"I'll show you a better way later."

She smiled. The truth was, he could show her anything he wanted. "Uh-huh. Promises, promises."

"What does that mean?"

"That I'm thinking you're all talk and no go."

He slid her a look.

She nodded.

"You're going to be taking that back."

She smiled, like that had been her goal all along, and images of taking her right here and now in the Jeep flooded his mind.

"Take the next exit," Lilah said. "Echo Canyon."

He shook his head. "Granite Flat is faster."

She didn't protest, but she did give him a long look.

"Problem?" he asked.

"No. I don't have a problem with your control issues at all."

He rolled his eyes.

"In fact," she said, "in certain areas, your control issues are kind of hot."

Again his gaze swiveled her way. "Certain areas?"

"In bed, for instance." She sucked some melted cheese off her finger.

Slowly.

"Lilah," he said, voice a little lower now.

"Yes?" She sucked on another finger.

"Stop."

She kept sucking. "Stop what?"

Without warning, and gaze still on the road, Brady reached out with quick, accurate precision and wrapped his fingers around her wrist. "What did I tell you about payback?"

"That I love it?"

He laughed softly, and sucked her last cheesy finger into his hot, wet mouth.

When her eyes drifted shut with a soft moan, he nipped her finger with his teeth, making her gasp. "And when I say later, I mean it." Smiling, he let go of her and turned his concentration back to the road.

They drove in silence for a while as Twinkles napped—and snored. Brady enjoyed the relative quiet.

Lilah was wearing softly faded jeans that whenever she leaned forward to adjust the radio, sank low in the back, giving him peek-a-boo glimpses of smooth skin and the very hint of incredibly sweet twin dimples.

He wanted to dip his tongue in those dimples.

As for that ass, he wanted to cup it in his hands and—

"You're on the shoulder of the road, Brady."

Fuck. He swerved back. "Well, if you'd stop distracting me . . ."

"Distracting you?" She pulled one of her legs up and beneath her, twisting to smile at him. Her shirt gaped a little, revealing a curve of breast and another hint of baby blue silk. The lingerie from the Pharmacy. "How can I be distracting you? I'm just sitting here," she asked, the picture of innocence.

"I'll pull over," he warned her.

Damned if she didn't look intrigued, making him both groan and laugh at the same time.

"No," she finally said. "I don't think you will." She ran a hand up his thigh, found him through his jeans and outlined him with a finger.

He nearly jerked them off the road again. Luckily the narrow two-lane highway was utterly deserted. He pulled over so fast they both were rudely yanked back by their seat belts.

Twinkles scrambled for purchase on the backseat.

"Wha—" was all she got out before he'd unhooked her seat belt and hauled her over the console and into his lap.

He had his mouth on hers and his hands in her pants in one heartbeat, and in the next he had her whimpering for more. He kept that up for long minutes until she was rocking her hips and panting.

"Oh God." She arched to him. "Please . . ." She was breathless, head back, eyes closed. She was the most beautiful thing he'd ever seen. "Come for me," he whispered in her ear, stroking her in the way he knew made her crazy, making her gasp and cry out his name.

And she did. She burst and shuddered in his arms and while she made her way back to planet Earth, he held her close against his chest, face buried in her hair. She would probably call it cuddling.

He called it regaining his sanity.

Holding her was his sanity.

Before she'd stirred a muscle, her cell phone rang from somewhere in her purse on the floor. She lifted her head and stared at Brady, hair all wild, face flushed, mouth open. "My ears are ringing."

"It's your cell."

She looked so adorably, gorgeously befuddled. "Oh. I knew that." Feeling around for it, she finally got it open. "Hello? Yes, ma'am, we'll get there before dark." Craning her neck, she looked out the window.

It was already dusk. Her eyes caught on his obvious erection straining the denim, then met his, and in them was an apology but also amusement.

He pushed her back to her side of the Jeep and put it into gear before pulling back onto the road.

"I'm sorry," she said. "I owe you."

He liked the sound of that, but it didn't help his condition any. He shouldn't have touched her, but he couldn't help it—she was the hottest, sexiest thing he'd ever seen, and watching her come was his new favorite drug of choice.

"Don't you think we should fix this before we get there?" She reached out to touch, stroking him through the denim, making him groan. "Later," he said.

"You've got a lot of laters."

"Don't worry, I always collect my debts."

They got to the ranch fifteen minutes later, right at sunset. Years before, the owners had given up the actual ranching to their kids, and then their kids' kids. Mr. Leo Johnson was a big guy, but it was clear that his wife, Ellen, was completely in charge. She took one look at Brady and raised a penciled-in brow. "Dr. Death! Honey," she said to her husband, "look, it's Dr. Death! Nice article."

"Thank you," Brady said, sliding a glance at Lilah, who was grinning. He wanted to be annoyed, but the sight of her genuine amusement always derailed him.

Ellen introduced them to the three homeless dogs she'd found, each a Collie mix and probably litter mates as well. They were clearly neglected but dying for affection and made immediate friends with Twinkles.

Lilah said she'd have little trouble finding them homes, but before Brady could help her load them up, Ellen had dinner on the table and refused to let them go without eating.

Leo said grace and thanked God for the food, the house, the ranch, and every single animal on the ranch, and then his children, and his children's children, and then for the past fifty years with a great woman, and just before Brady fell asleep at the table, his ears pricked up as Leo added, "and for bringing a new couple by for company tonight."

Brady turned his head to meet Lilah's wide eyes. *Couple?* she mouthed, looking so horrified he nearly laughed.

Leo smiled. "Sorry, it's just very obvious that you two are recently together."

"Yes," Ellen said. "You keep staring at each other or touching in some way."

Brady looked down and noticed that indeed he was thigh to thigh with Lilah, and even more telling, he had an arm draped over the back of her chair, his fingers tracing absent circles on her shoulder. His fingers froze midtrace.

"So, how long has it been?" Ellen asked, passing around the thick pot roast and heart-attack-in-the-making mashed potatoes that were the best mashed potatoes Brady had ever tasted. "I mean, I assume this is brand-new," she said with a secret smile at her husband. "Since there was no mention of a relationship in the Dr. Death article, and we all know how thoroughly invasive that gossip rag can be."

"Um," Lilah said, looking uncomfortable. "Well, to be honest, we're not—"

Brady reached under the table and squeezed her knee. He didn't know what came over him, probably retribution for how she'd mercilessly teased him in the Jeep, but he heard himself say, "Don't be shy, honey."

She stared at him, clearly concerned he'd lost his marbles. And he had. The day he'd met her.

"Oh, tell us the whole story," Ellen said, clapping her hands with glee. "I love a real-life romance."

Brady smiled at Lilah. "Go ahead, darlin'. You tell it."

Lilah's eyes narrowed on Brady. Her fork was still in midair, full of potatoes that he suspected she might want to fling into his face as she contemplated him. "Well, sweetheart," she said, "it's just that I don't know where to start."

Ellen was smiling so eagerly. "At the beginning!"

Lilah looked at her and hesitated. Clearly, she was willing to go head-to-head with Brady in a battle of wills, but she wasn't so willing to be rude or cruel. But she must have gotten over that because she said, "We met at the beauty salon in town."

Brady had been smiling, feeling pretty damn pleased with himself for one-upping her—until this.

"Yeah," Lilah went on, clearly gaining steam. "Brady was at his weekly grooming session." She leaned into Ellen as if departing with a state secret and continued in a stage whisper, "He's very hairy, you see."

Brady choked on his peas.

"Wax or laser?" Ellen whispered. "My son-in-law swears by his monthly male Brazilian."

"Brady, too," Lilah said, patting a still coughing Brady on the back. "You okay, baby?" She smiled sweetly at him and began shoveling her food in as if she hadn't eaten in a week. "Oh, Mrs. Johnson, this is all so delicious!"

Brady finally recovered. "Lilah cooks, too, Ellen. Actually, she's an incredible baker. She makes the most amazing desserts."

Now it was Lilah's turn to go pale. The only thing she baked was store-bought cookie dough.

"Oh, that's lovely!" Ellen exclaimed.

"And you should see her on the fly," Brady said. "That's her specialty—improvising."

Lilah narrowed her eyes at him but before she could respond, Ellen spoke again. "Oh, that is a talent. Maybe you can demonstrate," she said hopefully. "I have just about everything you could need for any recipe."

Lilah sent Brady a look of sheer, undulated panic, followed by a look that promised her own payback.

That was okay. After the male Brazilian thing, he was pretty sure he could take whatever she dealt out. Smiling, he leaned back and shot her his best *your turn* look, which she returned with a *you-are-so-going-down* volley.

Fine by him. He'd go down with her any day. With her, on her . . . however and wherever she wanted.

# Seventeen

A little while later, Lilah escaped to the Johnsons' very small, slightly fussy bathroom at the end of the hallway and stared at herself in the mirror. Her eyes were bright, and there were two spots of color on her cheeks. She looked under the influence.

And she was.

She was under the influence of lust. Damn Brady for baiting her, for making her feel . . .

Alive. The man made her feel so alive.

She was still staring at herself when the door opened. A big, warm, built body nudged her over, making room so he could squeeze in behind her.

"What are you doing?" she whispered.

Brady gave her a look that made her nipples pebble up against her shirt as he reached out and hit the lock.

Click.

It echoed over the pounding of her heart. Staring at him in the mirror, she shook her head. "Brady—"

"Lilah," he said calmly. Stepping closer, he forced her up against the sink. His hands gripped the tile at either side of her hips, trapping her in. "A male Brazilian?" His voice was that deep half growl she'd heard only when they were naked and he was whispering erotic, explicit promises in her ear, the ones that never failed to make her blush.

"Well, hey, for all I know you really do wax."

He pressed himself against her butt. He was hard.

"Oh no," she whispered on a laugh even as she rocked back against him, causing him to hiss in a breath. She stopped breathing entirely and went damp. "We can't."

Seeing right through her, he smiled into the mirror, slow and extremely badass.

Oh no. No, she wasn't going to melt just because he was giving her that look. "You have to go," she whispered, attempting to elbow him away. "Shoo."

He made a sound that might have been a snort of laughter. "Can't."

"Why not?"

He grabbed her hand and brought it behind her to cup over his crotch.

"Oh my God." But her fingers stroked him. Bad fingers.

Brushing her hair out of the way, he leaned down to nibble on her neck. "Can't help it," he murmured against her skin. "You have this effect on me."

Her eyes drifted shut, and a horrifyingly needy, hungry little whimper escaped her, loud enough that she lifted her own hands and clamped them over her mouth.

"Mmm," he barely breathed against her ear. "Love that sound." His hands slid from her hips upward, beneath her top.

"What are you doing now?"

"If you don't know, I'm doing it wrong."

Oh, she knew. And the truth was, she'd do whatever he wanted and they both knew it. Ever since he'd come to town with those sharp, assessing eyes and hard-but-oh-so-giving mouth and all that testosterone, her body had been a complete traitor. His tongue rimmed her ear and she had to lock her knees to remain upright. "Oh God."

"Give me a minute and you'll be saying 'Oh, Brady.'" He ran his fingers lightly down her arms and then encircled her wrists, setting them on the counter's edge, indicating she should keep them there. She wriggled back against him, grinding her bottom into his erection. "Hold still," he commanded softly in her ear.

She shivered and it was entirely possible she had a mini-orgasm. If he hadn't been pinning her between the hard sink and his even harder body, she'd have slithered bonelessly to the floor.

Then his hands slid beneath her shirt and ran up her rib cage, stopping just short of her breasts.

She held her breath but couldn't quite keep quiet. "Touch me!"

He pushed her shirt up and the cups of her bra down and, watching her reaction closely in the mirror, palmed her breasts. Then one of his very talented hands slid slowly down her belly and into her pants. "Oh Jesus." His breath was hot against her ear. "You're ready for me."

She'd been ready for him since she'd first laid eyes on him, and she didn't see that changing anytime soon.

His hands went to her hips and before she could draw her next breath, he'd shoved her jeans to her thighs, groaning softly in her ear at the sight of the baby blue thong he'd bought her. There was something incredibly thrilling about being so exposed while he was fully dressed behind her, watching himself touch her in the mirror.

"I—" She gasped when he gave one quick yank and ripped the underwear off her.

"I'll buy you more. Hell, I'll buy you an entire Victoria's Secret store," he promised, his voice a rough, barely there growl as he slid his hand between her thighs. "I can't get enough of you, I can't."

She met his gaze. His eyes were no longer playful but dark and filled with a dangerous emotion. Dangerous, because now it wasn't just her good parts aching. No, the nameless ache spread and hit her heart with deadly precision. Turning in his arms, she twisted her hands into his shirt, and then their mouths connected, hot and demanding. His tongue touched hers at the same moment his fingers slid home. Her toes began to curl, but he slowly withdrew, making her whimper.

"Later," he murmured, but continued to hold her close.

Panting, Lilah dropped her head to Brady's chest. "I hate later." After a minute, she pulled her clothes back into place. Without panties. God. She slumped back against Brady. Beneath her cheek, his heart was thumping steadily. Definitely faster than his usual near-hibernation beat. Lifting her head, she flashed him a tight smile. "I get to you."

"Are you kidding? You own me," he said, his voice running over her like silk.

And with that startlingly revealing statement, he unlocked the door and slipped out, leaving her leaning against the sink, heart still pounding, nipples hard enough to cut glass.

"What are you doing?" Brady demanded an hour later when they were finally back on the road heading home.

The four dogs were in the back, sleeping in a relaxed pack. Outside, the night was dark and chilly, but inside the Jeep it felt warm and toasty, and by the light of the dash, Lilah was moving around, driving him crazy as she pulled off her sweater.

"Just getting comfortable," she said. "I have a long night ahead of me. I still have hours of studying once we get back. I have a big advanced chem midterm tomorrow."

"You should have told me." He glanced over at her. "I'd have gone and gotten the dogs for you. And that's a little revealing."

She looked down at her shirt and laughed. "It's a man's cut beefy T-shirt, and I'm wearing a bra beneath it—as you already know since you had your hands on me earlier. If you're going to worry about something, worry about the fact that I'm commando."

His dick jerked inside his jeans.

"And that I'm commando at all is all your fault."

True. He had the tiny blue scrap of panties in his pocket to prove it. At the thought, he let out a frustrated groan. "And if you could stop saying commando, that might help."

She laughed again. She was laughing, and all he could think about was getting back into her pants. Where she had no panties. Nope, just warm, wet flesh. He scrubbed a hand down his face and tried to steer his mind to something else. Multiplication tables maybe. *Twelve times twelve is—*

"You're going to get a ticket," she said, glancing at the speedometer. "You in a hurry?"

He knew that she knew damn well he was in a hurry. In a hurry to get her home and naked to finish what they'd started.

Because when she was in his arms he was content, as he so rarely ever felt. He didn't want to examine that too closely, because if he did, he'd have to face that not only was he thinking about Sunshine as "home" but that he was also thinking about a future. In one spot. *Twelve times thirteen is—*

"You seem a little on edge," she said.

Yeah, he was on edge. On a very narrow one, too. Because he could get her home as fast as he wanted, but it didn't matter. She had to study and sleep. "I'm on edge, yes. Because I've been hard for hours."

She laughed. "Poor baby."

He was beginning to wonder if he was addicted to her. There'd been times in his wild, misspent youth where he'd tried just about everything under the sun—all manner of drugs and alcohol. It was amazing he'd never become addicted to anything, but how ironic that after all that he was addicted to one little woman.

Not that she had the same problem with him, of course. Nope. She was over there cool as a cucumber, looking like some kind of hot, sexy trouble.

So what the hell was bothering him? She was a dream lover, wanting nothing from him but mutual sexual bliss. No strings . . .

Perfect.

Only it wasn't. Not even close.

Lilah turned to Brady as he drove them through the dark night toward Sunshine. The mountains were nothing but black inky silhouettes, the moon a solitary half orb hanging overhead, casting Brady's face in its glow. He was in his driving zone, giving nothing of himself away.

As if sensing her interest, he glanced over, his features softening when he saw her looking at him. "That dessert you came up with was genius," he admitted.

It had been genius, if she admitted so herself. She'd seen the little pretzel twists on Ellen's kitchen counter, next to a bowl of Hershey kisses. Lilah had taken a baking sheet, spread out the pretzels, put a chocolate kiss in the center of each and then baked. When the kisses were just slightly melted, she'd pulled them out and added a single M&M on top of each, pushing down, spreading out the kiss over the pretzel.

Better than any candy bar at 7-Eleven.

"And I bet no one but me knew you made that up on the spot from the crap she had out on the counter," he said, sounding amused.

"Hey, you loved that crap. You ate like twenty of those pieces of crap."

"I did." He was leaned back, utterly relaxed as he drove, the annoyingly sexy alpha.

"You didn't do so bad yourself," she admitted. "Telling her that I could bake. We're even now, right?"

"Oh no," he said silkily, his voice like warm butter. "We're not even. Not even close."

There in the dark interior, with the darker night all around them, surrounded by the wilderness and four adorable dogs in the back, she shivered. "Don't tell me you're going to hold a grudge."

He slid her a glance. "Weekly grooming sessions? Male Brazilians?" He smiled evilly. "Yeah. I'm holding a helluva grudge. If I was you, I'd be worried. Very worried."

"I'm pretty sure they knew we were making all that up." She nibbled her lower lip. Okay, maybe she'd taken it a little far. "And I was really torn between the Brazilian and saying that we met at the dog-grooming place, where you were having your Pomeranian groomed. The one with a jeweled collar."

"Christ."

She smiled. "I've got to ask—why did you go with the whole couple thing in the first place?"

"Because they wanted it to be true."

She stared at him. "So you told a whopper to a very nice, kind middle-aged man and his wife for altruistic reasons? That's . . . sweet," she decided.

"I am sweet."

She laughed, and he smiled wryly. "Okay," he said. "Maybe sweet is a bit of a stretch."

"I don't know," she murmured, feeling herself soften inexplicably as she thought of all the little things he'd done for her. Giving the woman who'd crunched his bumper a ride home, leaving her breakfast, carrying her to bed when she'd literally fallen asleep on her face. Driving one hundred miles for a dog rescue just to keep her company . . .

"You have your moments."

\*   \*   \*

It was midnight when they pulled back into Sunshine. Brady walked Lilah into the kennels and waited while she got the dogs in and settled, spending a few minutes with each of them, making sure they were calm and had what they needed even though she was yawning widely every two seconds and clearly dead on her feet.

With good reason, he knew. She'd been up since before dawn. He stepped in and helped her, a physical ache in his heart, the one that he was getting used to when it came to her.

"What's the matter?" she asked when they were done.

He'd just realized what else was really bugging him. She was there for everyone and everything, and yet near as he could tell, it didn't go both ways. Not because people didn't love her and want to help her. They did. Everyone loved her. Everyone wanted to help her.

But she didn't let them. She was the most independent, feisty, sexy woman he'd ever met. "Nothing," he said, and walked her to her cabin.

"Want to come in and look beneath my bed? Or better yet, in my bed?"

He wanted her, bad. Beyond bad. But more than getting her naked and making her scream his name, he wanted her rested. She worked so damn hard, was clearly exhausted . . . "I'll tuck you in."

"I'm not going to sleep."

"You've had a long day."

"Yes, but that chem test I'm taking tomorrow counts for half of my grade. I have to burn the midnight oil." She turned in the doorway, clearly expecting him to leave.

Instead, he caught her close, lowered his head, and kissed her, and for a moment she clung to him. It was sweet and warm, and like always when he was within two inches of her, not enough. Gently he nudged her farther inside her cabin. "Get comfy."

She smiled, and he laughed. "Not that kind of comfy. I'm going to help you study."

"What? Why?"

"Because I can."

"What do you know about animal reproductive physiology?"

"I'll be holding the book," he said. "I'll know everything."

Her smile was gone, and so was the warmth in her eyes. "I can do it by myself."

He cocked his head and studied her. "What just happened, what nerve did I step on?"

"Nothing. But I can do this on my own."

That wasn't an answer to his question and they both knew it. "Of course you can do this on your own. But why should you have to if someone's willing to help? Oh," he said, nodding when she didn't respond to that either, "I get it. You don't want help."

"I don't need help."

And in her mind, he knew, there was a huge difference. "Everyone needs help sometimes, Lilah. Except for you, apparently, because that would signify some kind of weakness, right? Not accepting my help allows you to lump me in with all the other men in your life. The ones who, like everything else, are to be taken care of, not vice versa. Because no one's allowed to take care of you."

"That's . . . stupid."

"I might be temporary, Lilah, but I'm not stupid. And I'm not one of your pets, either." He nudged her to the kitchen table where her books were spread out, waiting. "Sit down. The professor is here to make sure you pass."

"Brady."

"That's Professor Brady to you," he said.

She arched a brow and gave him a level look. No longer defensive but not yet willing to concede surrender. "So is this some kind of sexual fantasy? The beleaguered student servicing her professor for an A?"

"Hmm, sounds promising." He nudged her into a chair, smiling when a trickle of good humor came into her eyes. "We'll get to that. For now, crack that book, woman. Don't make me show you what happens to naughty schoolgirls."

# Eighteen

Three hours and lots of caffeine later, Lilah walked past a sleeping Twinkles and Boss and threw herself on her bed. She was frustrated and near comatose and also quite possibly close to jumping Brady's bones.

"What type of uterus is found in mares?" he asked, following her from the kitchen to stand at the foot of her bed, staring down at her in a very intense professor sort of way.

She wanted to strip him naked and lick him like a lollipop, and he wanted to know what a chemical element was.

He nudged her foot. "Lilah."

"Bipartite. Sir," she added with a little smart-aleck salute.

"I like that," he said with a firm nod as he consulted her review notes. "More of that. Now chemically, FSH is what?"

"A protein."

"A protein, sir," he corrected.

She rolled her eyes while he turned her pages. "An oocyte that is surrounded by several layers of cells but does not contain an antrum," he said.

He'd stripped out of his sweatshirt, leaving him in a

loosely fitted Henley and a pair of cargo pants with more pockets than she could count. He looked edible.

"I can see you need incentive." He got on the bed and crawled up the length of her, spreading her legs with his knee. "An occyte . . . ?"

"Secondary follicle . . ." She broke off as he rested his forearms on either side of her head, his face just inches above hers.

"And the structures on the chorion that interlock with the uterine endometrium in the ruminant?" he asked, pulling off her clothes, brushing kisses to every part of her that he exposed, making her mind go blank.

When she didn't speak, he raised his head, his eyes dark with concentration. "Lilah . . . ?"

"Um . . ." This was supposedly all review for her, but she couldn't remember. She blamed his sexiness. "I'm—" She moaned when he drew her breast into his mouth and struggled to think. "I— God, Brady."

He switched to her other breast and slid a hand between her thighs. His breath caught and he made a distinct sound of male pleasure that made her inner muscles contract.

"Brady?"

"Shh." His voice was low and delicious. "I know what will help." And he shifted, kissing her belly, her hips, a thigh . . . and then between them. "This." He rubbed his jaw to her inner thigh. "And this." He stroked her with his tongue and she promptly forgot the question.

"Oh, please," she whispered.

And he did. In a shocking short time, he had her crying out, shuddering with the surprise release. When she'd recovered she found him leaning over her, playing with her hair, face smug.

"Okay," she admitted. "I needed that." She pushed him to his back, pulled off his clothes, and climbed on top of him. "Now you, Professor Know-it-all. Your turn to beg."

"I'm not much for begging."

"Hmm." She started at his throat, working her way down, tasting every inch of him, stopping occasionally to nibble. By the time she got to his abs, he was alternately groaning her name in a plea and in warning.

But not begging. Not yet. Drunk on her own power, and also how he felt shifting restlessly beneath her, she continued southward.

"Christ, Lilah," he grounded out when she finally drew him into her mouth, his hands sliding into her hair. "Christ, don't stop."

*Close enough*, she thought, and didn't stop.


A long shower and another cup of coffee later, Lilah smiled softly at Brady. "Cotyledons."

"What?"

"That's the chorion that interlocks with the uterine endometrium in the ruminant. Thanks for helping me, you're my hero."

"I'm no one's hero." He pulled on his jeans by the first light of dawn slanting in the opened shades, adjusting himself with a scowl.

Either he'd slept badly after he'd put her into a pleasure coma, or her "hero" comment had gotten to him. She was betting on the latter. "In a hurry?"

"I've got to go."

Yeah. Definitely, it'd been the hero comment. "Feeling claustrophobic?"

"This place isn't that small."

"That's not what I meant and you know it."

He ignored that and bent to lace up his boots. "I have a flight scheduled. I'm taking Dell to Idaho Falls for a business thing."

She nodded. "So go."

His mouth tightened, and he whistled for Twinkles, who leapt to his feet to follow blindly. As she was beginning to realize she would do as well.

At the door, Brady paused. "Shit," he muttered to himself with feeling. He turned back to her, staring at her for a long beat while she forced her expression to remain even. Then he closed his eyes. "Fucking sap," he said, and strode toward her, hauling her up to her toes to kiss her stupid. "Kick ass today," he said against her lips.

"You, too," she whispered, but he was already gone.

Brady walked through the chilly morning air, shadowed by Twinkles. It wasn't a month yet, but probably he should call Tony and at least get himself back in the queue to fly. Getting the hell out of Dodge ASAP would be a good thing.

Too bad he couldn't bring himself to do it. He wasn't ready to go.

It was as simple and terrifying as that.

"Arf."

"Yeah, yeah." He'd taken off on Lilah like a bat out of hell, and now all he could see was her face as he'd left. There hadn't been disappointment or irritation. She hadn't been offended the way any number of women in his past would have been when he did his usual vanishing routine. Lilah didn't get upset or withdraw. There'd been only those two words, her softly spoken "So go." And yet in them he'd heard all the damage, all the hurt, she felt.

She was prepared to watch him walk away.

God, he was an ass. He turned around so suddenly he tripped over Twinkles.

"Arf."

"We're going back. I don't know why, so don't ask me." Brady wasn't afraid of much. He doubted there was a boogey man left on earth that could scare him. And yet one woman from the middle of nowhere with heartbreaking eyes and the most courageous heart he'd ever known absolutely terrified him.

As he once again entered the clearing between the cabin and the kennels, Adam was just getting out of his truck, juggling two steaming drinks and a big bag of food from New Moon, the health food store in town.

"What are you doing here at this time of morning?" Adam wanted to know.

Brady shrugged. He'd asked himself that a hundred times in as many seconds. He still didn't know. "She doesn't like health food."

"Are you just getting here?" Adam asked. "Or just leaving?"

"Both."

Adam's eyes went to slits. "I usually offer the choice of death or dismemberment to people who mess with her."

Brady sighed, and Adam stared at him for a long moment, then slowly shook his head. "You poor bastard. You're as fucked up over her as all the others, aren't you?"

"I'm not—"

Adam arched a brow, and Brady closed his eyes.

He was.

He was totally and completely fucked up over her. Which settled it. He did not need to go back inside that cabin. Nothing good would come of him going back in there except muddying up the waters with more of his crazy-ass, confused emotions. Without a word to Adam, he turned around and began walking away.

"Was it the threat of death or dismemberment?" Adam wanted to know.

The truth was, he'd welcome either.


Six hours later, Dell had finished his business and Brady had the Bell 47 aimed back at Sunshine. The trip had gone well, rendering Belle Haven a new contract handling the vet care for a 250,000-acre ranch in the Idaho Falls area.

"This trip alone was worth having the chopper," Dell said as they headed into Sunshine.

Brady shrugged. "Anyone can fly you after I'm gone. Hell, you can hire a pilot right out of Smitty's if you want."

"Rather have you."

"You might want to check with Adam on that," Brady said dryly.

"Why, because he found you coming out of the woods suspiciously near Lilah's cabin at the crack of dawn looking like you'd had a long night?" Dell shrugged. "He's always a bitch when he's not getting any."

"What are we, sixteen?"

"If we were, then he would have threatened you with death or dismemberment. Which one did you pick, by the way? I always pick death."

"And yet here you still are."

Dell grinned. "Yeah. He's all bark and no bite. Probably you should just stick around and keep us in line."

"Stick around?"

"Oh, I'm sorry. You don't know those two words in that particular order. They mean stay. Unpack. Whatever you want to call it."

"I can't."

"Why not?"

Brady stared at him. "Because."

"I realize you're allergic to permanent," Dell said. "But so's Adam, and he makes it work. He travels everywhere all over the country all the time training and delivering the search and rescue dogs, but he always comes back. That's the trick. You could do the same."

"I could train dogs?" Brady asked.

"Travel, smart-ass. Go back and forth." Dell paused. "Be a partner."

"I don't work well with others."

Dell laughed. "Well, no shit. And here I thought your sunny disposition would be such an asset."

Brady let out a breath. "I'll think about it."

"You do that. I'm thinking if you turn us down, I'll hire a female pilot instead, maybe one who wears a short, tight uniform and greets me with 'How can I serve you, sir?'"

Four days later, Lilah was near the outskirts of the county, on the edges of a ranch about to rescue a raccoon mama and her cubs. It had to be close to a hundred degrees outside and she was hot, tired, and filthy. Despite the unseasonably warm day, she was dressed for work in Carhartts and a long-sleeved T-shirt meant to protect her arms. She was tired because she hadn't slept much. Midterms were over, at least for now, but it hadn't been studying that had kept her up the past few nights.

It had been Brady.

Or the lack of Brady.

As for the filthy part . . . well, that was part of her job. She'd been sent here by Dell, who'd talked to the rancher who owned the land and was mad as hell about the raccoons who were constantly stealing the fresh eggs from the hen coops.

Lilah understood the problem. Raccoons were messy and mischievous, and they made pests of themselves on small ranches like this. Certainly it was easier to shoot them, but she hated the thought. She and Dell had a friend in Lewiston who had three thousand open acres. The woman had previously taken in various wild critters and didn't mind doing so again.

Lilah had a pile of humane cages in her Jeep ready to go, and with the hope in mind that the raccoons would be fond of the canned cat food she'd brought as bait, she got out of the Jeep and headed to the front door.

No one answered.

Knowing that she had permission via Dell from the ranch owner to try and solve his problem, she walked around to the barn, which was opened from two sides. Standing in the first opened doorway, able to see clear through to the other opened door, she caught sight of a man out on a horse in a neighboring field.

Probably the ranch owner.

Not wanting him to think she was trespassing, she waved a hand and called out to him, but the sun was in his eyes and he clearly couldn't see her. Plus, she knew he was older and couldn't hear well. She turned back to the barn and went still as she caught sight of movement in the rafters.

The resident raccoons. One big masked head appeared, and then three little matching ones perfectly lined up beside their mama.

Her cell phone rang. "How's it going out there?" Dell asked.

"Working on it," she said.

"Yeah, well be careful. Newberry's pretty determined to shoot the shit out of them. I guess they got into his kitchen yesterday and completely destroyed the place. Remind him that I sent you, that he said it was okay for you to remove the raccoons if you can. He's an older guy and can be mean as a snake. Part of the reason I called you about this in the first place is because his neighbors are threatening to call the authorities on him for using whatever moves as target practice."

"He's out in his field right now but I'll flag him down before I leave." She disconnected and went to the Jeep for two of the cages. Using a ladder she found against the far barn wall, she climbed to the top of the rafters and then precariously balanced there as she came face-to-face with the big mama herself.

Who showed her teeth.

Lilah ignored her and set the traps. This took a few min-utes because she had to keep backing off to give the growling, snarling mama some space. "You'll be thanking me for this in a few days," she promised the pissed-off matriarch raccoon. "You'll—"

The crack of a shotgun ricocheted over her head and shocked the hell out of her, and she barely held on to the rafters. "What the—"

"Goddamn raccoons!" Newberry shouted, clearly frustrated that the sun was in his eyes and he was shooting into a dark barn, which didn't help his aim or his mood.

"Wait!" she cried.

But he'd already pulled the trigger and this time the bullet pinged somewhere just to her right, so close she felt it whizz through her loose hair. She flattened herself on the rafters so that she was lying belly down, and felt the contents of her pockets fall. Keys. Phone. The single buck she held in reserve for the swear jar. She gulped for air as the dollar bill slowly floated to the ground. Through the opened door she could see Mr. Newberry, still on his horse, closer now, once again sighting with his rifle through the opened doors.

He'd seen her shadowed movement, had known the raccoons were up here, and had started shooting.

Unfortunately, Lilah was a side dish on the same platter. Before she could blink, the gun went off again and this time she felt the impact jerk her body.

Fire blazed along her arm.

Barely managing to cling to her perch, she looked down the twenty-plus feet between her and the ground, which was suddenly whirling like she was on a merry-go-round. Through the spinning, she heard Mr. Newberry's horse gallop off. "Wait!" she called with a gasp, but he didn't hear her. She reached out for the ladder and then empty air as said ladder crashed to the ground. Alone, with no way down and no cell phone, she blinked past the sweat in her eyes.

Even the raccoons had deserted her. She set her forehead to the rafter she was clinging to. "Don't pass out," she told herself, knowing the fall would definitely be worse than the bullet wound. "Just keep your eyes open."

But that was hard . . .

The next thing she knew, she heard male voices raised in question, and she forced herself to lift her head. Either she was hallucinating, or the two tall, imposing figures in the doorway were Dell and Brady.

Yelling for her.

"I don't know why she wouldn't be answering her phone." This was from Dell. "Her Jeep's out there, but Mr. Newberry hasn't seen her."

"Here's why she's not answering," Brady said grimly, and crouched down to look at the pieces of her smashed phone.

Just as Lilah opened her mouth to say his name, he raised his head, his gaze landing unerringly right on her.

"Hi," she said, voice nothing but a croak.

He rose and strode toward her. "You okay?" His voice was calm. Maybe that meant everything was just fine.

"I-I think I was hit."

He was at the fallen ladder now, raising it with far more ease than she had. "Hit with what?" He broke off, focusing in on the drops of blood that had fallen from her to the ladder.

"What is it?" Dell asked, moving toward them.

"Blood. Hers, I think." He never took his eyes off her. "Hold on, Lilah," he said, climbing the ladder with agility and speed. "You hear me?"

She didn't answer because she was busy shivering. Odd to be so cold and hot at the same time, and as a bonus, someone was sticking her arm with a hot poker with every heartbeat.

"Lilah. Open your eyes right now."

Oh. Oh yeah, that was the problem. Still clinging to the beam, lying along it like she was on a balance beam, she tried to concentrate.

"Lilah, you hold on. Don't you dare let go," Brady told her.

That's when she realized that she was weaving. And the rafter was shaking, trembling beneath her. And look at that, her hands kept slipping . . .

Suddenly Brady was right there, wrapping an arm around her waist, drawing her up against his body, his free hand running over her as he balanced for the both of them. When he got to her arm, she cried out and his face went grim.

"What is it?" Dell called up.

"She's been shot and is going into shock."

"What the fuck?"

*Oh, look at that,* Lilah thought, eyeing her arm. There was blood dripping—everywhere. "Mr. Newberry thought he was shooting at the raccoons. It was an accident."

Brady cupped her face and forced it up so she could no longer see her arm. "Are you hit anywhere else?" Without waiting for an answer, he ran his hand over every inch of her, searching for more holes.

"Ouch," she said weakly.

"I'll kiss it later," he promised. "Let's go."

She relaxed her death grip on the rafters and wrapped her good arm around his shoulder, burying her face in his neck. Her world tilted as he descended with one hand on the ladder, the other wrapped tightly around her. As soon as their feet were on solid ground, he slid his other arm beneath her knees and carried her out of the barn to Dell's truck.

"Thought you weren't a hero," she murmured.

She thought she heard a rough, low laugh as he tore her shirt from her arm. "Christ." He ripped off his shirt and used it to staunch the bleeding.

"How bad?" Dell asked him, stroking Lilah's hair.

"Bullet's still in there."

"Fuck."

Lilah used Brady's now bare chest as a painkiller. As far

as narcotics went, it was good. She smiled at the definition of muscles, the light smattering of hair that tapered to a line, vanishing into the loose waistband of his cargoes. She wanted to run a finger along it to find the hidden treasure, but then he pressed down on her arm and she cried out.

"I know." Brady gathered her back into his arms, then sat in her spot, cradling her in his lap, pulling her in so tight she couldn't breathe. "You're my hero," he murmured against her temple.

"I want to go home now."

"You're going to the hospital, sweetheart," Dell said, getting into the driver's seat.

"No," she murmured. She hated hospitals. They reminded her of losing her grandma, but as she looked down, she saw that she was bleeding right through Brady's shirt, and her world spun.

"It's okay," Brady said, holding her close. "I've got you now."

That was a good thing, because that last little pinpoint of light faded, and Lilah fell into the darkness.

# Nineteen

Brady entered Lilah's bedroom balancing a tray. Nurse Nightingale, that was him. He set the tea and toast on her nightstand and eyed the white bandage on her arm, covering the spot where the bullet had penetrated her biceps.

"Lucky lady," the doctor had said, and the words rang in Brady's ears now as he sat at her side.

She was white, pasty, and out cold.

The eighteen stitches, she'd managed. Dealing with the police and their questions as she'd assured everyone that one, she hadn't been trespassing, and two, that Mr. Newberry had not in fact been trying to kill her, she'd handled as well. Sitting in a hospital room waiting to be released, though—that had been torture given how she'd hounded the hospital staff for her release papers.

The doctor had finally released her with a whispered "Good luck" to Brady beneath his breath as he left.

It had taken all three of them, Adam, Dell, and himself, to bring her home. And a silent battle of wills to see who would get to stay to take care of her. But then Adam had been called out on an S&R call.

"I'm not leaving," Dell said.

"Yes," Lilah said groggily from her bed where Brady had set her. "You are."

"Lil—"

"Don't, Dell. I'm too tired to fight with you, but if you want tears, I'll work some up."

Dell grimaced. "But—"

"I'll cry all over you," Lilah promised weakly as Brady pulled off her boots and covered her with a quilt. "Besides, you heard the doctor. I'm going to be fine. I just want to sleep off the drugs he gave me."

"Actually," Dell said, "he didn't say you were fine. He said you were a pain in his—"

"Go," Lilah said.

"You were shot because of me," he said tightly. "I sent you out there."

"I was shot because I didn't realize I looked like a raccoon from fifty yards. I want to be alone, Dell. That's all."

Dell looked pointedly at Brady.

Brady stared back at him evenly. He wasn't going anywhere. Not with the fury still churning within him.

She'd been shot.

She was the best thing to ever happen to him, even though he'd tried like hell to push her away. In fact, he'd very nearly succeeded at that, and she could have died today.

"Oh, for God's sake," Lilah burst out. "If you both don't get the hell out of here "—she looked at Dell—"I'll sic Lorraine on you."

Dell paled. "That's just mean. If he's staying, I'm staying."

"He's not." She held her ground. "Lorraine," she said again, softly, with a steel undertone.

Brady was impressed. Especially when Dell caved like a cheap suitcase, giving in with gracious defeat as he kissed her cheek and made her promise to call him if she needed anything.

He passed Jade coming in at the doorway. Jade had the latest issue of *Cosmo*. "It's what I brought my sisters when they had babies," she said to Lilah. "Wasn't sure what to bring for a gunshot wound. Which, by the way? Pretty damn cool." She eyed Brady. "Do you think if I get myself shot, I can get a bodyguard that looks like him?"

Brady decided to ignore that. "See if you can get her to agree to rest. She's not real good at that."

"No kidding. She thinks she's the Energizer Bunny." Jade looked Lilah over, still speaking to Brady. "You could try bribing her. Your woman has a love affair with crap food. You try that yet?"

"Excuse me," Lilah said. "His woman?"

Jade grinned and dropped the *Cosmo* on the nightstand. "I can see you're well taken care of here. I'll see you tomorrow, Lil."

"I'm my own woman!" Lilah yelled after Jade, who merely laughed and shut the cabin door.

Alone now, Lilah turned her glassy eyes on an admittedly smug Brady.

"You heard me," she said. "Out with the others."

"No."

She arched a brow. Or she tried. But she was doped up pretty damn good. Finally she gave up with a sigh and rubbed her forehead as if it hurt. "I don't want to hear no. I want to hear the sound of the door hitting you on your very fine ass as you follow everyone out."

"Yeah, that was pretty impressive how you managed to kick them out." He sat in the chair in the corner of the room and crossed his arms.

She attempted a glare but she was drooping. "Dammit. My eyes keep closing."

He blew out a breath and leaned in to stroke her hair from her face. "Let them."

"You . . ."

She drifted off before she could finish the sentence, which undoubtedly was for the best. He waited another five full minutes to be sure, then pulled the quilt off her. Without hesitation, he stripped her out of her bloodstained clothes. He went through her dresser for something comfortable for her to sleep in.

One of his T-shirts lay neatly folded on top of her pj's. He stared down at it for a beat, discombobulated by the sight.

She had one of his shirts.

Something happened inside him at that, a warmth spread through his chest. It felt good and hurt all at the same time. "You're killing me," he murmured.

Turning back to the bed, he slipped the shirt—his shirt—over her head, taking care of her arm as he tucked her in.

"Glad you stayed," she murmured. "You're the only one who can ever make me feel better."

He stared down at her pale, beautiful face, unable to think past the surprise of that. Surprise and . . . satisfaction and pride as well, that he'd given her something, after all.

Himself.

He hadn't meant to, God knew he'd tried not to, but he had. He sat on the chair again, and with Twinkles at his feet, settled in to watch her breathe.


Lilah woke up disoriented and groggy. Her clock said four, and given the blackness at the window, it was A.M. and she'd just slept for twelve straight hours. There was a dark figure sitting near her.

"Just me," Brady said.

She let out a breath and swiped a hand over her face. "I was having a weird dream. I was shot—"

"Yes."

She let out a breath. Right. Not a dream.

He rose and offered her a pretty pink pill and two white chalky ones. "Take these and go back to sleep."

"No, I don't need them." Her arm was throbbing, but she hated the way they made her feel.

"You're taking the antibiotic, Lilah."

"Fine." She swallowed it with the water he handed her, then grabbed at him when he started for the door, ridiculously panicked over the thought of him going, when earlier she'd wanted nothing more than to be alone. "Don't." To make sure, she pulled him over her.

"Careful," he murmured, holding his weight off her by the palms he had planted on either side of her hips. "I don't want to hurt you."

She ran her good hand over him, humming in pleasure at the feel of his biceps, taut and straining. Yes, she needed more of that. She tried to pull him closer, but he held back from full contact.

Stubborn man.

She tugged again, wanting a kiss. Needing a kiss.

"Lilah—"

"Please," she whispered, her hand curling around his neck, pulling him in. "Please, Brady."

"Just one." He let their lips meet, lightly.

"Mmm," she murmured, the small brushing closed-mouthed kisses warming her from the inside out. But then it wasn't enough and she opened her mouth and touched her tongue to his lower lip.

A rough groan rumbled up from his chest, as if she were causing him physical pain. She closed her eyes and let herself live in the moment, in the delicious sensations as their tongues touched and explored with increasing pressure and hunger. His scent, his taste, the heat, everything, she loved it all, and it swirled around her like a spell, draping over her like a magical coat, suspending any ability to think.

Okay, that might have been the last of the drugs leaving her system.

But he was the best drug of all. "You take away my pain," she whispered. He also took away her ability to think straight. And she wasn't the only one affected, either. From deep in his throat came another low, masculine sound and she slid her hand down his shoulders to his chest, feeling his heart beating solidly beneath her palm. Below that, where their lower bodies were pressed together, he was hard. "You're better than pain meds, Brady."

He shifted and rested his forehead against hers, sliding his hands into her hair, his fingertips shockingly gentle against her scalp. "You're not all the way here with me."

How to tell him she was more with him than she'd ever been with anyone in her entire life? "I am. Trust me, the meds have worn off. Please, Brady, I need—"

"Rest."

"I can rest when I'm dead."

He let out a long breath, clearly fighting with his old-fashioned male moral ground. "Go back to sleep for a while." His mouth was at her ear, his breath hot against her skin.

"Can't."

Leaning over her, he rubbed his jaw to hers. "Close your eyes."

When she did, he ran his hand over her body, a light touch, caressing, teasing. She rocked up for more, but he held her down. "Just relax," he murmured, his mouth leaving hot kisses along her throat.

Her nipples were hard and pressed against the soft fabric of the shirt—his shirt, she realized. He must have removed her bloody clothes. His eyes went heavy-lidded and hot at the sight of her nipples. Then he slid his fingers beneath the cotton and desire shot through her, centering between her legs.

"Is this what you need?" he asked, strumming her like an instrument. "This?"

"Yes," she gasped, rocking into him.

His other hand went to her hips and held her still. "Don't move, you'll hurt yourself." With another long, deep kiss, he lifted the shirt up and over her head, taking great care with her arm. Then he bent to her breasts, the tip of his tongue stroking her nipple as his other hand slid between her legs.

She gasped again, writhing beneath him.

"Stay still," he reminded her sternly as his fingers worked their magic. "God, you feel like silk." He stroked her and she moaned. "Wet silk." And then he slid lower on the bed and gently pulled the material aside, out of his way. Holding her legs open with his broad shoulders, he put his mouth on her.

At the first touch of his tongue, she started to shoot straight up, but his hands caught her before she could. "No moving," he reminded her, gently holding her effortlessly immobile as he not so gently took her straight out of her mind with pleasure.

Afterward, he held her while she attempted to get herself under control. Or as under control as she could get for someone who'd been shot, drugged, and had just had the mother of all orgasms. He was sprawled on his back. She lay curled at his side, one leg and her bandaged arm over the top of him. She had no idea why having his arms tight on her calmed her more than anything she'd ever known. Maybe because she'd never let herself be vulnerable before, with anyone else.

Ever.

Even thinking it had peace settling in her heart, and she knew that she was right where she belonged. She tilted her head up to study him. His eyes were closed but she knew he wasn't sleeping. "Brady?"

"Yeah?"

She sighed dreamily. *I love you*, she thought.

He ran a hand over her, scooping her hair from her face. "Now you'll be able to sleep."

Yes. Yes she would . . . But she forced her eyes open one last time to make sure he was still there.

His arms tightened on her and he nuzzled his face in her hair. He breathed her in, his arms tightening on her. "You'd make a shitty soldier. I'll take care of you."

She knew that all his life, people had needed him in one form or another, and he'd taken care of them. He'd always come through.

But who took care of him? She wanted to be the one. "Stay," she said, knowing that if he'd only let her, she'd give him as much comfort as he always gave her.

"Yes."

"Promise?"

She held her breath when he cracked open an eye and leveled it on her. He wasn't big on promises, she knew this. But if he gave his word, it was as good as gold.

"Promise," he said, and brushed a kiss against her jaw. "Now close your damn eyes and zip it."

She closed her eyes and fell asleep smiling.


The next time she woke up, her arm felt like fire, her mouth was drier than the Sahara Desert, and . . .

And she was in Brady's T-shirt and nothing else. The sun was peeking through the blinds, casting shadows on the sheets. The other side of her bed was empty and she rolled over and took a deep breath, inhaling the scent of Brady.

He'd slept with her.

A smile broke on her face, but then it all came back to her. Being shot. Getting stitches while pretending she didn't have a needle phobia. And then . . .

Nothing.

Wait—Brady, Dell, and Adam had taken her home, then argued over who was going to stay. She remembered Adam leaving, and then Dell, and Brady covering her with a blanket. She remembered his delicious method of helping her sleep . . . That had ended well for her, very well.

She looked at the clock. It was nine. In the morning!

She'd never slept past six thirty before, never, and suddenly her grogginess was gone, replaced by panic.

Cruz was on vacation, and she had the animals!

Struggling out of the covers, she staggered across the room, tripped over a startled Boss and jammed her legs into sweats. The best she could with one arm. She looked down at herself. More disconcerting than her commando status was the fact that she couldn't rein in her hair.

Glancing fondly at the painkillers sitting by her bed, she bypassed them for Motrin instead. She wouldn't be able to run the kennel if she was high as a kite, so she was going to have to suck it up, bad hair and all. Jamming her feet into boots, she bent over to tie them, got dizzy, and nearly fell on her head. Note to self: no bending. Which meant no lacing her boots.

She was going with the thug look today.

Moving as fast as she could without tripping over her own laces, she hit the bathroom and brushed her teeth—about all she could manage. She ran out the door and into the kennels, and skidded to a shocked halt.

Brady was behind the front counter. He had a cat on his lap and another at his elbow. Abigail stood guard at his feet next to Twinkles. In front of him was a short line of people and pets, waiting patiently to check in.

Actually, not quite patiently. Mrs. Lyons was in Brady's face, waggling a finger at him. "You'd best be good to my babies," she was saying. "I hear what they call you, you know. Dr. Death. Honestly, I don't know what Lilah was thinking, letting you work here."

Brady shoved his hand through his hair. "Your animals will be fine."

"My babies."

Brady looked at her, and with an utterly straight face, nodded. "Yes, ma'am."

Lilah covered her mouth and bit back her laugh as her heart slid to the floor at his feet. She couldn't help it. Watching him so completely out of his element and yet trying his best to run her world for her when he had no idea what he was doing, was it for her.

Even as she thought it, he looked up and frowned. "What are you doing out of bed?"

"No rest for the weary. Thanks for opening for me. I can take it from here."

He put his hand over hers when she tried to scoot behind the counter. "I'm also closing, Lilah."

"I'm fine."

"Yeah, maybe, but you're still going back to bed."

Everyone in the place was swiveling their heads back and forth between them like they were at a tennis match.

"Brady," she said, the voice of reason even as her legs were wobbling wildly with the need to sit down. "There's too much work to do. There's the billing, cleaning cages, feeding—"

"I'll figure it all out."

"I can't ask that of you."

"Then don't ask."

"I—"

"Stop." Dislodging the cats, he came around the counter and scooped her up into his arms.

She felt the silly little flutter deep in her belly. She had no idea what it said about her that she was enjoying his bossy, know-it-all attitude.

"You're done here," he said and turned to the room. "I'll be right back. No one move."

No one did, but the entire room gave a collective sigh, including Lilah.

One minute later, Brady set her on her bed and stood there, hands on hips, a stern look on his face. "Stay."

"Brady," she said very gently. Stupid, stupid man. "You can't tell me what to do."

"The doctor said you were to be kept quiet and still for a few days, even if I had to handcuff you to the bed myself."

Well, if that didn't cause a hot flash. "The doctor isn't trying to run his own business with his partner on vacation now, is he?"

Brady gave her a long look, then let out a breath. "Okay, I give. What'll it cost me for you to promise to stay here today, right here, all day?"

"Dinner," she said without pause.

"And?"

"Dessert."

"Goes without saying," he said, the very corners of his mouth twisting into a smile. "And?"

"And the handcuffs you just threatened me with."

The rest of his temper faded from his face, leaving something much, much better, something that nearly gave her a mini-orgasm.

"You're only teasing me," he said, eyes dark. "But I'm going to remember you said that."

Gulp.

# Twenty

After being confined to the cabin, Lilah tried to keep busy while imagining the hell that Brady was going through. By the time that Adam came by to see her, she nearly pounced on him. "Oh, thank God. Would you please go help Brady at the kennels?"

Adam laughed. "Just came from there." He plopped next to her on the bed and grabbed the TV remote, flipping through the channels with male single-minded purpose. "Trust me, Dr. Death is doing better than Dell."

"What does that mean?"

"Your kennels are full up, since Brady's in the paper again—"

"Again? Why again?"

"Yeah front page this time, for being the big hero yesterday. There's some talk of featuring him weekly."

She choked out a laugh.

Adam grinned. "And Dell's all butt-hurt because he didn't make the cut. Anyway, now Brady's got chicks from three counties over dropping off their pets. You're making

a mint." He tossed the remote aside. "Daytime TV is shit.
You need pay-per-view."

An hour later, Jade and Dell brought Chinese for lunch.
They were scowling at each other when they walked in.

"What's wrong?" Lilah asked.

"Nothing," Jade said in the tone that of course meant the
exact opposite.

"I said I was sorry," Dell said to Jade, tossing up his
hands. "Christ, it was just a little harmless flirting. Women
generally like it."

Lilah divided a look between them. "Who was flirting?"

Jade jerked her chin in Dell's direction. "Stud man here."

"With whom now?" Lilah asked.

Jade snorted. "Exactly."

Dell looked confused. "You. I was flirting with you."

Lilah felt her brows raise at this.

Jade shook her head. "Me," she repeated, irritated.

Which clearly didn't help Dell's confusion any. "I said
it was harmless!" he said, the picture of male exasperation.

"That," Jade said, poking him hard in the chest, "is the
problem." She glared at him as she sat on the bed.

Lilah decided maybe they needed a moment alone and
tried to get up, but Dell sat next to her and threw a leg over
hers so she couldn't move, then carried on like she wasn't
even there.

"You don't like when a man flirts with you?" he asked
Jade over Lilah's head.

"It's the harmless part that chaps my ass." Jade grabbed
the food, shoved a container and chopsticks at Lilah, and
grabbed the next container for herself, closing her eyes as
she chewed.

Lilah glanced at Dell and was startled to see . . . hurt and
longing? But when she blinked, it was gone. "Dell—"

He grabbed the third container. "We checked on Brady."

Lilah recognized the subject change as a diversionary

tactic and was just enough off her axis to let it go for now. "And? How bad is it?"

"He's running the place like boot camp. Even Lulu is behaving, though it's probably out of fear that she'll have to run laps if she doesn't." He laughed at the look on her face. "He's doing fine, Lil, stop worrying. In fact, he was telling Lorraine where to stick it," he said. He smiled. "Best moment of my day."

Shit. Lilah tried to get up, but Dell's leg was still over her. "Relax. He's got it all under control." He had the fried rice, and Lilah knew from experience if she didn't demand her share pronto, he'd eat it all in less than two minutes. "Gimme," she said.

After she'd filled her belly, she felt better and tried to get up but Dell shook his head.

"I'm getting up, Dell."

"No you're not."

"Yes I am."

"Christ, what is it with all the stubborn women today?" He spared a glance at Jade, who merely narrowed her eyes at him.

"I feel just fine," Lilah said.

"No go." Dell held firm. "If I let you up, you're going to go check on him."

"Yes."

"You're still on bed rest."

"Since when did you talk to my doctor?"

"Not your doctor, your keeper."

"Yes, well if you want to keep your pretty face, get off me."

Jade snorted and kept eating.

"Sheesh," Dell said, moving. "You're grumpy when you get shot. And I don't know what your problem is," he said to Jade.

"I'd tell you to think about it," Jade said. "But that might be a stretch for you—" She broke off, staring at him. "Are you kidding me? What, are you twelve?"

"What?" Dell said, looking around. "I didn't do a fucking thing."

Jade pointed to his Levi's, which were low slung and had sunk far enough on his hips that when he'd sat, they'd revealed the waistband of his boxers, which were pink and covered in little red lips. He looked down at himself and shrugged. "They were a gift."

"Pig," Jade said.

Later, when Lilah was alone again, she fought with discomfort and discontentment and told herself it was from being cooped up.

It wasn't from wanting things she couldn't have.

Except it was.

At eight, there was a knock at her front door, but before she could move, she heard a key in the lock.

Only three people had keys. Adam, Dell, and as of this morning, Brady. He had her set of keys, actually, so he could come and go between the kennels and the cabin. She listened as footsteps, sure and steady, came down the hall. "You're lucky I don't sleep with a gun beneath my pillow," she said to the tall, dark, built shadow who appeared in her doorway.

Brady propped up the jamb with a shoulder, and a smile flashed from him in the dark. Imperturbable as usual, the bastard.

"I think we've had enough accidental shootings for this week." He crossed his arms. "But out of curiosity, do you really think you could shoot me?"

She thought she could do a lot of things to him. Smack him for the smugness. Hug him for how hard he'd worked today.

Love him for exactly who and what he was . . .

"No," she answered honestly. "I don't think I could shoot you. But I could throw a gun at your head."

He laughed. "Now that I believe."

"Are you here with the handcuffs?" she asked hopefully.

That tugged another rough laugh out of him. "Thought I'd save that for when you're feeling better."

Heat slashed through her, pooling low in her belly. "You worked hard today."

"No harder than you do every day." There was admiration in his voice for what she did, and then there was a warmth inside her to go with the heat.

"I don't bring in women from three counties over," she said. "That's new."

Pushing off from the doorjamb, he came forward until his thighs bumped the bed. Leaning over her, a hand on either side of her head, he bent close.

It was dark, but she had enough of a glow from the moonlight outside to see his exhaustion, and concern.

For her.

"I'm okay," she told him softly. Reaching up, she cupped his face. "Really."

"Wanted to make sure." He kissed her softly, tenderly, and she kissed him back. The emotion rocked him, she could feel it in the fine tremor of his body. And suddenly it was all ferocious intensity, and she wanted to show him just how okay she was. She wanted to lessen some of the tension she felt in him, wanted to help him let go. Tugging his shirt up with her good hand, she smiled when he took over and yanked the shirt off in one fluid motion.

"Pants, too," she whispered, running her fingers down the center of his chest, past his belly button to the waistband of his cargoes.

Almost before she had the words out, he'd stripped down to skin.

And Lord, what beautiful skin.

With his careful help, she shimmied out of her pj's, then

lifted the covers to make room for him. Pulling him over the top of her, she sighed in pleasure, loving the way she felt when his weight pressed her into the mattress. Arching, she wrapped her legs around him, absorbing the groan that wrenched up from deep in his chest.

"Lilah—"

"In the bedside drawer."

He pulled out a condom and put it on before he came back over her. She rocked again, shifted strategically, and then he was inside her, the sensation taking her breath away.

"Christ, you feel good . . ." He let out a long, shaky breath and kissed her jaw, her throat. "So fucking good."

She tried to rock her hips against him but he wasn't budging. Not until he was ready, and as she already knew, wasting energy on pushing him was useless, his body was like steel. "Brady . . ."

"Shh. Give me a minute. Just feel."

She let her hand roam, she couldn't help it. His body was smooth and muscular. And scarred. Her fingers traced a few of those scars, memories of long-ago battles he never spoke of, and then she pulled his face to hers to nip at his bottom lip.

Growling low in his throat, he finally began to move, setting an agonizingly slow rhythm, his hips barely grinding in a circle as he did, careful not to jar or hurt her.

She heard herself whimper but not in pain. She was dying with each and every single rock of his hips. She dug her fingers into the cheeks of his perfect ass to try to speed him up, she tried words, she even bit his shoulder, nothing rushed him.

The sensations overtook her. The rush of pleasure at the top of every thrust he made had her orgasm building from her toes. Her eyes wanted to close, but she fought the urge, not wanting to tear her gaze from the look on his face. It was beautiful.

He was beautiful.

And then she was flying over the edge, coming hard. As she gasped and cried out, lost in the pleasure, his vivid blue eyes stayed locked on hers, his expression revealing every flicker of pleasure she gave him as he quietly followed her over.

The next few days were crazy for Brady, shuffling between kennel duties and the flying he did for Adam and Dell.

It was the nights, however, that stuck with him: the long, hot, steamy, tear-up-the-sheets nights.

The best nights of his life.

Three days after Lilah had been shot, he ambled over from the kennels, dirty from head to toe. He'd had a record day, including managing to be felt up by the seventy-year-old Mrs. Lyons. At the front door of the cabin he stopped to remove his boots, going still at the wild laughter from inside.

When he walked through, he found Lilah in bed, surrounded by Jade and three other women.

His gaze soaked Lilah up, the low-cut yoga pants and snug T-shirt she wore, the color on her cheeks that said she was feeling much better, the shine in her eyes that assured him she'd finally caught up on sleep and was no longer in constant pain.

Someone had brought pizza, magazines, fingernail polish, lotions, and a bunch of other frilly shit. There was so much estrogen in the room he almost couldn't breathe. He stared at Lilah in the middle of the bed, the center of attention, wearing no bra and a bandage from getting shot—

Christ.

She smiled at him and just about melted his bones away. "Hey."

"Hey right back atcha. Everyone out," she said, not taking her eyes off him.

No one listened. The talking and laughing continued.

Lilah put her fingers to her mouth and whistled, loud and long. "Party's over," she said into the ensuing silence, snagging Brady's hand. "Except you."

"I need a shower," he said inanely.

"Yeah? Well, it just so happens that I have one."

At this, there were hoots and hollers and whistles. Brady shook his head as the women gathered their things to leave.

"Here." Jade slapped a *Cosmo* up against his chest. "You might want to keep that one. Page fifty-seven, 'Fun with Handcuffs.'"

More laughter.

He turned and met Lilah's eyes. "Telling tales?" he asked.

She lifted a shoulder. "It might have come up in conversation is all."

"Uh-huh." When everyone had left, he stripped and showered until the hot water was gone. He came out of the bathroom for the duffel bag of clean clothes he'd dropped in the bedroom.

Lilah rose to her knees on the bed and gave him the "come here" finger crook.

Raising a brow, he walked forward until his legs bumped the bed.

She wrapped her arms around his neck. "Hi," she said.

He bent his head and kissed her until they were both breathless, and then he set his forehead to hers. "Hi."

She smiled and he got hard. Just like that. "Dinner," he said. "Out. You up for it?"

"Another date?"

"If I say yes," he asked cautiously, "are you going to tell me you don't have anything to wear?"

"Hey, you're the one nearly naked." She ran her hands down his chest, over his abs, and then played with the edge of the towel low on his hips, the one barely covering him.

"And you smell fantastic," she murmured, and took a bite out of his shoulder. "I could eat you up."

He was on board with that.

But she got off the bed. "I'll get dressed. I ordered something new." She stripped off the T-shirt and then the yoga pants as she walked to the closet in nothing but a teeny tiny black pair of bikini panties.

He groaned.

She shot him a smile over her shoulder. "You've seen it all before."

Yes, up front and personal. Three nights in a row, in fact, and he couldn't imagine ever getting tired of it. "Put clothes on," he said in a voice so low and thick he barely recognized it as his own, "or you'll be dinner."

Laughing, Lilah slid a halter-style summer dress over her head and slipped her feet into sandals, then twirled for him.

"Pretty," he said, and tugged her into him so that she fell against his chest. Sliding his hands down he cupped and squeezed her ass.

"Hmmm," she hummed, face against his throat as she rocked her hips to his. "Either you're happy to see me, or"— she rocked again, grinding into him, making him groan— "you're packing again."

Giving her a light smack on her ass, he pulled away and dressed, then carried her out the door.

"I was shot in the arm, not the leg," she pointed out. "And I'm all better. I can walk."

He didn't set her down until he placed her in the passenger side of his truck.

"Where are we going?"

"State secret."

She rolled her eyes, but she didn't ask any more questions until he'd parked outside of a steak house in Coeur d'Alene.

"I needed red meat," he said to her silence.

"Yes. It's because you're a caveman."

Smiling, he came around for her, but she shoved him in the chest. "Don't even think about carrying me in there."

"Some women like to be carried."

"I'm not some women."

"True," he said.

She waited until they were seated and had ordered before she asked, "Are we celebrating something?"

"Yes. The fact that I'm not wearing duck shit today and also that for the first time in days I'm done working before bedtime."

Some of her enjoyment of the evening drained. "I know. I know and I'm so sorry. I wanted to come back to work today, but you said you'd withhold sex if I got up."

He set his hand over hers. "I'm not complaining, Lilah. You work your ass off. I know you're still hurting some, and I wanted you to have one more day off."

She studied him over the candle flickering between them. "Thanks."

"For?"

"My life, for starters. I still can't believe you and Dell got to me so fast when I needed you."

His eyes softened and he set down his glass and reached for her hand. "You'd have been fine."

"It could have gone another way." She drew a shaky breath. "I should have been more aware of my surroundings. I need to be more careful."

"More careful would be good."

She scrubbed her hands over her face. "I was just so damn tired, and then I got that call . . ."

"So next time you'll take one of us with you."

"You won't be here next time."

His eyes were steady on hers. "You know what I mean. You'll take someone."

She stared into her wineglass and nodded, trying not to

think about how soon that might be. It'd already been close to a month, which meant it could conceivably be only a matter of days.

"What did you get on your test?" he asked. "Grades posted yet?"

"Got an A." She smiled. "Only two more semesters to go."

"And then what?"

And wasn't that just the scary part. She didn't know.

"You're awfully closemouthed about your hopes and dreams," he noted.

She raised a brow. "Recognize that, do you?"

Clearly not feeling playful, his eyes never wavered. "You must have ideas on what you want."

"Yes."

He waited for more, but suddenly she wasn't feeling like sharing. *Liar*, said a little voice. *You always feel like sharing. You're just afraid to give it all and then lose him. And you are going to lose him. Soon.*

He was looking at her, and when she remained silent, he said, "So you let me into your body but not into your head." He nodded but didn't look happy. "I get that."

"You don't want to be in my head," she reminded him. "And hell, Brady, half the time I don't want to be in my head."

His eyes were stormy. Filled with censure. Feeling like a jerk, she pushed around a piece of steak on her plate. She understood why she was feeling out of sorts. She'd started this whole adventure with him for fun, but then she'd gone and gotten her heart involved. Which didn't explain what his problem was. "Help me out here, Brady. I'm not sure exactly why we're doing this."

"Doing what?"

"Fighting."

"Are we fighting?"

She shrugged. "Feels like it."

"I'm just trying to get to know you better."

"But why? You're not long-term, remember?"

"Hello, pot," he said softly. "Meet kettle."

She stared into his eyes. "Not fair."

"No?" He leaned forward, intent and focused on her. "Then tell me why everyone and everything else in this town is allowed to take up residence in your fold, but you keep me out."

"You didn't want in, remember?"

"Christ." He sat back, his expression suggesting that maybe she was being an unfathomable pain in his ass.

Which was true. She was being a pain. It was called fear. Because she decided right then and there that she was absolutely not going to let herself ruin what very well might be one of the last few nights she had with him. No regrets, she reminded herself. Not ever again.


They left the restaurant in silence.

Normally that was Brady's favorite state of being but not tonight. Tonight he needed more.

And it pissed him off.

He opened the door to the truck and went to help Lilah in, but she gave him a long look and he lifted his hands in surrender, backing up to watch her struggle one-handedly.

"Goddammit," he breathed when she winced in pain from tweaking her still healing arm, and gave her a boost.

When he walked around and angled into the driver's seat, he felt her hand settle on his arm.

"Thank you."

Turning toward her, he stroked a strand of hair from her face. "For letting you hurt yourself trying to get into the truck?"

"For letting me be as stubborn as . . . well, you. Turn left," she said when he would have turned right to take her home.

He turned left and ended up at the convenience store.

"Wait here," she demanded.

He arched a brow.

"Please," she added so sweetly that he shook his head and did what she asked. She vanished inside, only to come back five minutes later with a brown bag and a smile.

"Ian was inside," she said. "He says if you strike out tonight, I'm to call him."

"Good to know," he said, wondering if he was going to indeed strike out. He reached for the bag.

"Nope," she said, holding it out of his way. "Surprise. Go straight."

He went straight.

"Now right again."

He slid her a glance, but in the dark of the night he couldn't see her expression. "Finally decided to take me to some remote area to off me?"

Her soft laugh was a balm to the soul he hadn't realized was aching. "You afraid of me, Brady?"

*More than you know.* "Should I be?"

She was quiet a moment. Then she let out a soft "yes."

# Twenty-One

Lilah took Brady to the lake, his earlier words echoing in her head.

*You're awfully closemouthed about your hopes and dreams.*

*You let me into your body but not into your head.*

*I'm just trying to get to know you better.*

The night was balmy, with a nearly full moon, and aware as she had been all week that her time with him was winding down, she took his hand, wanting to lose herself in him, wanting to feel connected.

They walked to the water's edge, sitting there, absorbing the night. The soft breeze rustling the hundred-foot pines. The distant cry of something looking for its mate. The water lapping near their feet.

He was right, she had held back. Big-time. She'd done so out of self-preservation, but that didn't make it okay. If she was going to have no regrets, she needed to be fearless. Because no way was she going to be the woman who couldn't—or wouldn't—let herself love.

She pulled the bottle of whiskey out of the bag and made him laugh softly. God, she loved making him laugh. He didn't do it often, but when he did it was a beautiful sound.

She went back into the bag for her second item—a deck of cards.

"Strip poker?" he asked hopefully.

She showed him that they weren't regular playing cards but the game Uno. "It's all they had." She shuffled and dealt, then took a swig of the whiskey and offered the bottle to Brady.

Eyes on hers, he tossed back a swallow, then smiled because she was still coughing. "So, you do this a lot," he said.

She laughed and picked up her cards. They played a round and she lost. She set down the cards.

"Strip Uno?" he asked this time, still hopeful.

When she smiled, Brady knew he wasn't going to get to see her strip.

"Something not quite as fun as stripping," she said. "But I hope you'll like it." She hesitated. "I'm going to tell you something about me."

He was surprised by this.

Lit by the glow of the moon playing off the water, she smiled at his expression. "I know, brace yourself. Are you ready?"

"Hit me," he said.

"I grew up out here."

"I already knew that." He eyed her sundress, knowing she wore only a pair of skimpy, mind-blowing panties beneath—which meant that he could have had her naked in two rounds of Strip Uno.

"Yes, but you didn't know that I grew up poor as dirt."

He stopped thinking about Strip Uno and met her gaze. "I guessed."

She nodded. "Of course at the time, I had no idea we were that bad off," she said. "My grandma never let on. She took on odds jobs like cleaning houses and sewing, taking me with her so I wouldn't be alone. She'd pretend we were going on a grand adventure, and I believed her until in second grade, when John Dayley told me I was poor white trash."

Brady's chest tightened, for her grandma, for the little girl she'd been.

Laughing a little, she shook her head. "I didn't even know what white trash meant," she said, not nearly as bothered as he. "When I got home, I asked my grandma and she said it meant that we were special. The next weekend she took me to the circus. One of her cleaning clients had left her the tickets. It was"—she closed her eyes and smiled in fond memory—"amazing. I wanted to be a circus ring leader. I wanted to grow up and have all those animals around me, and I wanted to take care of them." She paused, glancing at him to make sure he wasn't going to laugh.

But that ache in his chest had spread now, and he didn't feel much like laughing.

"It was my first personal goal for myself," she said quietly, hitting him with those mossy green depths that he could jump into and never come up for air.

He smiled past a tight throat. "I like it."

They took another shot of whiskey each and played a second round. He lost, but only because he forgot to say Uno. Lilah looked at him expectantly.

"I'd rather strip," he said.

"Don't tempt me. Talk. Tell me something about you. Something about when you were young."

He found it far easier than he could have imagined, which was no doubt thanks to the whiskey. "I was a punk-ass teenager when I landed at Sol's, and pissed off at the world." God, so pissed off. Even now he could remember the anger burning through him at every turn. "I'd just gone through a few different foster homes, each nicer than the last, and for various reasons, I didn't get to stay at any of them."

And he'd wanted to. Stay. He'd wanted a place where he belonged to someone.

"Why couldn't you stay?" she asked.

He shrugged, able to once again feel that bone-deep help-lessness at not being in charge of his own fate. He'd been through some hairy shit in his life, especially in the army rangers, where too many times to count death had been a certainty, and yet nothing had been worse than that helpless-ness he could still practically taste. "The first couple that took me in ended up getting pregnant, and she got too sick to care for a kid, even a nearly grown one."

"Oh, Brady," she said softly.

"The second family had four daughters of their own al-ready. They'd requested a girl, and when one came along, they traded me in."

"What?" She straightened, eyes blazing. "You weren't a used car!" she said in outrage, making him smile and reach for her hand.

"It's okay," he said.

"No, nothing about that was okay." She took a deep breath, clearly fighting for control. "What about the third family? And if you tell me that they traded you in, too, I'm going to go hunt them down myself."

"They got transferred out of state and didn't want to go through the paperwork to keep me. So I got dumped on Sol. By then my biggest goal was to get the hell out. I was done."

"Well, no wonder!"

Because she was a little drunk and a whole lot adorable in her righteous anger for him, he pulled her close to his side and nuzzled his face into her hair. "At that point, I had no particular destination in mind. I just wanted to be free, to go."

"So what happened?"

"Sol happened. He wasn't much on patience, but he knew enough about how a teenage boy's head worked. He put me on a horse and pointed me in the direction of more than seventy-five thousand acres of wild land to explore."

"Goal accomplished?" she asked softly. "You felt free?"

"Goal accomplished."

Again they took a shot, and Brady was glad they were within walking distance of her place.

They played another round.

Lilah lost. "By the time I got to high school," she said, knocking back more whiskey, "I had a good idea of what poor white trash was and I didn't like it. I'd never left Idaho, not once in my entire life. Can you imagine?" She shook her head in amusement at herself.

The moonlight touched over her hair, her face. Brady thought he'd never seen anyone more beautiful.

"All my life," she went on, "all I wanted was to go see the world. I mean I love the people here, love my life, but I wanted to see what was out there. College was my ticket out. I got a full ride at UNLV, and off I went."

She'd been a girl from the wilds of Idaho who'd never seen a big city much less left those wilds. He could only imagine how different Vegas must have seemed to her. "What did you think of the place?"

She laughed a little. "Culture shock. But it was a free ride, at least at first." She shook her head. "And it was a goal accomplished for me as well, and I never took that lightly. Ever."

He nodded. He understood perfectly.

"My grandma was so proud," she said softly, wrapping her arms around her knees, staring out at the water reflectively, remembering. "Everyone was. And I knew I had to do it—I had to succeed. But then my second year happened. My grandma got sick and I was coming back and forth, and my grades dropped. Because of that some of my funding fell through, and I had to take a couple of jobs to make ends meet."

His heart stopped. "Is this the part where you tell me you were forced to dance or strip for tuition? Because if so, I'm going to kick Dell's and Adam's asses and enjoy it."

"No, I didn't become good friends with them until after college." She laughed. "But sweet offer, thanks. I'll shelve that for the next time either of them pisses me off. I worked at night waiting tables at a club. It was fun but hard work, and I took on more hours than I should have. I fell even more behind and needed help. So the TA of my microbiology class offered to tutor me. Tyler—" She broke off, both the words and the eye contact, and dropped her head to her knees. "I fell for him a little bit."

He couldn't quite read her tone now and for the first time felt unsure as to her feelings since her face was hidden. "Is he still in your orbit like everyone else?"

She shook her head, her entire body tense. Clearly, this had not been a lighthearted fun relationship. He slid his hands to her shoulders, which were knotted tight. He worked at them silently, tugging a low moan from her before she straightened. "I fell in love with him. With Tyler. And he . . ."

Her sudden silence had his heart stopping again, because he could read her quite clearly now. He wasn't going to like this story.

"I thought he loved me back," she said very softly. "But . . . it turned out that he had this whole other life he'd hidden from me. He was a dealer on campus. Which sounded so crazy to me when I found out—he wasn't a guy you'd ever think was dealing drugs. He didn't do them himself, he was clean cut and well liked, but . . ." She shook her head. "One day he got wind of a police search at his frat house, and he got stupid."

"How stupid?"

"He panicked and planted all his stuff in my dorm room. He had to save his stash," she said. "Screw me, right?"

Brady drew a long, slow breath. "What happened, Lilah?"

"They couldn't find what they wanted at his place, so they thought they'd check with the girlfriend. The stupid, naïve girlfriend. I was arrested." She drew a shaky breath while Brady worked through the rage churning through him for what had happened to her.

"Everything eventually got cleared up," she said. "But the damage was done. I'd missed so much class time that I couldn't make it up, and even if I could have done so, I couldn't possibly have focused while working at clearing my name."

"Tyler," Brady said past a very tight jaw. "What happened to that asshole?"

"He got off on a technicality, something to do with the way the search had been conducted. He ended up skipping town without so much as a sorry or good-bye."

Since she was facing away from him, he couldn't see her expression. Which meant she couldn't see his, and that was a good thing. He knew she was used to keeping the people in her life close, developing real, deep, lasting relationships that stuck. It was a comfort to her and made her feel like she had a full family at all times. This, he was certain, had completely devastated her on all levels. "Tell me you taught him a lesson involving your boot and his nuts before he left."

"I thought about it, but no." She paused. "I tried to shake it off, tried to go on and not think about it, but . . . well, I guess I got a little depressed."

He pulled her into his lap and hugged her. "I'm sorry."

"In the end, what happened with Tyler didn't matter. I was too busy dealing with my grandma. I came back here to take care of her."

Which is how she'd ended up not finishing school at all,

he realized. "Was there no one else?" he asked. "No one to help you?"

"No one really knew how bad it was. And it didn't matter because shortly after that, I was too busy to worry about it because the doctors wanted me to put my grandma in a nursing home. I . . . couldn't. I just couldn't do it to her. She was so independent all her life, so feisty and strong . . . I just couldn't." She paused, pressing her face into his throat. He tightened his grip on her and she burrowed in like she'd been made for him.

"When she died," she said very softly, "I should have gone back to Vegas, but I couldn't even think about it. The joy of it was gone for me. I didn't want to leave Sunshine anymore. I felt like a failure."

Given how hard she worked at getting her degree at night, and how equally hard she'd hid it from everyone, she still did. "You have nothing to be ashamed of, Lilah."

"Are you kidding? I fell for the oldest trick in the book— the TA seduction. And the arrest and all that—I was so stupid."

"Not stupid," he said quietly, with rage seething through him for what had happened to her.

"Naïve then," she said. "I wasn't ready for the hurt. It surprised me and turned me off on the whole relationship thing."

"What about Nick and Cruz and Ian?"

She shrugged. "Nick's a good guy, but he's got weird feet."

Brady arched a brow. "Weird feet?"

"And he's allergic to dogs and cats."

He nodded. "And Cruz?"

"Hates junk food."

"And Ian?"

"I never got to see his feet."

Brady fought the urge to remove his boots and ask her if

he had weird feet. "So you've been using excuses on why not to have a relationship. Got it. But why me?"

"Well, for starters, you're not allergic to animals." She smiled and kissed him. "That's a point for you."

"And I like junk food." Another point.

"Yeah, that was a biggie." Her smile faded as she got serious. "But mostly it's because you were a complete stranger, someone new, someone who didn't know me, someone who maybe in the end wouldn't hurt me because I'd keep it light." She smiled again but minus her usual wattage. "I was wrong about that, by the way."

She was so strong and fierce and loyal and sweet and even though she'd made it perfectly clear all along that she didn't want to keep him, that he was held in her heart but not owned, he'd let her inside him. So who was the stupid one here? Him.

Because even if she changed her mind about wanting a future, there was no future to be had. He was leaving. In a few days, as a matter of fact. Trying not to let the pain of that show, he tucked a strand of hair behind her ear and traced his finger down her soft cheek. "Lilah—"

"I don't know if you know the rules of Uno," she said, extricating herself from his lap and standing up. "But if you lose twice, there's a penalty." She looked down at him, eyes shiny but smiling.

She was trying to lighten the mood, and he was game. "What kind of penalty?"

She tugged on the halter tie of her dress and it slipped over her breasts, then her hips, and dropped to the ground, pooling at her feet, leaving her in nothing but those very tiny black panties.

"God bless the penalty," he whispered reverently.

She hooked her thumbs in the strings at her hips and let those fall as well.

Brady tried to say something but found he couldn't speak

because his tongue had stuck to the roof of his mouth. He couldn't breathe either. "You are so beautiful, Lilah."

She smiled, and he felt a helpless one curve his mouth as well. "Come here," he said.

Shaking her head, she turned away, giving him a heart-stopping view from the back as she took a few running steps and then a very neat dive into the water, vanishing beneath the surface.

# Twenty-Two

When Lilah surfaced and shoved her sopping wet hair out of her face, she found Brady right where she'd left him, sitting on the edge of the water.

Watching her.

If she had to guess, she'd say that his expression was an intriguing mix of dark desires and warm affection. If her nipples hadn't already been hard from the shock of the cold water, they'd have tightened simply from looking at him.

When he remained still, nothing but that unfathomable stare that was alternately turning her on and making her want to stick out her tongue at him, she dunked.

When she surfaced again, farther out this time, barely able to touch her feet down, he'd gotten to his feet.

Eyes narrowed.

"What are you doing?" he asked.

He hadn't raised his voice. He knew the water carried sound with ease, as if he were standing right in front of her instead of thirty feet away. "Skinny-dipping."

"By yourself?"

"Well," she said, "I'd hoped to have company."

"Your arm—"

"Doesn't hurt." *Much.*

"You're under the influence," he said.

She smiled. "Are you worried you'd be taking advantage of me?"

"Hell, no. I'm worried you'll take advantage of me."

She laughed and he smiled, and the knot that had been tight in her chest since she'd opened up to him far more than she'd ever intended to finally loosened.

He bent and untied his boots, then kicked them off, and her pulse kicked into gear. She'd wanted this, had hoped to goad him into it, but now that the moment was here, her belly quivered and heat bounced through all her good parts like a Ping-Pong ball.

When he straightened, he pulled his shirt off and tossed it aside. "How cold is it?"

"Like bathwater."

"Liar."

She smiled. "Didn't want to scare you."

"I don't scare easily."

"Uh-huh, and now who's the liar?"

His eyes never left hers as he unbuttoned, unzipped, and shoved down his cargoes.

Her tongue was still hanging out of her mouth when he dove in. Choking back her laugh, she whirled and started swimming, hampered by her bad arm. She'd been raised out here and had swum almost as soon as she could walk, but her arm slowed her more than she'd planned on.

And sure enough, in less than five seconds Brady came up alongside of her, tempering his pace to match hers.

She flipped to her back and used her legs. And still he remained with her. She kept it up for a few more minutes, swimming as hard as she could, enjoying the exertion. After a quarter of a mile or so, she turned and headed back.

Brady beat her by a length.

Treading water about fifteen feet from where their clothes lay, she shoved her hair out of her face and breathed heavily, watching him.

He shook his head, sending water flying. His eyes were dark and hot. God, so hot. His breathing was labored, too, but not nearly as much as hers. "Cocky," she complained.

"No, I've swum in waters much colder than this, and for much farther."

"Hmm. So you're a better swimmer than me."

His smile was slow and sure as he dragged her in close against him, taking away her need to tread water as he did it for the both of them. "Maybe we could find an area where your talents exceed mine," he said, all low and sexy.

"Hmm."

"Lilah."

His voice never failed to give her a secret little rush. She found that there were things that she desperately longed to hear from him, things she'd told herself she didn't need, but she'd lied to herself.

She needed.

So damn much.

So she pushed even closer, craving the contact, craving the connection, because when they were together like this, his body said things to her that his voice never would. She ran her hands up his chest and let her legs drift around his waist. The contrast of the cold water lapping at her with the warmth of his hard body made her shiver.

"Are you cold?" he murmured.

"No." She slid her hands into his hair and stroked his scalp with her fingernails. A sound of sheer male pleasure, nearly a purr really, escaped him, and his hands went to her ass, a cheek in each palm. He was hard against her belly. Moving them toward the shallower water, he dropped to his knees with her so that she was straddling his lap, the water at their chests. Her legs were spread by his thighs, his hands tightening on her as he stared into her face. "Every time I look at your mouth," he said huskily, "I want it on me."

With a soft smile, she pulled his head to hers and kissed him, long and deep, feeling him pulse against her. Mmm. Reaching down, she stroked him, making both his breath hitch and her inner muscles contract. "In me," she whispered against his mouth.

His face was etched in pure desire, but he shook his head. "No condom."

"Just for a minute." It was reckless, and she didn't care. Dammit, for once, she wanted to do something wild, something without thinking about the consequences. So she wrapped her fingers around him and guided him home, burying him inside her in one long fluid motion.

He choked out her name in a rough groan and then again when she lifted up until he almost came out of her. Slowly she sank back on him, the angle of their bodies pushing him even deeper. Still gripping her ass tight with one hand, his other came around and lightly stroked her where they were joined.

And then again. And again. Until she felt like she was going to burst. "Brady," she gasped. "Stop— I'm going to . . ."

"Do it," he commanded softly. "Let go for me, Lilah."

The timbre of his sexy voice alone nearly sent her over the edge. Combined with his caressing thumb as he thrust upside her with every other heartbeat was all it took, and she burst, collapsing into him.

He held her tight through the trembling. He was still rock hard inside her, and she arched her hips, eliciting another rough groan from him. "Don't." Tightening his hands on her, he pressed his forehead to hers. "Don't move. Not even an inch."

His voice was rough and strained, even lower than

normal, and she wrapped her arms around his neck and pressed her mouth to his. He took control of the kiss, his fingers digging into her hips to hold her still, the muscles in his arms quaking with the effort not to move, not to take his own pleasure. She kissed his shoulder, his throat, his mouth. They were drenched from the water, but there was a heat coming from him, as if he had a fever.

Slowly he pulled out of her, closing his eyes when she made a helpless little sound of loss. Gently she kissed his jaw, then gave him a not so gentle shove toward shore. And then another. Eyes locked on hers, he let her, and when she had him in the very shallow water, he also let her kick his feet out from beneath him.

Laughing, he went down to the sand, bracing himself on his elbows, the water lapping at his thighs. She crawled between them and lapped at him, too.

With a low groan, his head fell back as she worked her way up until she came to his most impressive erection. Kissing the very tip, she absorbed the way he breathed her name. "Trust me," she whispered again.

"Already there."

When she drew him into her mouth, his fingers slid into her hair, guiding her into the rhythm he wanted, until with a deep breath, he lifted his head. "Lilah—"

"Shh."

He made a sound of frustration and closed his eyes when she resumed, his hips rocking up to meet her every move on him now. He said something completely unintelligible, gasping, his hands curling into fists in her hair. His eyes were shut tight, his teeth gritted. "Lilah—Christ! I'm going to—"

"Do it," she commanded, mirroring his words back at him. "Let go for me, Brady."

He shuddered and came hard. While he struggled to regain his breath, she kissed his thigh, his hip, the spot low on his ridged abs where his skin was so satiny smooth.

He was still laying there, eyes closed, still as a rock, as if he couldn't possibly move a muscle. She lifted her head. "You okay?"

The sound he made might have been affirmation or maybe evidence that his brain had been thoroughly scrambled. Feeling quite pleased, she sat cross-legged by his hip and waited for him to collect himself.

The water lapped at them gently. From a distance came the hoot of an owl and the song of crickets. Finally Brady turned his head and met her gaze.

She grinned.

A soft smile curved his lips as he took in her naked form by moonlight. "So who's cocky?"

She laughed, and his smile deepened as he pulled her close, pillowing her head on his shoulder. Pulling her in closer, he brushed a dazed kiss to her temple. "You undo me, Lilah. Every time."

"Do you like that?"

"You nearly rendered me unconscious with pleasure. I fucking loved it."

"Can you move yet?" she asked.

"That would be a firm negative."

Nodding, she rose and gathered all their clothes. And then started walking back to the cabin.

"Hey."

When she didn't stop, she heard him swear, heard the sounds of him staggering to his feet. "You took my clothes."

She kept going.

"We left my truck—"

"It'll keep."

"Lilah, Jesus. We can't walk through the woods naked."

"You trained for all conditions, soldier," she called back. "Keep up."

He didn't respond to that, but she could hear him right behind her, silent as they walked buck-ass naked beneath the moon.

"That was crazy," he said a moment later as they walked into her cabin. "Anyone could have seen."

"But no one did." Turning to him, she dropped their clothes onto her couch and smiled. "You swam in the magical waters, Brady. At midnight. You know what that means?"

He was very busy running his gaze over her body like a caress.

"The myth says that now you're in danger of finding your true love," she reminded him.

He snagged her by the hips and rubbed his naked body to hers. "I don't buy into myths. I buy into realism. I make my own fate."

"Yeah? And what does your fate say?"

"It says I'm about to make love to an amazing woman, right here . . ." He dragged her down the hall, grabbing a condom out of her bathroom drawer as they went. Then he wrestled her onto her bed and covered her body with his. "Right now."

When he put his mouth to her breast, she cried out in sheer pleasure. She'd barely recovered from that before he was inside her, whispering in her ear to give him everything she had, every little piece, that he wanted no less.

She had no choice but to give it to him, give him everything, her only solace was in knowing that he was doing the same.

## Twenty-Three

B rady woke the next morning alone in Lilah's bed with Boss on his chest and Twinkles on his feet, both of them staring at him balefully. He scrubbed a hand over his face and let out a breath. Alone again.

"Arf," Twinkles said.

"Mew," Boss said, and turned in a circle on Brady's chest, using claws.

"Jesus!" Brady pushed the kitten off of him. Bare-ass naked, with all the blankets and sheets tossed to the floor, man and kitten stared at each other. The kitten's eyes narrowed in on Brady's morning wood and crouched, butt wriggling, ready to pounce.

"Do it and die," Brady said, and rolled out of the bed. "Just once," he muttered on the way to the shower, followed by both animals like they were all in a parade. "I'd like to be the first one up."

He'd always been the first one awake in the past. Hell, he'd never spent much time sleeping with a woman period. But Lilah seemed to throw his entire universe into a tailspin.

Setting the shower tap to scalding, he climbed in and put his hands on the tile. Head down, he let the water bead down over his shoulders and back.

The icy spray hit him without warning at the three-minute mark, and he swore the air blue. Christ, Lilah shouldn't have to live like this. He was taking a look at the hot water heater himself before he left town. He dressed and headed down the hall, tripping over Boss, who yowled his feelings on the matter and vanished under the couch. Brady sighed and dropped to his knees, bending low to peer into two pissed-off glowing eyes. "Well, you can't run in front of me, dammit."

"Arf."

"Stop it," Brady told the dog, who was trying to lick his face. "You're not helping. Boss, out now."

Nothing but daggers coming his way.

"Nice view."

Brady straightened and met the amused eyes of Lilah as she came in the front door. She was carrying two coffees and a donut bag, and right then and there, he fell in love. "If you tell me you have a chocolate-frosted," he said with great feeling, "I'll give you my life's savings and anything else you want."

"What if I brought something healthy, like a wheat-grain muffin."

"Then forget the life savings."

She laughed. "What if all I want is a repeat of last night?"

He grinned. "Then I'd say you're easy."

"When it comes to you, anyway." She set the bag and coffees on the counter. "Enjoy."

"Wait a minute," he said as she started out the door again. "Where are you going?"

"It's this little thing called work."

"You can't just show up and go."

"Sure I can. Watch me." She pulled open the door, then looked back. "But thanks for last night."

"Oh no you don't." He snagged Boss by the scruff of the neck and dragged him from beneath the couch, cradling the pissed-off kitten to his chest. Then he grabbed Lilah, too. "Thanks for last night?" he repeated, suddenly feeling a little pissed off and not sure why. "What exactly is it you're thanking me for, Lilah?"

She opened her mouth, but his cell phone rang. Ignoring it, he kept hold of her and reeled her in closer. And because he was also pretty fucking pathetic, he pressed his face into the curve of her neck and breathed her in. "You smell so damn good you're making me hungry." He licked her throat and felt her shiver.

"New lotion," she said. "Mango peach. Aren't you going to answer that?" she asked of his phone.

"No."

"It might be important."

At the moment he couldn't think of anything more important than making her respond to his question, but the moment had passed and she was looking at him as if he'd lost his marbles.

And it was entirely possible that he had. Swearing, he let go of her, yanked his cell phone out of his pocket and glanced at the screen. "It's work."

"Dell or Adam need a pilot?"

"No. Tony."

"Oh," she exhaled, taking a step back. "He's calling because—"

"Because it's been a month, which is what I said I needed. He's been calling me every day for a week telling me to get my ass back to work."

"You're leaving."

"I should have already left, Lilah."

She swallowed. "When?"

"Like I said, he wanted me yesterday."

"When, Brady?"

"Today or tomorrow maybe. Depends on what he says."

She nodded. "I see."

Yeah, except she couldn't. She couldn't possibly see, not when he couldn't. And he honestly couldn't see how the hell he was supposed to go. He answered his phone with a terse "Miller" and watched as Lilah grabbed one of the coffees and walked out of the cabin.

Lilah entered the kennels, made her way through the rooms to her office and stopped before sitting at her desk.

No.

Not where she wanted to be. She swiveled and walked out the door again and alongside the back of the building, where no one could see her. Slowly she slid down the wall, giving in to her weak knees.

Brady was leaving.

She could still see him coming out of her bedroom wearing only a pair of jeans that molded his sculpted legs to perfection and cradled her favorite part of his anatomy, a part that had never failed to deliver on its promise. His feet had been bare, his chest, too, and just looking at him laid her heart bare as well. He'd looked as if he'd belonged there in her place. Just as he'd made himself at home in her heart.

And he was leaving.

His month was up and now work was calling him. She'd known he'd already turned a few jobs down over the past few weeks, but she'd also known that he wouldn't do that forever.

Maybe he was even packing at this very moment.

She heard a car drive up and, realizing she had tears on her face, rose. Dammit. Swiping at them, she headed back inside, where she got busy fast with the usual drop-offs, feedings, walking, and general care of the animals, not to mention the dreaded paperwork.

At lunchtime Cruz showed up, tanned and rested from a week on Maui with friends. They caught up with each other, and Lilah showed off her new scar from being shot. Cruz was suitably horrified and impressed.

Later, when she was off shift, Lilah made her way to Belle Haven for a late lunch with Jade, walking in the back door before remembering that Jade had taken today off to visit an old friend. Redirecting, she turned around to leave and passed Dell's office.

He was behind his desk on the phone, looking his usual easygoing self, even though his other phone was ringing off the hook and the sounds from the waiting room and patient rooms related more to a mob scene than a veterinarian's office.

That's when she remembered that Adam was gone, too. He'd left last night for a trip back east to an S&R conference. "Need help?" she asked.

Dell nodded in relief and pointed to the waiting room.

She walked into chaos. There were dogs and cats, several birds, and a lamb. None were particularly calm, and neither were the humans that went with the pets.

Brady stood behind the reception desk, scowling darkly at the computer as if he were considering tossing it out the window. Which was undoubtedly why everyone waiting was giving the front desk—and him—a wide berth.

It didn't surprise Lilah that he'd obviously stepped in to help. Or that he'd worked as hard as he had from the moment he'd arrived in Sunshine doing whatever was needed or asked of him. Because for as big and tough as he was, he'd pretty much dedicated his entire life to others' safety and/or well-being.

What did surprise her was how well he fit in. With the town, with Adam and Dell. With her. For all that he wanted to be the lone wolf, he'd made sure to have their backs, all of them. He had a real bond here, one that she knew startled him.

And made him uncomfortable.

Well, it startled her, too. But it didn't make her uncomfortable. It made her feel good, feel connected. It made her feel happy.

That would change, very soon, when he left. And yes, she'd known this day would come, but she wasn't ready. And worse, she didn't think she ever would be.

How scary was that? The room was so noisy she had to come up very close to him to be heard. "Problem?" she asked in his ear.

He barely looked at her. "What makes you think that? The fact that my head is spinning around and around, or that there's twelve people in the waiting room here for the same appointment block and only one doctor?"

"Ah. A scheduling snafu."

"That, or someone's messing with me." He gave her a second, longer look, eyes narrowed and dark. Very dark. "It's not you, is it?"

With a low laugh, she lifted her hands and shook her head.

"Don't even try that look of innocence. I know better."

"Hey. I've never messed with you."

"I have one word for you." He gestured with his chin beneath his desk. "Twinkles."

Lilah bent low and saw Twinkles sprawled out and fast asleep on Brady's boots. "Aw. And clearly, you're both hating the situation."

The phones were still ringing.

People were still glaring at him.

That's when Brady did something Lilah knew he rarely, if ever, did. He sank to a chair, put his hands on her hips, dropped his head to her belly, and said, "Please help me."

"Sure." She'd have even done it without the please, but he didn't need to know that. Because she couldn't help herself, she stroked a hand over his hair. "Move over."

He stood and gave her the chair. She tapped her fingers

on the keyboard and pulled up the schedule. "Well, damn. You're double-, triple-, and quadruple-booked."

He came up behind her, a hand on either side of her, braced on the desk as he looked over her head at the computer screen. "Tell me something I don't know."

If she turned her head, her mouth could brush the inside of either of his biceps. His skin would be warm, and just beneath, the muscles would be taut with strength. She could smell his deodorant and, beneath that, the soap he'd used.

Hers.

Unable to stop herself, she did it, she turned her head in the pretense of trying to see his face and let her mouth brush his biceps.

And maybe the very tip of her tongue.

"Lilah," he said warningly, his voice barely audible, rumbling from his chest through her back.

"It's your turn to smell like a piña colada," she whispered softly.

Bending his head, he put his mouth to her ear. "And does it make you as hungry for me as I always am for you?"

Yes. Yes, as a matter of fact, it did. "It's the soap."

"I love the scent of you," he whispered. "I love the taste of you. And it has nothing to do with the soap."

"The scheduling problem," she said unsteadily as one of his hands dropped down to squeeze her hips.

"Uh-huh." He made sure to brush his lips lightly against that spot just beneath her ear. The one he knew that melted her bones away. "I'll start pulling files," he said. "And taking the animals to an examining room. You man the desk."

"No, we should switch that," she said. "I can do the preliminaries in the exam room and speed things along for Dell."

His eyes never left hers. "Yes, but that would leave me behind this desk."

Which he was clearly hoping to avoid at all costs. "It would," she agreed, and smiled.

He arched a brow. "You'd throw me to the wolves?"

She turned and eyed the waiting room. Mostly women, looking Brady over in various degrees of interest, from hunger to outright lust. "Poor baby. Must be tough, having all these women want you."

"And how about you?" he murmured in her ear, taking a quick nip out of it. "You want me?"

*Always . . .*

If anyone happened to look over at them it would appear as if they were both intently studying the computer screen—which had gone into save energy mode and was running through a slide show of Belle Haven's animal patients.

Brady's pictures, actually, from the past month. They were great shots, but Lilah wasn't absorbing a single one because Brady was whispering a lurid suggestion in her ear, which made her both gasp and weak at the knees.

Forcing herself out of the chair, she avoided Brady's hot, knowing eyes. She grabbed the sign-in sheet and called the first name. "Toby?"

Shelly and Toby stood up.

Lilah turned to Brady, who wasn't saying a word, just watching her. The lion keeping its eyes on the prize. "Pull the file and bring it into me?" she asked.

Looking both hungry and amused, he turned to the files. Her last view of him was of his fine ass when he bent to the bottom drawer.

In the exam room, Shelly fanned herself. "Damn, Dr. Death is hot."

"That's the general consensus," Lilah murmured, resisting the urge to fan herself as well.

"And your consensus?" Shelly asked slyly.

Lilah sighed. "Same as yours," she admitted, and turned to go get Dell but instead came face-to-face with Brady, who stood in the doorway, holding the file, eyes unreadable. She bit her lower lip and flashed him a quick smile.

He didn't return it, but the very corners of his mouth

quirked slightly and his eyes promised retribution. Which worked for her, because she'd learned she really liked his forms of retribution.

It was two very busy hours later before there was any sort of breather. Lilah finally dropped into a chair beside Brady at the front desk. "And I thought my life was crazy."

"Your life is crazy." He got to his feet.

"Where are you going?"

He gestured to the waiting room, which was blessedly empty. "Things are under control again."

"Yes, but I have to get back to the kennels."

"No you don't. Cruz is there." He let out a breath. "I have to go."

"Seriously, you—"

"I mean I have to go, Lilah."

*Oh. Oh, damn.* She'd managed to work her denial up good, almost forgetting this fact. Slowly she rose to her feet, unable to sit while facing this. "You're leaving right now?"

His eyes said it all.

"But how can they expect you to just up and go at a phone call?"

"That's my job, Lilah. Pilot for hire. I go when the call comes."

Legs wobbly, she plopped back into the chair and put a hand to her aching heart. This isn't about you, Lilah. "Tell me."

"I'm needed in Africa by the end of the week. And I have to go to L.A. first."

"Oh."

"I'm sorry."

She let out a purposeful breath and tried to shake her head, but her body felt locked up tight. "Don't be. You were up front and honest with me. You weren't meant for a home base or growing roots. I've always known that." Listen to her, how mature. Even as she thought it, her eyes filled.

"Lilah," he whispered softly. "Don't."

"I'm not." She shook her head and was proud of her smile. She stood and went up on tiptoe to set her hand on his chest, brushing a kiss over his mouth.

His lips were set to grim, but she knew they could soften in a smile when he chose or drive her straight to heaven without passing Go!

What they couldn't do, however, was tell her everything was going to be okay.

Because it wasn't.

She didn't feel like she'd ever be okay again.

# Twenty-Four

Since packing wasn't an issue—Brady had never really unpacked—he went to Smitty's and tuned up the Bell 47 even though it was running perfectly and didn't need to be tuned up. He didn't want whomever Dell and Adam hired to have any problems. He was still sitting in the pilot's seat tinkering with the Bell's instrument panel when he heard footsteps. Something in his chest kicked hard, but as much as he'd hoped otherwise, it wasn't Lilah coming his way.

"We're not replacing you."

He turned to face Dell and Adam, who boarded looking unusually serious. Well, Adam always looked serious, but there wasn't so much as a glimmer of a smile on Dell's usually good-humored, affable face.

Brady shook his head. "You spent a lot of money for me to fix up the Bell. You've had an average of three calls a week where it's beneficial to take it up. Any of the pilots housed out of here or Coeur d'Alene would be happy to hire on and fly for you."

"Sure," Adam said. "And we'll use them as needed. But we're not hiring anyone on full-time."

"You guys want and need a third partner. You're over-worked, you need—"

"You," Dell said.

Brady shoved his fingers through his hair and stared at them, frustrated at all the unexpected things he was feeling at leaving. "This was always going to be temporary." How many times had he said that in the last day?

"It could stay temporary," Dell said, "if that's what your pansy ass needs. A word. A fucking word to make it okay for you to use this place as a home base. Let's call it temporary, then."

"He's going to do what he has to do, Dell," Adam said quietly. "He's—"

Running footsteps sounded, and again Brady's heart kicked. Because this time it was Lilah.

She came rushing up to the opened door of the Bell, her cheeks flushed, out of breath. When she saw Brady, she put her hand to her chest and sagged, out of breath. "I thought—I heard the engine start—I was afraid you'd left."

"Not yet," Adam said and turned to her, brushing a kiss to her jaw, giving her a quick squeeze. With one last long look at Brady, he left.

Dell came forward and hugged Brady, slapping him on the back. "I'll miss you, you chickenshit bastard. Be safe up there." Dell looked at Lilah, and then he was gone, too, leaving the two of them alone.

The silence was heavy. Not awkward, just . . . weighted. Unable to mistake the emotion coming from her for anything other than temper, Brady let out a breath and removed her sunglasses.

She blinked up at him from eyes that were clear and . . . not full of temper, as it turned out.

But sorrow.

And somehow that was worse, far worse. "I have to go," he murmured, hating himself in that moment.

"Yes," she said, crossing her arms. "You have to go."

He hadn't expected her easy agreement and didn't believe it. "It's my job," he said carefully.

"I know that, too."

"I—"

"Shut up, Brady." She uncrossed her arms, grabbed his shirt, and yanked him in. The first brush of her lips was soft, gentle. Tender. As if she'd put her entire heart into it. Then she settled in and the kiss deepened, a hot, intense tangle of tongues that nearly brought him to his knees. Before he could recover, she gentled the connection again, retreating in slow degrees until her lips were nothing more than a barely there butterfly kiss. "Be careful with yourself," she whispered huskily against his lips.

He didn't move, his body still a breath from hers. She . . . wasn't going to devastate him with guilt? For a moment he couldn't quite wrap his head around that. Or the fact that she wasn't going to even ask him to stay.

And suddenly he remembered how he'd reasoned with her when she'd had to give up Toby and then Sadie. He'd told her that if she'd found a loving place for the animals to live where they could be happy, it was okay to let them go. That haunted the hell out of him now, because apparently she'd listened and taken his words to heart.

Only she wasn't a fraction as devastated at letting him go as she had been the animals. "I'm leaving," he said again, just in case she hadn't gotten the right idea.

"I know," she said softly.

He just stared at her, and then shook his head. "Okay, wait a minute. Why is this so easy for you, letting me go?"

"What?"

"You've made a career out of holding on to everything, pets, people . . . You gather them all to your side, in your heart, but when it's me, you give me a smile and a kiss and tell me to be careful?"

She opened her mouth, then closed it. Then stabbed him in the chest with her finger, hard. "Well, what would you have me do, fall at your feet and beg you not to go?"

*Yeah. Actually. A little bit.*

*Maybe.*

Christ, he was one pathetic asshole.

She let out a mirthless laugh. "I care about you. I want you. And neither of those two things change whether you go or not. Do you understand the helplessness of that? And even then, honestly, I wouldn't change any of it if I could." She stabbed at him again. "So don't you tell me I'm just letting you go. I hate that you're going, but I'd rather have the pain of that than not having had you in my life at all." She glared at him from brilliantly shimmering eyes, breath coming hard. "You going will leave a huge gaping hole." She pressed her open hand to her chest. "Here. You're in my heart, and there's no way around that. I consider you mine, Brady. Mine." A single, devastating tear fell and she swiped it angrily away. "But you need your happy place. If it's not here, you have to go to it. And I need to let you." She paused, let out a soft broken breath. "You taught me that."

While he was still absorbing her words, and the utter anguish in which she'd spoken them, she stood up on tiptoe and brushed another soft kiss across his lips. His hands went to her hips to hold her against him and he closed his eyes, burying his face in her hair. "Lilah." His voice was raw and matched his throat and the burning in his chest.

Her arms slid around his neck and for a moment she clung, hard. He felt a tremor go through her and then she whispered against his jaw. "It's okay to go if that's what your heart is telling you." She pulled back and cupped his face, staring into it as if to memorize his every feature. "I'll take Twinkles back when you go," she whispered. And with one last long look, she left.

Shaken to his core, he sank to the pilot seat.

He'd gotten what he wanted.

He was free to go.

Shaking his head, he hopped down out of the helicopter and whistled.

Twinkles leapt to his feet from his spot under a tree in the shade and came running. Together they walked to his truck. Brady patted the passenger's seat and Twinkles hopped up, taking the shotgun position. Brady had been left behind enough in his life to know that it sucked. No way was he doing it to the dog—his dog. He was taking Twinkles.

So why it still felt as though he were leaving his entire life behind, never mind his fucking heart, he had no idea.

This was his choice.

It was always his choice.

Nodding, he drove, refusing to look back in his rearview mirror.

Except he did.

He kept looking into his rearview mirror the entire drive to L.A. It took him all night. At LAX, just before dawn, he parked in long-term parking and started walking with Twinkles toward the terminal where the charters flew from. Tony had booked him a ride from here. "Not sure what our choices are going to be for you," he told the dog. "Or exactly where Tony has booked us a ride to. But there are rules for four-legged creatures, so you'll probably be crate-bound for this next leg of the trip."

Twinkles didn't look concerned, he was just happy to be involved. Brady shook his head and let himself run Lilah's words back through his head.

*I consider you mine, Brady.*

*I need to let you go. You taught me that.*

She'd set free what she loved. She'd done so without knowing that she was his happy. She was his everything.

Christ, he was a total and complete jackass. Leaving her wasn't going to make him happy at all. It was going to make him a very sorry sack of shit with too much pride for his own damn good.

He looked down at Twinkles, who was sniffing everything in his path. "I don't want to do this."

Well, that wasn't quite true. He still wanted his job flying to all corners of the earth. He just wanted something else to go along with it.

A life.

He no longer wanted to work 24/7, never stopping or slowing because he had no reason to.

He had a reason. A five-foot-four, messy-haired, mossy-green-eyed reason named Lilah Young. He stopped walking. "Dell was right," he said to Twinkles, who stopped, too, then sat on Brady's foot. "I am a chickenshit bastard."

"Arf."

He choked out a short laugh that was completely devoid of humor and pulled out his cell phone. "I can't make this job," he said to Tony.

"Where are you?"

"L.A., but I'm cutting out."

"Again? Christ." He gave a big sigh. "And the next job?"

"Maybe, but I'm going offline for a few days."

"You've been offline for a month."

"I need a little bit more time."

"And then?"

"I'll get back to you."

Brady and Twinkles got a hotel room to catch up on some desperately needed sleep, then got up at dusk and once more drove straight through the night. As Sunshine came into view around dawn the next morning, Brady stopped at the 7-Eleven to fortify his nerves for what he was about to do. "Breakfast?" he asked the dog.

"Arf."

"Something with sausage. Got it." He went inside and loaded up with breakfast burritos, bagels, and donuts.

"Looks like you're buying breakfast for a crowd today,"

the young woman said. She was the same woman who'd been manning the cash register his very first day in town, when she'd asked him if men really thought of sex 24/7.

"It's actually more of a bribe than breakfast," he said.

She popped a bubble with her gum and adjusted her purple and black polka-dotted glasses frames. "For Lilah?"

He'd almost forgotten that there were no secrets in this town.

"Honey," she said, leaning on the counter, "I'm going to help you out." She added a package of donuts and two bags of chips to the stack. "Trust me." She patted his hand and gave him his total.

"That can't be right. It's not enough," he said, looking over all the loot in front of him.

"Oh, the donuts and chips are on the house," she said, bagging it all up. "You make our Lilah happy, and that's worth more than the snack food."

He didn't know what to say. He wasn't used to people knowing his business, but the reality was that here in Sunshine, Lilah was everyone's business. "Thank you."

She nodded and handed him his bag. "But you should know, screw up with her and I'll never sell you another piece of crap food. Ever. And let me tell you, from one junk-food addict to another? Ever is a damn long time."

"Understood," he said, not telling her he'd already screwed up. Because he was going to do whatever it took to rectify the situation. As he turned to walk out, she tossed in an extra package of donuts.

"Just in case," she said.

In case of what, he wasn't sure, but he'd take all the help he could get.

# Twenty-Five

Lilah stood in front of her outside kennels, hose in hand. The duck and the lamb she'd been boarding had left a mess. She was literally elbow deep in things that she didn't want to think about. It was a very attractive look for her.

Not.

Adding to the stress level was the fact that today was the first Saturday of the month. She had only a few minutes before she was due to work at Belle Haven's monthly animal adoption clinic.

"My life," she said to no one in particular, "completely sucks."

Because he'd done it.

He'd left.

Brady had taken him and Twinkles and her shattered heart, and without even realizing that he had pieces of her with him, he'd gone.

She hadn't slept, she hadn't eaten, and it was all so ridiculous. She'd known he would go.

But she'd hoped . . .

The tears that she'd managed to hold at bay clogged her throat and, dammit, fogged up her sunglasses.

Stupid sunglasses.

And perfect, now her nose was running.

She tried to shove her sunglasses to the top of her head with her forearm but succeeded only in making them crooked on her face and she sighed deeply.

And maybe a tear slipped.

This was all her own fault. She hadn't told him she loved him. She hadn't told him what it would mean for him to stay. She hadn't let him know.

The thought brought a few more unwanted tears and further fogged her lens. She couldn't see a thing. So when the hose hit a corner of one of the kennels and splashed up, it thoroughly drenched her with icy water and God knew what else.

"Crap!" She dropped the hose and reached out blindly for the towel she'd set on the railing behind her. Except her feet landed in something slippery and down she went.

For a stunned beat she just sat there on the ground, absorbing how bad every inch of her felt.

A truck rumbled up the road and she went still because she knew the sound of that truck. Great, and now her mind was playing tricks on her. It had to be Adam or Dell. Or maybe a customer. She sneaked a peek and gasped out loud.

It was Brady. He'd forgotten something. Dammit. She couldn't take another good-bye. Keeping her back to the direction of the clearing where he was parking and—oh God—turning off his truck, she scrambled to her feet and grabbed the hose. *Must. Look. Busy.*

Even when covered in dirt and gunk.

No, scratch that. She hosed herself down as fast as she could because no way was she going to let the last view he had of her be like this. Because looking like she'd just been in a wet T-shirt contest was ever so much preferable. Damn, why hadn't she put on a black T-shirt instead of a white one this morning? Now she looked like she was on spring break in Florida. Or on *Girls Gone Wild*.

*Eat your heart out, Brady, this is what you're leaving.*

Shading her eyes from the sun, she aimed the hose at the kennels to look busy, refusing to turn and look at him as he got out of the truck.

She heard Twinkles's little paws pounding the ground as he bounded through the open gate to her, butt wriggling happily along with his tail.

"Aw," she murmured, hugging him close with her free hand, feeling her throat tighten when he licked her chin. "What did you guys forget, huh?" she murmured, cupping his face. "What are you doing here?"

"Lilah."

Her heart dropped to her toes. Keeping her back to him, she concentrated on hosing out the kennels as if it was brain surgery.

"Can I come in?" he asked very quietly, pausing at the opened gate.

He'd never asked before. He bulldozed, quietly demanded, or just did whatever the hell he wanted.

But now he was asking . . .

Oh God. She couldn't do this. She'd gotten used to the fact that he was going, and now he was standing here being sweet and gentle.

Okay, she hadn't gotten used to the fact that he was going, and him being sweet and gentle was killing her.

"Can I come in," he repeated.

She shrugged. "The gate's open."

"I don't mean into the yard, Lilah."

No, she really couldn't do this. She was miserable and she'd lost sight of any positive reasons for him to go. If she had to say good-bye again, she was going to throw herself at him and cling. She nodded, swiping her eyes with her sleeve, probably smearing the last of her mascara while she was at it.

A big hand pried the hose from her fingers. The water shut off, and then that hand was back, turning her to face him.

Fingers slid along her jaw and forced her head up. He looked . . . wary. Not something she expected. He was dressed for the job, or so she assumed, in his usual cargoes, boots, and a nondescript button-down with the usual myriad pockets. He was carrying something, but she couldn't pay attention to that at the moment.

And if he was trying to intimidate with the solemn expression, the sunglasses were a nice touch.

Reaching up, she took them off of him.

He stood still and let her look her fill, his mouth unsmiling. He had a network of fine lines around his eyes, more from the sun than age. His eyes were stark and clear.

And utterly implacable.

He reached for her sunglasses, but she needed the barrier, the wall to hide behind, so she took a step back.

"Lilah."

She closed her eyes behind the lenses. Which, oh good, were still crooked on her nose. And here she'd thought she might feel stupid.

"Look at me."

She opened her eyes and saw what he had cradled between his free hand and his chest.

A box of goodies from 7-Eleven. Be still her heart. "Breakfast?" she asked, and look at that, her voice was perfectly clear. No way to tell that she was broken.

"I was thinking more along the lines of a bribe," he said.

"For what?"

Ignoring her question, his gaze searched her face with that quiet intensity of his, the one that made her heart roll over and expose its tender underbelly. "Are you crying?" he asked.

"No. I just cut up an onion. Yes, I'm crying, you big, unfeeling, insensitive . . ."

"Chickenshit bastard?"

"I was going to say ass, but okay."

He nodded and set down the box of food on a fence post, lifting a hand to sweep his thumb beneath one of her eyes. "I'm sorry," she whispered. "I didn't mean the ass part."

Though his eyes remained very, very serious, his mouth twitched. "Just the unfeeling, insensitive part?"

Again she lifted a shoulder. "If the shoe fits."

With an exhale of air, he took her hand. "I'm in."

Confused, she lifted her face, forgetting for a moment that she was a complete disgusting wreck. "What?"

His eyes were dark and still very solemn. "I'm in this," he said.

She stared at him. "Define 'this,'" she said very carefully. "Because if you mean you're here, in the kennels, I'm going to hurt you. Badly."

"Let's start with where you are," he said. "You're here." Taking her hand, he pressed it to his chest above his heart.

Beneath her palm she could feel the reassuring heat and strength of him.

And his heart, beating steady and sure.

"I haven't had enough caffeine for this," she whispered. "And I'm easily confused. I'm going to need more words here."

"I love you, Lilah."

Her heart stopped dead in her chest. "Okay," she said shakily. "Those are some damn fine words." She swallowed. "You came back to tell me you loved me?"

He nodded.

"And . . . that's supposed to make it easier to let you go again?"

"That, and the fact that I intend to come back. Every single time. If you'll have me. And plus," he said, suddenly sounding uncharacteristically unsure of himself, "I brought junk food."

"True," she managed, nodding, throat so tight she struggled to speak. "And not that the junk food isn't perfect, but the other thing. I need you to explain the other thing to me, Brady."

"I thought the I-love-you was self-explanatory."

"Oh my God. The coming-back thing! The every-single-time thing!"

Some of the wariness drained and he tugged her close, hauling her up against him, making her gasp. "Oh, don't! I'm wet and very possibly wearing doggie puke—"

Ignoring that, he wrapped his arms around her and buried his face in her hair. He was taking comfort in her, she realized with a shock, something he'd never done before, and it touched her deep to her core. "Oh, Brady." Unable to hold back, she hugged him as tight as she could. "I love you so much."

He kissed her. It was a really great kiss, too, deep and soul searching, and by the time he lifted his head, he wasn't breathing any more steady than she. Dropping his forehead to hers, he closed his eyes. "For as long as I can remember," he told her, "from the time I was just a stupid little kid, to being in the military, to working as a pilot for hire, I've lived my life as purposely uncomplicated as possible. You changed that."

She winced. "Because I'm . . . complicated?"

"Yeah." He smiled, and it spread to a grin when she frowned. "Turns out, I like complicated," he assured her. "But I've always thought of myself as a wanderer, a guy with no roots, no home base."

Maybe even a guy who couldn't be saved.

He didn't say those words but she felt them from him, and it broke her heart.

"It changed," he said before she could speak. "It changed because Adam and Dell nag like a couple of old women. It changed because of one silly dog. It changed because of a woman with a fierce, loyal, warm heart, a woman who refuses to back down for anything."

She melted against him. "I back down for donuts. I'm a 'ho for donuts."

A smile crossed his face. "I know, I count on that."

She smacked him and he smiled and took her hand. "What's it going to be, Lilah?"

It wouldn't be easy. Despite how much she loved him, he came with flaws. He was impatient, gruff, demanding . . . but she kind of liked the demanding part.

Besides, she was no picnic herself. She was flawed, too, as flawed as they came. He was waiting for her answer, his eyes holding more emotion than she'd ever seen from him. She rested her cheek against the soft cotton of his shirt. "You were never lost," she whispered.

"I know that, too. Now. Thanks to you." He drew a long breath. "My home base is here, Lilah."

"In Sunshine."

"No. With you. It's you, you're my home base, wherever you are. In the damn magical lake, cleaning shit out of the stalls, playing Uno. It's all you. You're it for me."

"You're good at this," she murmured.

He choked out a laugh. "If I were good, I'd have done this before driving all the way to L.A. and back." Cupping her face, he caught a tear on his thumb. "I've always been on my own. I liked it that way. No one waiting on me, depending on me in any way. I thought that meant I had it all, but that's not how it works. You taught me that. You showed me what it means to belong. I need you, Lilah. I need you with me, loving me. I didn't realize how much until I tried to go."

"Sort of like home is where the heart is?"

"Yes. And mine is in the palm of your hand."

She slid her fingers into his hair as the last piece of her broken heart clicked together. "Oh, Brady."

"I mean it. Life before you . . . It wasn't the same. I wasn't the same. I can't imagine being without you."

"That's good, too," she whispered. "That's probably going to get you good and laid."

"I'm counting on it."

She laughed and he lifted his head, his eyes fierce and intense on hers. "I always thought love was a weakness," he said. "That might still be the case, but I don't want to be without you. You're it for me, Lilah. You make me a better man, you make me feel . . ."

"What?" she said breathlessly when he paused.

"Everything. You make me feel everything."

# Epilogue

They showed up for the animal adoption clinic at Belle Haven together, hand in hand. They were late, because Brady had taken Lilah back to her cabin for a little review session on exactly what loving each other meant.

In the shower, of course, since she'd been such a mess.

Now she was clean but flushed, and her heart rate was still a little bit elevated as they walked into the reception area and stopped traffic.

Jade's fingers were a whirl on her keyboard. Dell stood in the doorway holding a file. They both went utterly still.

Jade took in the look on Lilah's face, the one that no doubt said *Just Fucked*, and let out a slow smile.

Dell's brow shot up.

Then the door opened behind them, hitting Lilah in the butt.

It was Adam, holding a handful of leashes, surrounded by a pack of golden retrievers, all suited up in their S&R vests. He was clearly in the middle of a training session and was followed by one of his students—the ever-uptight Holly.

Even attending a dog-training class she was wearing a business suit and heels. She was frowning, and when Adam stopped so suddenly, she plowed into the back of him.

"Adam," she started. "You can't just walk away in the middle of a class. You—"

"Shh," he said, and they all shushed.

Every single one of them in the place shushed.

Adam locked gazes with Brady.

"Dr. Death!" someone whispered from a waiting room chair.

Beside her, Lilah felt Brady tense. She knew it was important to him that Adam and Dell accept him. And the town, too.

"You forget something?" Adam asked.

"Yes," Brady said. "A few things, actually."

When he didn't expand, Dell laughed softly from across the room. "You going to fill us in or just stand there blocking traffic?"

"I forgot to tell you that the Bell sticks at two hundred and fifty feet," Brady said. "You have to baby the throttle, ease into it. Anyone who flies it should know that."

"We told you," Adam said. "We don't have plans for anyone to fly it except you."

"Well then, I'll make a note of it," Brady said.

Dell was smiling as he came close and clapped Brady on the biceps hard enough to knock him back a step. "You didn't come back for the Bell. You came back for the girl. Our girl."

"Yes." Brady wrapped an arm around Lilah's neck and pulled her in, pressing a kiss to her temple. "I came back for the girl."

There was a collective "awwww" from the waiting room. Mrs. Sandemeyer stood up and pointed at Brady. "I'm first in line for you."

"He's taken," Lilah said.

"I meant for him to see my baby." Mrs. Sandemeyer gestured to the dog at her feet.

"You do know he's not actually licensed in anything animal related," Dell said. "Right?"

"I don't care. He helps out, I've heard he helps out. He escorts the patients into the exam rooms. I'm ready to be escorted."

"What if I live up to my nickname?" Brady asked.

"I'm more afraid this line will take too long and I'll miss bingo tonight."

Dell grinned and reached behind the desk for the sign-up clipboard. "You in?" he asked Brady, holding the clipboard out.

Brady cupped Lilah's face with one hand and held her against his body with his other as he kissed her, sending a bolt of happy right down to her toes. "I'm in."

# headline
## ETERNAL

# FIND YOUR HEART'S DESIRE...

VISIT OUR WEBSITE: www.headlineeternal.com
FIND US ON FACEBOOK: facebook.com/eternalroman
FOLLOW US ON TWITTER: @eternal_books
EMAIL US: eternalromance@headline.co.uk